THE REALITY SHOW

BY KATE L. HART

BOOK ONE

Jacob Marley PUBLICATIONS

Books by Kate L. Hart

The Reality Show Series
The Reality Show – Book 1
The Whole Package – Book 2

Voices of Victorian Women Series
The Lark – Book 1
High Bred Rose – Book 2
The Basra Pearls – Book 3

Table of Contents

CHAPTER ONE

I stepped out into the plaza. Noise erupted all around me. Disoriented, I stopped. Skyscrapers pinned the noise in so it echoed all around me. Hundreds of people I never met jostled each other to get my attention.

All these people waited in the muggy August heat to meet me. They waved to me, shouting out greetings from behind a metal barrier. Stunned, I waved back stupidly. The camera operator gave me an encouraging head nod, so I started toward them, trying to look appreciative. Thick, boiling air hit me harder with every step I took reminding me of my exhaustion – I couldn't focus. The wet heat intensified the smell of baked bus exhaust mingled with boiling asphalt, grease frying from the corner vendor, and whatever was coming up from the subway grates.

A teenage girl stood in front of the crowd and yelled, "How could you leave Ethan? He's soo cute. You should've fought Tess for him."

Startled, I squinted at her. I did fight. I lost. Ethan wasn't in charge of his life: he didn't get to decide who to love. Julian, the producer of the reality: the wannabe god of his own little world, he decided. Not me, not Tess, certainly not Ethan. Julian sat upon his dais and ruled anyone weak enough to bow down before him.

No, I couldn't think about it.

I forced a smile on my face. My auburn hair cascaded in heavy curls that bounced down my back as they had when I was a little girl. The loose lilac dress of a sheer material that ruffled delicately with each step inside the studio started to wilt onto my legs in the humidity of the plaza. Julian wanted me to look soft, wounded and now wilted. That is why I forced a confident, carefree smile on my face. I wanted to be powerful, not wounded.

It didn't matter how I tried. Nobody cared. Nobody actually saw me. They already knew everything there was to know about me.

I am a reality show star, and they want to meet me.

I responded stiff and automatically to people calling out my name. I reached the crowd and people grabbed for me. I hadn't realized so many people loved me. I began touching people's hands as they reached out for me as if I were a rock star. One man proposed to me. I laughed at his joke, but couldn't be sure he was kidding.

I talked to as many people as I could. I tried to give them part of me, but there wasn't much left. I moved toward the young woman who'd yelled so desperately at me. Her pleading, dark eyes needed closure that I didn't have, but would fake for her. My romance was her romance and it ended, and we were both broken-hearted. Something inside me needed to soften this for her.

"Ethan loves you," she said when I finally reached her. "How could you leave him?"

"I had to go," I said.

"You could of stayed," she said, "You could go back again."

"No, no, I can't. Watching the show, you can't understand what's really happening."

"But Ethan loves you!"

"It was the million dollars I competed for, not Ethan."

"Come on Zoe, it's all faked," said a young woman in her early twenties standing next to her.

2

"Shut up, Mia," Zoe said.

"You're so gullible. How could he love her?" Turning to me, she said, "He played you, girl."

The statement stabbed straight into my heart. I closed my eyes and nodded in agreement. I put a hand over my microphone. I'd be sued if Julian heard me, but I had to tell her something.

"She's right, it's choreographed."

"I... I'm so sorry," Zoe said.

Mia butted in again: "You played it too cold, too long. I would have...."

My mouth dropped open, but she still rambled on. She openly admitted the show staged, and yet contradicted her own point. She could have kept Ethan? How? I clenched my jaw shut, trying not to look wounded.

"Carrie!"

Television personality Samantha Prowers stepped toward me. She interrupted the stream of advice now being spewed at me from many of the women in the crowd. They talked at me, arguing over my failure with Ethan, most implying I hadn't been promiscuous enough. Didn't they know I hadn't been cast in that role?

"Ladies, here are a couple of complimentary tickets to the Reunion Show in four weeks. You can see the finale live if you're available," Samantha, said cutting off the comments as many hands shot forward.

"Oh, I'll meet Ethan. I'd give him what he wanted," Mia said, taking one of the slim white envelopes. Appalled, I shook my head at Zoe. That's not what happened. Was it?

3

"Carrie, if you'll follow me back into the studio, you're up next," Samantha said. I nodded and followed her still waving and forcing a smile for my fans. The relief of the air conditioner hit me when I walked back into the building, and I shoved my shoulders back feigning confidence. Samantha indicated I should settle into one of two matching armchairs in front of the ever-probing lens of the cameras.

Samantha, an extremely thin woman with short hair framing her face, perched herself on the end of the other chair like a delicate bird. She talked to someone about her coffee while a man touched up our makeup and hair. All while she watched herself in a monitor that hung below one of the three cameras aimed at us. As an afterthought she asked if I wanted to get the Barista back, I shook my head in the negative. Watching myself do it.

I'd never watched myself perform on *The Whole Package*. Mesmerized, I shook the drooping ringlets that spilled over my shoulders. The defined muscles on my arms and crossed legs stood out somehow, but the subtler features of my light beige face disappeared in the monitor like an instant airbrush painted somewhere inside the camera. Two perfect blush lines moved from my cheekbones toward my hairline, but they looked dulled compared to my richly enhanced auburn hair. My rosy brown eyes were meant to stand out with globs of mascara, but even they disappeared as I squinted in the studio lights.

4

I hated lights in my face. I hated trying to look normal with the glare bringing on a hot flash and a headache while the mask of make-up I wore melted.

A man behind the center camera pointed at Samantha. She turned to me. I nodded. The man put up three fingers, then two then one. Samantha addressed the camera while I fidgeted unsure what to do:

"Welcome back. We're here live with *The Whole Package* contestant Caroline Carnegie. Following her, Mark will cook with French pastry chef Abril Durand."

After she said this, the monitor showed Mark at a stove from the other side of the studio. Then our cameraman nodded to Samantha. She turned and focused on me entirely.

"Carrie, thanks for coming. How does it feel to be home?"

"A little strange, actually... I don't think I've acclimatized yet," I said.

"I'm sure. For those of our viewers hiding under a rock, Carrie is the daughter of renowned architect Arthur Carnegie. Have you read the extremely flattering article coming out in *Architect Digest*, about your father?"

"No, my mom got an advance copy while I was on the show. I'm excited to read it," I said.

"I read it; it is mostly based on the article in *Places* Journal," Then she turned to the camera and said, more for her viewers benefit, "the educational journal that published an article claiming your father should be considered one of the most influential architects of the twenty-first century. How does it feel to be the child of a cultural icon?"

"I don't think about it like that, I guess. He was just my dad who went to work like anyone else's dad," I said. She continued, "He was taken too soon."

"Yes, he was," I agreed calculating the amount of respect my father's mention should inspire, and allowing it to show on my face.

"But having been cited as one of the greatest modern architects of our time, he lives on with us all. Do you feel like he would have approved of your going on a reality show?"

"Maybe not," I said with a laugh, which she copied.

"So, we want the dirt," Samantha said, her cobalt eyes bright with interest. Her hands folded across her legs leaning toward me like she just had to know, "Why did you leave *The Whole Package* in such a dramatic fashion?"

"Oh, I didn't mean for it to be dramatic. At a certain level, I always knew I was on TV. You know – you're always kind of on edge – but it was more like with all the drama around me, I reacted."

"You definitely reacted."

"Well, it's hard not to when you're immersed in something like that. It wasn't at all what I thought it would be."

"Every reality show contestant I interview says that, but *The Whole Package* has been around for five years. You knew what you were getting into," Samantha said.

6

I stammered, unsure what to say that wouldn't make me look like a hot, emotional mess.

When I only shrugged to answer, Samantha paused, scrutinizing me. I could feel the burn of her next question in her eyes before it even left her mouth.

"Did you know polls had you winning five to one?"

"No. We were so isolated I didn't know anything."

"Well, let me tell you, people believe you have recovered from the hand fate dealt you better than any of your housemates. Your fans would have crowned you *The Whole Package* if they could have. The million dollars by all accounts was yours."

"I didn't know how many people were rooting for me," I said.

"Maybe so, but you've won your fair share of the competitions. How could you walk away from a million dollars?"

"I guess two million is the going rate for my self-respect," I said. Then I laughed to cover up my defensive tone. No amount, I promised myself. I would never again be driven the fool by money.

Samantha continued to question me about me about leaving Ethan, but she couldn't ask much beyond what aired on the show. Julian had to save the real drama for the reunion show. She asked about the other contestants, and I refused to bash on anyone. She briefly asked about my fiancé's death, not even calling Gordon by name, and she didn't linger on the topic. After poking me over and over with a sharp stick about the stupidity of my choice, Samantha finally said, like we were best friends, "Well, Carrie I think considering what you've been through, we can all agree you were one of the more resilient women in the Manor House, and I am sorry you left."

"Thank you," I said feeling a bead of sweat trickle down my neck.

"Let's take a look back at Carrie's time on the show."

A fifteen-foot screen set between us showed highlights of my time on *The Whole Package* put to music. I turned trying desperately to disconnect as it showed me climbing out of the limo, I could hear the people out in the plaza reacting. They made some kind of a muffled positive cheer when I turned to George instead of Ethan. I hated the vintage lace and silk dress I'd been wearing when I first met Ethan, but the plum color contrasted dramatically with my coloring and didn't look too bad on screen. I crossed my arms in on myself when the screen showed Ethan's amazing eyes laughing at something I said.

The screen blipped to the opera house. Ethan took my hand warmly in both of his to help me out of the limo. A trick, a device contrived to trap me into performing. It wasn't right. He shouldn't have closed both his hands around mine like I was special – like I was the only one. Oh, why did I smile at him like such a goof?

Then the screen showed me rock-climbing. I threw my arms up when I made it to the top of a cliff. I didn't win that competition, but I made it to the top – my arms up in the air, raised in triumph for some reason. Everything I did on the screen was artistically beautiful, and a worthy of the two Emmy nominations Julian often bragged about.

The screen showed Ethan kissing me. I could still taste his minty kiss. I focused on the corner of the screen, not looking at the image, trying not to remember. Ten women for one man – it wasn't right. No – it was all a game for a million dollars. Nobody told me to fall in love.

Watching the screen, I knew they'd encouraged it. One girl and one boy – that's the way it's supposed to be. That's what the enormous screen showed – my made-for-television romance in little blips. It didn't show what actually happened. On the screen, it all seemed so high class—wholesome family television. Julian hid all my awkward moments, my fumbles. He dressed up his hooker to look like a princess. I fought to keep the emotion in my chest. They didn't get any more of me. They wouldn't get any more of me!

Finally, it showed Ethan's heartbroken face as I walked out the door.

Despite everything, it made me sad. Could love grow in such a situation? The memory of the sweet emotion washed over me, begging me to believe in it.

No! Love turned me into a crazy person; it made me a reality TV star. I wanted nothing to do with it.

It seemed simple enough, quaint little segments set to music. A month and a half, my mini-life, all packaged up. Little slices, entertainment for the masses. But then, why did he look so sad when I left? Ethan. Oh, what really happened? I stood abruptly as the screen went dark.

Samantha also stood, trying to figure out what I was doing.

"Thanks so much for having me," I said. I stuck a hand out to her and smiled.

"Thanks for coming." As she released my hand she said into the camera, "We will return right after this."

The camera operator nodded we were clear and she asked:

"You okay?"

"Fine," I said turning to the stage manager. He invited me to stay for the next segment. I declined. He directed me back into the green room, a large lounge area with huge pictures of Samantha and all her fellow co-hosts along the walls.

As I entered the room, Julian, my puppeteer stood, casting himself in the role of a gentleman from another era. Julian, a middle-aged man with ever-moving eyes, a short, grey ponytail, and a closely cropped beard, scrutinized me as I walked through the room.

He drew breath as I swiftly passed him. He said something but I didn't stop. I stayed calm and drama free – I hadn't looked wounded. I ruined the picture he created. It was my choice how I presented myself to the world – not his. Never again!

"You weren't supposed to leave yet," Julian said louder this time. I didn't respond, but felt very conscious of where he stood behind me. Feeling his obsessive stare on my back, my neck crawled, waiting for him to pounce. I sped up toward my best friend, Andrea. Her peaked nose upturned slightly, giving an air of being unapproachable. She sat on a puce-colored sofa, her ever- moving foot impatiently waiting for my interview to end. She held up the bag containing my shorts and tee shirt. As I passed her I grabbed it.

I changed quickly, unhitching the microphone pack easily; I was so practiced at it. Getting out of all the body altering undergarments was harder. I came back walking even more swiftly than before.

10

"I left the microphone taped to the dress, everything's in there," I said pointing to where I changed.

"I think you can keep the dress," the stylist said, looking to Julian. I forced myself to look at him.

"Carrie, I can still fix this," Julian said.

"There's nothing to fix," I said.

"You were so close to the million dollars. I think –"

"Never to my benefit. I'll be at the reunion show to fulfill my contract, then we will never see each other again."

I turned before Julian could say anything else. Cut him off before he opened his mouth – that is the only safe way to interact with Julian Morrows.

I pulled Andrea up from her waiting. I hated waiting. They never showed how much waiting the contestants of *The Whole Package* did. Five seasons and nobody watching the show had any idea of how much waiting we did. A month and a half of my life wasted waiting on Julian.

I walked away while Andrea tried to keep up. We said nothing as my leather flip-flops smacked the smooth glossy floor. Andrea and I climbed into the elevator and pushed the button for the parking garage.

Andrea eyed me – waiting.

"It wasn't what I thought it would be," I said as we glided downward.

"It never is," Andrea said.

"What happened?" I asked as the doors slid open.

"I have no idea, but we'll figure it out," Andrea said. She put an arm around my stiff shoulders. I crossed my arms over my chest and said:

11

"Do you know how much waiting we did? You couldn't possibly understand what we... or I mean what I went through by watching the show... that woman...."

"She doesn't understand," Andrea said.

"I don't even know what happened. How could she?" I asked.

"We'll figure it out. Start from the beginning," Andrea said.

"I don't want to talk about it!"

"You're just going to let this happen to you? Without a fight?"

"Fight?"

"You just said you don't know what happened to you, Carrie, you have to figure it out. You have to look at this," Andrea insisted.

I said nothing. She was right. I couldn't even remember how I knew she was right. Somewhere along the line I promised myself I would no longer stand on the sidelines of my own life.

"That day, I got into the limo, I knew I shouldn't have, but I did."

"Limos are kinda fun," she said.

"Not for me," I said.

"No, no. I guess not," she said looking at me with the pity I always saw when people remembered how many cemetery curbs I'd pulled away from in limousines.

"Carrie – from the beginning," Andrea said.

CHAPTER TWO

In the distance, frothy fog spilled down the side of the tall northern California hills. Between the hills a valley bordered the ocean. The valley grew wild with no interference. A hapless, meandering road slid aimlessly out of an opening between the hills and wound through the isolated little valley where Julian Morrow taped his reality show *The Whole Package.*

That day twenty contestants stood off at the side of the road which turned and shifted at the convenience of the landscape. I was contestant number sixteen, which means I watched fifteen women climb into a limo and disappear around a bend in the road.

With every woman who left, reality came clearer into focus for me. I was about to appear on television. The act of fate I expected to rescue me from appearing while I ignored it for six months wasn't coming. No one stood between me and my limo ride, and I was stuck. Unprepared for what came next. Then and only then did it occur to me to ask myself:

"How did Adam talk me into this?"

Then realizing I was in fact talking to myself, I looked over at the other contestants to be sure they hadn't heard me.

"So, I guess I'm next," I said, looking over at Erin and Sandra who stood behind me in line. Contestant Seventeen, the woman who stood directly beside me, refused to even talk to us, so I didn't know her name.

"Good luck," Erin said politely looking me up and down. She'd almost laughed at a few of my jokes in the last hour and a half but caught herself and instead looked at me suspiciously. What ulterior motive I had

13

for trying to make her laugh, I have no idea, but she seemed determined to think I might pull a fast one on her if she let herself like me.

"What are you guys going to say to the judge again?" I asked.

"Just introduce yourself darlin'," Sandra said, exasperated, making me feel small.

"My best friend Andrea wanted me to tell him I'm a Capricorn and the stars foretold good things for me this month," I said.

"I'm not sure that's the best—"

"Now Erin, let her express herself however she sees fit," Sandra interrupted.

Sandra winked at Erin.

"It was a joke," I said, feeling my face grow hot, despite the chilly coastal breeze.

"Of course, it was," Sandra said in perfect condescension, pulling up the collar of her double breasted pea coat.

The limousine coming into view silenced us. Slowly, it came toward us on the old worn road where we stood waiting. I clasped my hands in front of me. I breathed deeply trying to calm down. I closed my eyes.

When I opened my eyes, the limo stopped in front of me. I stood frozen, stiff, and unprepared. Up to this point, the whole idea of my going on a reality show had been funny. I'd found it a topic on which mirth could not help but flow.

Now, living the experience, nothing funny swam among the scattered thoughts floating around my head;

14

in fact, I couldn't get anything to land long enough to think of what to say. I found, though social in nature, I did not care for the intense clenching of my stomach and the slight shake in my body this experience gave me. Then and there I decided I'd be home by morning.

In fast forward, the kindly old reaper appeared too suddenly. With his watery brown eyes surveying me, instead of piercing me with his scythe, he took my suitcase.

"Whenever y'all are ready, he's waiting," Sandra said in a strong southern drawl, breaking the spell. The man was indeed waiting for me, but I couldn't see why.

"I'll need everything," said the attractive retired-aged man whose healthy glow only made his gray hair look good.

"Oh," I said, and handed over my handbag and wrap as well.

"You're going to be fine, Missy," he said quietly enough that the other contestants didn't hear him. I smiled to oblige him and he walked back to the trunk with my accessories. I paused in front of the door waiting. The man slammed the trunk shut and started back toward the driver's side.

"I think you have to get your own door," Erin half whispered as if Sandra might not hear.

"Oh, right," I said. I quickly pulled the handle and slid into the back of the limousine almost expecting to see my mourning family in there waiting for me.

Instead, I found a doe-like woman with the glossiest lips I'd ever seen. Her brush and make-up kit were poised at the ready. She started trying to fix my wind-swept look while a man sitting next to her prodded me to turn on my microphone under the tight lace of my grandmother's dress I wore.

"Why did Julian make us stand out there on the road for so long if he cared what we look like?" I asked. She focused on the brush, pulling it harshly through my thick tangled auburn waves.

"It's a matter of timing," she answered.

"Timing? Most of us would fit in this limo and it wouldn't even have to move to get to the next contestant."

"Well," she glanced over her shoulder to make sure the sound operator who sat back talking loudly into his walkie-talkie, wouldn't overhear. She said quietly, "it makes for a great before-and-after shot for your designers. It's a compliment you're one of the last. It takes longer to make you look... well, run down. It's supposed to be a dramatic difference kind of thing."

She threw her arms out, "Women taken from hard circumstances and given a new look. But with you being a socialite I wouldn't be surprised if your designer goes more modern with you." She eyed my dress. "Like an update instead of a –"

The stylist stopped talking abruptly. The sound operator scowled at us. The limo angled its uncomfortable straight length past a hill and into a thin, curved lane. We passed a little pool house, with a huge free-standing satellite dish. Someone liked their HBO, yet my cell phone and wireless internet wouldn't find a signal?

The woman next to me tried to calm my long thick waves with something that smelled like peaches and

16

cream. She formed a thin tight braid that acted like a headband holding in the waves. With no mirror, I pictured myself looking like a red-headed Alice in Wonderland.

We came upon a cream-colored mansion, failing to imitate the famous Victorians thirty miles north in San Francisco. It squatted too low to be a stately old dame painted up for tourists. Instead, it looked like a massive, misshapen butter cube. A lone house isolated along the coastline would've given me the creeps, but this one didn't even accomplish that. The nearer the limo came, the more the hill sloped away beneath the mansion and exposed the clashing gray foundation.

Ah, the recoil my father would have felt if he lived to see his oldest child on a reality television show taking place in such a sadly crafted mansion. My ever-nagging inner glimpse told: life would never be this complicated mess had he lived. I pushed away the regret and focused.

Towering lights and cameras on tripods formed a little cove around two men past the house. Even from a slight distance, I could distinguish the host from the twenty-nine-year-old pediatrician who would judge the resiliency of the contestants.

The host spoke to us that morning. With the intensity of a coach calling plays at the Super Bowl, he taught us how to be attractive and confident on camera.

"Talk slowly, no big arm movements, make eye contact, and don't look directly into the camera. Okay break!"

I thought it overkill when I saw one woman taking notes. Now I tried to remember the rest of his tips.

Bumping and jolting, the limo rattled over the badly paved road. The stylist finally satisfied with my hair renewed her assault on my face. When she reformed my eyebrows, I could feel her recreating my face as a fifties star. She must have realized my sheath style dress with an illusion lace neckline was created in dark plum so it didn't mimic Grace Kelly's wedding dress too obviously. My grandmother tried to get a maid to, "do up my face" in the same way when I wore the dress to my engagement party.

It wouldn't be hard for some designer to update my look.

The limo came to a stop with an ugly scraping sound of hubcaps on the curb. Fed up, I swatted at the stylist. I didn't have a mirror, but I could tell by the satisfaction on her face she'd achieved my outdated look. She moved to the other side of the limo, next to the scowling sound operator, so the camera didn't see her when the door opened.

I turned to the door waiting for it to open, but nothing happened. I examined my supposed judge, a doctor, wondering what I would say to him. He stood bent, leaning his head toward the host to hear something he said. He was too handsome. His appearance held nothing understated or even distracting about it.

Slender and about six feet tall, with dark hair and chiseled features, the judge filled out his black tux as a made-for-television hero should. My peevishness stopped briefly as I wished I looked over his bio at least a little. By studying it, I may have used it to get off the show in the opposite manner other contestants would use it to stay on.

"They need you to say something into your microphone," the sound operator said.

"Testing," I said wishing something funny would pop out of my mouth. A man wearing huge headphones outside the limo gave a thumb up. Watching everyone bustle around to make ready for the moment the door opened made me frantic for a better strategy.

This is a comedy, I reminded myself, not a horror film. My dress was funny. I wore the last symbol of my grandmother, the dress she bought me for my engagement party, and I wore it on a reality show. My grandmother would have passed out and needed salts to revive.

I could hear her patronizing voice saying, "Oh Carrie! How could you do this to me, to the family, to your dead father's memory?"

The limo driver finally opened the door for me. Everyone in the space backed out of the camera's sight line.

Lights and a camera were in my face as I emerged. After I made it out of the limo the host backed up. He waited for me to come over. The judge fidgeted in his tux.

In that moment, frazzled humor took over. I turned to the limo driver and said, "Hi, I'm Caroline Carnegie. You must be the judge, Ethan?"

Everyone stared at me until I heard the host of the show and Ethan burst out laughing behind me. The limo driver scratched his eyebrow.

"I'm George. That handsome young fella over there is Ethan."

I glanced sidelong at Ethan, after purposefully putting my back to him. Then I said, "Ah, break my heart, George."

George laughed and walked to the trunk of the limo. He unloaded my suitcase, handbag and wrap as though

19

he didn't have any idea cameras poised to take every television in the U.S., including Puerto Rico any tiny misstep he made.

"Okay, let's try this again," the host, Lance, said. An average built man, he had enough charm radiating from his rounded face to make him moderately good looking. He had an arm over Ethan's shoulder. "We need you to introduce yourself to Ethan, Caroline." I nodded, walking toward them noticing the strange angle of the house completely blocked out the wind.

With the idea of "mock it until they ask me to leave" I walked toward Ethan, still deciphering in my head what to say. I would not tell my sob story. All the heartache I'd endured – all that I overcame to become *The Whole Package*.

Ethan smiled at me. I smirked sweetly back trying to ignore the cameraman and the tremor running through my body.

"Hi. I'm Ethan Stewart."

"Caroline Carnegie."

"What makes you *The Whole Package*?" he asked. I looked up at him.

I stopped.

His amusement showed clearly in the most amazing silver eyes I'd ever seen. Brightness peered through them and somehow lit his whole face. This made him distracting.

"I... uh I deserve a million dollars because I'm disorganized, and you know redheads don't age well. Without it, I'm probably in trouble."

"Well, that's something to think about," Ethan said looking at the host to see if I was joking. Instead of responding

20

he said; "Was it an older man thing – you hitting on the limo driver?"

"No, no. It's the hat."

"I'll make a note of that," Ethan said, like he could find one.

"I'm not sure you could pull it off." I shook my head at him like he was a dork. He grinned. Then he looked as though he wanted to say something else, but the host cut him off. "Time. Sorry, you took too long with the limo driver. It'll be the most ... interesting intro we've ever had, but now the next contestant's coming."

"All right," I said, but didn't move. Intrigued, I paused to examine Ethan's eyes. As he shifted to grin at me, they gleamed silver to blue, segmented by miniature lightning. I hadn't anticipated this anomaly. I begrudgingly admitted his eyes brought his appearance into the realm of interesting. No. Stop staring at him. I turned. What if he interpreted my pausing to examine him as interest? I walked away – fortunately inside my head this time – I asked myself for the second time in six months:

"How did Adam talk me into this? How do I get out of it?"

I hurried toward my suitcase, purse and wrap George left piled on a little path leading to the house. If I had opened the folder labeled "Ethan Stewart's bio," I would have seen his picture and known about the eyes. Scolding myself for not being more prepared I barely heard Ethan call to me. I turned and said:

"Huh?"

"My grandma was a redhead," he replied. "I only saw pictures of her like that, but after it turned white, she looked

21

like all the other kids' grandmas. You're going to have to step
it up if –"

"So bluntly honest didn't work for you," I interrupted.

"You're lucky I'm looking for *The Whole Package* and not
the best sob story or you'd already have lost."

"I'll try to get a little weepy next time," I said.

"Or a better delivery," he said.

"Ah, no, my timing is impeccable," I said grinning at his
warmth.

Wait, was I flirting?

Before he could respond I waved and nodded while
turning abruptly, breaking away from his gaze. I concentrated
on the sound the wheels of my suitcase made every time they
clicked over a tile in the sidewalk. I could feel Ethan's amazing
eyes still on me, but the clutching in my stomach had turned
into more of a pleasant bubbling.

Trying to exit in the most unfeminine way possible, I
started shrugging my shoulders with each step. It made my
wavy hair ripple. My internal panic blared in my head. The
openly-displaying-my-faults approach may not have been the
best way to go after all. However, even among my alarmed
thoughts, I didn't regret it enough to wish I had said I was a
star-reading Capricorn.

CHAPTER THREE

I walked clumsily, dragging and bumping my suitcase up three rounded steps. Then I pulled open the foggy glass door of what the host referred to as the Manor House.

I stopped in the tight entryway, blocked by two men carrying a stack of long, thick planks of metal.

"I'm losing it, can you…" one called to the other.

"Just stay there. Stay there," the first man snapped at me as if I would try to duck under his load.

Feeling rather useless I waited for the two men to stabilize the planks. I saw most of the twenty women competing for the million dollars already sitting or standing around the main area of the house. Weary glances indicated contestants worked hard to stay out of the way the production crew, who moved aimlessly like wind-up toys on unknown errands.

The whole ground level could be seen from my vantage point, except a boxed-out space on the opposite side of the room from me. That must have been the kitchen. Usually, the concept of open floor plans opened up the kitchen space, but not here for some reason. The corner of the boxed-out kitchen naturally cut the open space in halves. A large sitting room and dining room spread to one side. The space around the other side of the boxed-out kitchen lay empty except for a rug and a few tables with vases on them.

A man with a large rounded nose on an incredibly thin face walked up to me expectantly before I made it to a seat.

"Can I take your suitcase and purse?" he asked.

23

"Oh," I said.

I squinted at him. My handbag contained credit cards, cash, and ID's, not to mention it was my little sister Addie's Hermes Birkin.

"I'll keep my handbag, thanks."

The man nodded curtly and took my suitcase up a staircase that curved off to the left.

Again, I headed for the love seat, but slower this time, glancing at all the women assembled. I wouldn't call the other contestants my competition as I had no intention of getting onto the show. Then, I suppose I'll own, that despite this firm resolution, the need to self-affirm took over.

All the women looked like models. Not the too-thin runway models, but wouldn't-you-like-to-buy-this-sweater, department store models. All the contestants were beautiful, but many were also understated, almost like they were meant to blend in. Almost like they were … living props.

I stood out. Shorter than the other contestants, my deep copper hair shined brighter than even the brightest clothing. My eyes wandered the room confidently, always on the lookout for something funny. My oval face curved upward in a natural smile. I couldn't suppress my lips even when I was uncomfortable. I could see that, among the other contestants, I came off as a bright blaring light without even trying.

I sat on the unoccupied edge of a cold leather loveseat. I smiled at the tawny haired woman with big teeth and an expressionless face I sat next to. She squinted at me suspiciously, and I could see, like Erin, she tagged me as Julian's spy.

24

That morning, Julian Morrows, the producer of *The Whole Package*, noticed me only moments after I walked into the hotel conference room. He left the women he was helping mid-sentence to greet me. He stayed with me pretty much the rest of the morning. Grandmother would have been pleased.

The love seat started to vibrate, pulling me from my thoughts. The woman next to me moved her nervous leg so fast I said:

"And we're off."

She looked confused.

"Because it feels like the love seat just started its engines?"

She glared at me and abruptly stopped moving her leg.

"I was just kidding," I said grinning, "keep going, you were giving me a back massage."

She squinted at me, staying still.

The strange configuration of the couches allowed the woman to turn her whole body from me toward the huge picture window as if nonverbally reprimanding me. Didn't I know better than to stand out in a crowd? I turned to see what she looked at and found a strange solace in the view.

The windows looked down on a path. The path curved through a lush emerald lawn. The land extended into the distance, then abruptly ended and dropped off to the Pacific Ocean. The ocean rolled familiar, it carried a friendly buoyant feeling to it. Without meaning to I sighed, and it felt like taking a deep breath after being oxygen deprived.

I tried to lean into the couch to give my back a rest. Between the dress, the microphone pack, the cold leather I sat on and the cold women I sat next to, I had no luck

25

getting comfortable. I stood up. Visible relief slumped the woman's shoulders as I walked away.

"Op, coming through," the makeshift bellhop said carrying a long pole.

I moved quickly to the far side of the room. I found a narrow hall under the curving staircase. A woman I recognized balanced on this stool in front of a camera. This little out-of-the-way cove made the perfect quiet spot to interview contestants. The cameraman interviewed a woman named Serena, who was anything but tranquil, but A Ball of Cunning Energy wouldn't make an appealing name. The long woman with strawberry blonde hair stood a few spots ahead of me waiting for the limo. She had not blended in.

I tried many times to talk to her, but Serena never warmed up to me, even a little. She kept asking how I knew Julian Marrows so well. I assured her I didn't know him. She did not believe me. She openly encouraged all the contestants around us to distrust me.

I quickly stepped back into the main part of the house, not to catch her attention. I took two steps and almost smacked into a horizontal tripod

"Excuse me," a man said as he shoved me back into the entry way.

The door swung open and caught the heel of my extended foot. I yelped a little. The whole room turned. At that moment, it would have been nice to blend in.

"Oh, sorry y'all," said a sweet southern drawl as I leaned down rubbing my ankle. Sandra leaned forward waiting for me to say something. Her unreal morning glory eyes looked a little bloodshot, and the trail of mascara down her cheek looked poetically beautiful as it ran after the million dollars. She wore a tight silver dress, and her faultless beauty made her intimidating. But she also had this cool girl quality about her that brought out the well-hidden insecurity in me. She definitely didn't blend in.

"Hey, Sandra," I finally said.

"Carrie, it is unwise to stand behind a swinging door."

"Right –"

She cut me off by looking over my shoulder and squinting at the space behind me. I turned to see the man who took my suitcase ogling Sandra.

"Hey," he said, with a cool guy head nod. Sandra gave a bit of a not-a-chance exhale.

"Carrie, whenever y'all get a minute, would yah mind handing this to him?" Sandra said nodding at her suitcase, refusing to look back at the man.

"Oh yeah, sure," I said.

I swung the suitcase to the makeshift bell hop giving him an encouraging smile because he turned beet red. He smiled back shyly, and his breathing eased up. I turned back to Sandra, but she left the tight entryway. I saw her heading for the cold couch I'd vacated. I hoped cool girl didn't want to chat.

I glanced at my image in the mirror across from the door, and, following such an encounter with beauty, I looked like the incredible hulk after he morphed and his clothes no longer fit. The muscles on my arms bulged out of the lace sleeves of my dress; I started running 10K s after Gordon died.

Acknowledging that I was wrong in thinking I had the smart factor over the other women who clearly knew to stay out of the path of swinging objects, I moved back to the large empty room. I stopped when I overheard the two women whispering to each other:

"I know how to get the million dollars out of him, no problem."

"I don't even care about the money. He looked at me with those eyes of his and well... he's enough of a prize for me," the other woman shot back.

Since everyone seemed leery of me, I didn't attempt to talk to these women. I feared something meant as a joke would backfire. Instead, I zeroed in on the lone woman blending in, despite her amazing beauty. Her perfect olive skin set off her dark hair that gleamed with garnet red when it hit the light. Yet another red head? Except to compare myself to her wasn't fair: I looked like a cartoon character next to a classical work of art.

"Hi. I'm Carrie," I said before I fully made it into the woman's space.

The woman looked at me with shocking green eyes. Her eyes darted the surrounding area for a moment to be sure I spoke to her.

"Oh, um, I'm Veronica... Fodor," the woman finally said with a very gentle lift on her vowels indicating she was from the Northeast. Veronica went quiet, leaning back against the wall to hyperventilate.

"Are you all right?" I asked, wondering if she needed medical attention.

"I'm gonna throw up," Veronica said.

"Yeah, maybe you should lay off the liquor. I know this is television, but I'm not sure you've delved far enough in yet to qualify for rehab," I said.

She stood in confused – stunned silence – that's all she gave me.

"I'm kidding," I said.

"Oh, right," she said.

"You're funny, I'm not. I'm going to be eliminated tonight I bet."

"Oh uh…" I trailed off. With such a look of defeat written on her face, I couldn't disagree. I wondered if I could somehow teach her face to be confident. Someone nature thought so highly of, to endow with such a unique beauty, should not waste her loveliness drooping as Veronica did. With ever the eye of the artist, I felt her beauty, like viewing a master's work.

"Do you think Ethan will be in soon?" Veronica asked. "I wanna get this over with."

"I'm sure. I'm Number Sixteen. I got pelted with the door by Eighteen."

Veronica had a question in her eyes, but it was too fresh a humiliation to joke about yet.

"Look! There's Nineteen now," I said. A strong-looking woman opened the door, her fair chin-length hair speared off at the ends. Her delicate almost mousey features made her look small even though she stood taller than me.

"She looks nice," Veronica said.

"Her name is Erin. She would be a good friend for us if she didn't think I'm part alien," I said grinning at Veronica. Veronica shyly grinned back.

29

"Or maybe she noticed how much Julian likes you," Veronica said looking to the ground.

"Nonsense. She's a conspiracy theorist."

Veronica laughed for me, almost drying up the shine of extra moisture in her eyes.

Erin tugged on her heavy suitcase. She planted her backside against the door and pulled, but the suitcase was jammed on the stairs.

"Okay, she's going to need help," I said. I unceremoniously handed my wrap and handbag to Veronica.

"Here, Erin. Let's lift it up," I said jogging over to her, barely avoiding the cameraman setting up his tripod.

"Oh yeah, it's stuck," she said.

After a jarring lurch that stretched my ill-fitting dress to its full capacity, the suitcase jumped through the door.

"Thanks," she said, but she looked me up and down like I may have brethren being held in area fifty-one.

I grinned at her, determined to win her over. She spoke intelligently and would have laughed at my jokes if Serena hadn't glared at her every time she started to.

She walked away from me trying to look composed. With simply a glance she handed the trunk-like suitcase off to the man responsible for it. Then she walked toward Serena, who waved from the cove where she'd been holding the camera for her.

The wiry makeshift bellhop stared at the black baby elephant of a suitcase before him. He looked up the stairs and then back at the suitcase a few times.

"You could put it in the kitchen until you see if she even makes it onto the top ten," I said.

"Genius," the man said, his bony face turning to smile at me. He balanced the enormous suitcase on its little wheels, like a large woman teetering in high heels. I would've helped, but Veronica slipped back into her corner to have a panic attack.

"I can't do this," Veronica whispered as she handed me back my accessories.

"Of course, you can," I said, "You're a beautiful woman who obviously has a lot to offer, or you wouldn't be here. They pressured you to have a good audition tape. You must've done really well."

"My best friend, Sue, shot it, but it was just the two of us." Then after a pause and an agonizing look, she owned up: "We shot it twelve times."

I willed myself to choke down the comment trying to come out. I didn't know what to say – well, that wouldn't offend. My own video had been a big joke and I'd never seen the finished product. Adam did it all.

Veronica took long, deep breaths. If only I could figure out how to help her relax. If she could stand up a little straighter, and smile, pull away from the wall a bit maybe I could….

No, Veronica would be eaten alive if she made it on the show. A few of the other contestants behaved like overly confident piranhas. As if to prove my point, the flirty contestant called;

"I need a drink here." She whipped her straight, wheat-colored hair over her shoulders.

"Okay, I'll have something uncorked," the makeshift bellhop said. In his defense, he tried not to stare at her bulging chest as he said it.

"Unboxed more like," a stagehand said to another, not observing Veronica and me in the corner.

"I prefer a white," the woman said.

I couldn't help staring. How had gobs of thick black mascara and bright ruby lips made it through the makeup artist? Julian instructed us to look natural, toned down even. She looked like an old-time Vaudeville star. If my Grandmother had seen the Vaudeville star, the look on her face would be something akin to smelling rotten milk.

No – no! I hated thinking like that. I did not want my grandmother in my head.

"I'm feeling a bit parched myself. Perhaps y'all ought to serve everyone," Sandra said. She used her cool girl shrug and the makeshift bellhop dropped what he was doing. He headed for the boxed-out kitchen area immediately so she didn't have to wait.

"Does anyone else need anything?" the Vaudeville star called, re-establishing herself as the hostess. From that point on Sandra started fighting the Vaudeville star for some undefined dominant position.

"I'll have the waiters start coming around," the makeshift bellhop said after he handed Sandra a drink. He walked over to the men closest to us and nodded.

"How are we supposed to get the risers up and serve drinks?" the man asked him in a hushed voice.

"Well, if Julian weren't so cheap, we could've started yesterday," the other said.

"Then he'd have to pay us," the makeshift bellhop answered.

"Wasn't happening," the second man said.

"What you're saying is stand on the bottom riser so it doesn't hurt as bad when they fall," I asked.

All three men turned startled. The makeshift bellhop came in closer and glancing over his shoulder said quietly with half a grin:

"I'd stand on the highest riser, always best to be on the top of the doggy pile."

I laughed. Then he said to the men:

"Finish what you're doing. I'll start serving."

"Right. Wouldn't want anyone to sober up from brunch," I said.

"Nope," The man grinned at me and disappeared.

I silently observed the stage hands, the Vaudeville star, Sandra, and Veronica, in turn. Would Ethan prefer the Vaudeville star over someone so classically beautiful, but shy, like Veronica? But then in between the two, there was calm and confident Sandra.

Finally, the last contestant entered the house. Twenty women crammed into the main area perked up as the host came in. Sandra and the Vaudeville star popped back into view. Sandra didn't seem as collected as she had been.

"Okay, ladies, Ethan's getting some instructions from Julian then he'll be right in. In the meantime, we are going to review the rules one more time."

"Oh, come on," the Vaudeville star said.

"You are evaluated on the six traits of resiliency developed by Ph.D. television personality Dr.

Patricia Corbon. She initially created this show as a branch of her talk show. Her mission is to help people like you who have overcome misfortune to be recognized and rewarded. The first trait is –"

"Your ability to work as a part of a team – resilient people know how to collaborate," Sandra recited.

"Second, Perspective. Resilient people know that unpleasantness will end eventually. They can keep a certain amount of grace under pressure, and even tend to find a positive lesson in misfortune," the Vaudeville star joined in.

"Third. Resilient people practice healthy habits. They are able to keep themselves physically and emotionally strong. They laugh often," Lance continued as if he hadn't been interrupted.

"Fourth. Resilient people stay positive. Resilient people have an inner strength that teaches them to believe in themselves and sluff off discouragement," Sandra said.

"Yeah, like staying positive while living in a house with a bunch of women and no outside contact," Veronica whispered to me. I nodded. Veronica couldn't help her nerves no matter how many times she stood up after being knocked down. I wondered if being an introverted person was a resilient trait in Dr. Corbon's opinion. That woman seemed more like the Wizard of Oz than a psychologist.

"Fifth," Lance continued, "Resilient people focus outside of themselves. They care for the people around them."

"Sixth. Resilient people set goals and achieve those goals. They know what they want and they know how to get it, no matter what gets in the way," the Vaudeville star finished. She looked like she knew how to get what she wanted.

"Each competition will test your resiliency. You are rated twice a week, on a 1-10 scale, by our impartial judge. First, on your resiliency after a competition, and second, after volunteer opportunities. Extra points are awarded throughout the week for outstanding shows of character. The woman with the most points stays in the competition, the woman with the least points is eliminated. Only Ethan, Dr. Corbon, Julian and the audience will ever know at any time how many points you have."

"How do you know how well you're doing?" Serena asked.

"You should know by the way you feel inside while striving to live the attributes of resiliency," Lance said as if reading off a cue card. The makeshift bell hop handed him a clipboard and his focus shifted from us to it.

"That was vague," I whispered over my shoulder to Veronica.

"Everyone could see the points when Dr. Corbon ran the show," she whispered back.

"What do you mean?"

"I read online that the producer Julian Marrows and Dr. Corbon had a falling out. Contestants who were losing wouldn't even try and the show lost ratings. Julian took over to bring them back up. Dr. Corbon won't have anything to do with the show anymore."

"I wonder why?"

"I don't know. She wants them to stop using her name in it, but they won't," Veronica whispered.

"Really?"

"Yeah, I guess Dr. Corbon and Julian hate each other."

"That does not bode well for us, does it?"

"I don't know," she answered, and may have said more but Lance handed the clipboard back and said:

"All right, if some of you could go out into the garden or around the pool area. Everyone will get a chance to talk with Ethan." Then, looking straight at me, he said, "Remember this is the time to get personal. Let Ethan get to know the person you've become despite all you've overcome–"

"Well, it's a little chilly out for me," the Vaudeville star interrupted loudly, "I'm staying in."

"I suspect if you'd put on a little more dress you'd be comfortable darlin'," Sandra said, following her.

"Would you come outside with me?" Veronica said leaning over to my ear, "I'm hot. I can't breathe too well."

"Well, I'll go, but I have to throw on my wrap so I'm not chilly," I said loudly. A few of the women giggled sucking up to me as I flamboyantly threw my wrap around my neck for dramatic effect. This may have been more triumphant a moment if I hadn't heard a small ripping noise as I swung my arm.

"Oh, Grandma's going to kill me," I said.

"What?" Veronica asked.

"Nothing. Let's go through the dining room doors," I said moving quickly toward the exit.

Grandma was dead. What was the matter with me? I tried not to care that my expensive designer dress ripped. Why didn't I sell it online to pay my car insurance when I had the chance? No one would buy it ripped. We walked to the other end of the large dining room table. Veronica slowed, glancing at the front door Ethan would come through. She came to a complete stop, pausing in the propped-open French doors.

The French doorway led to a garden with sculpted bushes and a gaudy gold dragon fountain. The appalling dragon sculpture leaned over spitting water into a basin and staring at me through its greedy ruby eyes. The disturbing dragon eyes clashed dismally with the little buds of pink roses climbing the lattice arch over the doorway.

At the sound of Ethan's voice at the other end of the house, Veronica flinched like she'd felt an electrical shock. I forced myself to keep looking out into the garden. It occurred to me that the design of the house and garden looked like a variety of backdrops, without any interconnected design. The architect and designer were at war. Like the avid theater lover who worked as a stagehand, I couldn't enjoy the play unless the scene changes were flawless.

"Somebody with an awkward taste took free rein to this house," I explained to Veronica.

"I guess you're right," Veronica said looking at me, her face bright red, and her eyes darting all over the place. No doubt she accidentally managed to make eye contact with Ethan. I tried harder to ignore him. Ethan's silver eyes hit my back like the sun's warming rays. Still, I refused to turn.

"I never notice things like that, but it is... kinda," she said.

"Like a pet python in a little girl's bedroom?" I asked, opening my arms to the statue among bushes of pink flowers and the garden table covered in purple glass stones.

"Yeah, where did you learn to pick up on things like that?" Veronica asked.

"My dad was an architect on the East Coast. He was a purist," I said.

"My dad's a structural engineer. He keeps up with the architectural world. What's your dad's name?"

"His name was Arthur Carnegie," I said.

"Like Carnegie Hall?"

"Built around the turn of the century, so no, but he's a distant relative. No. He built a skyscraper in New York near 57th and Central Park. The Carnegie Building, they renamed it for him after... anyway it's his most famous," I said. "He has a lot of other impressive buildings, but people only remember the skyscraper."

"He died, didn't he," Veronica asked.

"He passed away when I was fourteen," I said.

"I'm sorry."

"Thanks. We were close."

I would have said more, but two high-pitched female voices interrupted us.

I turned when one woman screeched:

"What do you mean a hairdresser can't be with a doctor – is that written somewhere?"

"I meant he needs someone –"

"Do you see me? You don't know what I've been through in my life. I can have any man I want."

The two women, forming an alliance only a short time earlier, stood in front of a fake Grecian pillar. Ethan stood between them. He looked like he had no idea what to do. He connected eyes with me. I covered my open mouth trying not to look stunned. I gave a lame cough so the action wouldn't look weird.

38

Ethan opened a hand to me, and his look asked me what to do. I gave a slight shrug and head shake because I had no clue. He said uncertainly:

"Ladies, I've been instructed to find the ten contestants most worthy of a million dollars. No matter what walk of life they come from."

He looked straight at me as he said this. Then he turned away from me to focus on the women. He reminded them romance wasn't on the table, but neither heard him. I didn't like his back to me. It bothered me. I liked to see the way his eyes looked when he spoke.

Veronica and I crossed a faux stone path away from the dragon to the small garden table. We sat among dwarf Magnolias exploding in varied shades of pink like a display of miniature, living fireworks. Few of the other contestants opted to come outside.

"There are a lot of redheads here," I said. "Us, and I saw at least two others. Four out of twenty is unusual," I said.

"Most people don't consider me a redhead," Veronica said.

"Oh yes! The red in your hair is pronounced. Ethan must like redheads," I said fingering a piece of hair over my shoulder.

"Must," she said.

"It's kinda weird there're so many redheads, and yet, not one African-American. That's weird, right?"

"Yeah, I didn't see any Hispanic women, either; plenty of blondes, though."

"Living in New York, it's almost uncomfortable not to have any ethnicity around. It feels too –"

"Pod people," Veronica said.

"Right?"

She nodded.

I turned and again came face-to-face with the ruby-eyed dragon, reminding me a million dollars was no slight prize.

CHAPTER FOUR

An equipment handler, recast as a waiter, came around with snacks and wine. Both Veronica and I refused the wine. Veronica did because she counted calories obsessively. I abstained because rule 101 of recruiting; don't ever get tipsy in front of your clients. In this case, America watched me, and I'm sure that included some of my clients. I had to be sharp. Many of the women who had been working hard to blend in partook excessively to ease their nerves. No one had eaten since the hotel's brunch.

The atmosphere quickly became spring break-like among the blending contestants. Some of them behaved so ridiculously I wondered if maybe they were paid actresses trying to liven us all up. The few contestants I would consider competitors didn't seem to drink much over the afternoon.

In silence, I ate strawberries, crackers, and exotic cheeses. It wasn't enough, but I didn't want to go looking for more because Veronica only took small dainty bites of a strawberry.

"I didn't eat much at brunch," I said.

"Oh, me neither," Veronica said, "but if I eat too much I'll just puke it back up."

"Okay, I'm going to bite, Sweetie. Why are you doing this to yourself?"

"Well, my friend Sue married this guy she's dated since middle school. I go out with Sue and Joe and I'm the third wheel."

"You know this isn't a dating show, right?"

41

"Yeah, right. The highly successful judge always ends up dating the woman who becomes *The Whole Package*. How can he help himself?"

"Ethan just said he wasn't looking. Plus, Julian insisted no one feel pressured into being romantic with Ethan. That's not what being resilient is all about."

"I don't see it that way; I see it like they've done the pre-screening process for me. The judges on this show are always amazing, successful humanitarians. Ethan donates his Saturdays to a free clinic. How else would I meet someone like that?"

"I can't believe you have a hard time meeting men."

"Yeah Peter Pan boys I can find, but a man who is driven and committed –"

"Not to an asylum," I said.

"Right. Not a crazy, and that's not easy to find where I come from."

"But on a reality show?" I asked.

"Did you read Ethan's bio? He's kind of amazing," she said.

I shrugged. The conversation lagged. Veronica took on a shy and humiliated silence. Veronica's internal conflict between wanting more than she was born to, and having pride in where she came from was foreign to me. Having been born to nobility – if the country has such a concept – I couldn't see the big deal either way. In my social scenes, my native refined circles, men were driven – mostly by chauffeurs. I'd never really taken the time to decide what I wanted in a relationship like Veronica seemed to. I thought her too eager for thinking about it, let alone saying it out loud.

"What's your angle, you know, your sob story?" I asked breaking the tense silence between us.

"Immigrants' granddaughter works her way from extreme poverty to a Master's degree in Computer programming by the age of twenty-two."

"Good for you – you're not twenty-two, now right?" I said.

"No, it's been a couple years – although I was just out of school when I applied to be on this show," she said.

"How long ago did you apply?" I asked.

"Over two years ago," she said.

I stammered. A few of the contestants mentioned waiting for two years to appear on the show. I couldn't figure out the application process in my head. Adam only sent my application in six months ago. Veronica waved a hand in front of my face and asked:

"Everything okay?"

"Yeah. Sorry, um," I said, "where's your master's from?"

"Rutgers."

Silence again.

"Do you have an education?" she finally asked.

"Uh, yeah MBA from Harvard," I said my cheeks glowing.

"Oh, that's really impressive," she said. She looked away and blinked tears out of her eyes. I didn't know what to say to make her feel better. I couldn't help where I'd been educated; I was a legacy.

"How did you get here?" Veronica finally said.

"My co-worker Adam nominated me –"

"No, I mean what did you –"

"Adam's single, by the way," I quickly interrupted.

"You don't think I can get Ethan?" Veronica said looking away and blinking hard again.

"Oh, no, it's just – I've been in love before; I don't think this can lead to that kind of an emotional bond. For anyone, you know?"

"It has to; I'm so tired of being alone. How else would I meet a single guy who's so amazing?"

I shrugged.

"What am I going to do?" she asked.

"Maybe I can help. It's what I do for a living," I said.

"You get people onto reality shows?" she asked.

"No. I'm a headhunter," I said feeling the burn of a challenge.

"Oh, is that like –"

"A recruiter," I said.

I could see how badly she wanted to get onto the show. I'd seen this kind of want only a few times. Getting her on the show looked more like fulfilling a dream than grubbing for money.

"You know," I said, "you should try to think up a few really good questions to ask Ethan. Finding a connection will help you get his attention."

"Like what kind of questions?"

"You read his bio?" I said.

"Yeah – uh, I memorized it," she said.

"Okay. Let's sit here quietly while you think up some questions you could ask based on it. Make them personal, something you'll have in common with him that the other contestants won't. It should help if he has to think about an answer," I said.

" 'Kay," she said.

I watched her think. If the right situation presented itself, I could get Veronica on the show. It remained my priority to get off, the sooner the better. But I liked Veronica.

People recruited by my firm are poised to succeed from infancy. Top of the class, with the right connections, and trained to put forward genial, outgoing personalities—even if they have to be medicated to do so. Veronica wasn't any of these. She was the rare gem, the graduate who worked hard for every slight success she achieved.

Recruiting self-made applicants gave me the only satisfaction I found in my job. I worked a little harder helping them along their way. In my mind, they deserved more because they worked harder for it. Granted, this wasn't a fortune five hundred company, but still, it offered a certain amusement for me.

After some time, Veronica looked to be working backward into a distress.

"I'm sure you have some good ideas. Don't disregard them," I said.

"I'm not sure it's –"

"They'll be fine; no one here has come up with Einstein questions to ask. Trust your instincts. They'll draw you to good questions when your interview comes," I said.

"Is that what Adam does, recruiting?" She became bright red and shook, embarrassed about something. Veronica was so shy and yet determined.

"Um ... he works directly with the companies. I find applicants he needs to fill their positions. We're kind of a team," I said.

"That's cool," she said.

I nodded. She looked at me expectantly.

"This Adam – how old is he?" she finally asked.

Didn't she want Ethan?

"He's older than you, by a bit. I mean, Ethan – he's closer to your age. You're only twenty-four?" I said, feeling combative for some reason. I tried to tell myself Adam would be good for Veronica, but like any tightrope walker, I needed my safety net. Adam always caught me.

Again, I found it a little odd he insisted I come on *The Whole Package*. He assured me he'd manage to recruit for his own accounts so we didn't lose business while I competed.

When we first started working together I thought he had a crush on me for all the interest he took in me. But then, he wouldn't have sent me on a reality show where I had to impress a handsome single judge if he had a crush on me. Apparently, my answer didn't satisfy her because Veronica, in her quest for details, helped me along;

"What does he look like?"

"Adam?"

"Yeah," Veronica rolled her eyes.

"He... I guess he's really good looking."

"As good looking as Ethan?"

"Adam's handsome in a more mature way than Ethan," I said. "Adam looks like a cologne ad whereas Ethan is more of a romantic lead or a boy band wannabe. Anyway, I don't think you should give up on Ethan yet. You're seriously so pretty."

"I'm smart – pretty only gets you so far," she said.

I stammered. She was looking for a man on a reality show, how smart could she be? Veronica read my face.

46

"It's okay. My dad already informed me this does not make me look smart," Veronica said.

"Sorry," I said.

She laughed. I love people who can laugh at themselves.

This opened an onslaught of joking about reality shows and our being on one. I didn't even stop to realize no cameraman bothered to interrupt us. Veronica pulled more personal information from me, talking straight into my microphone, than any of them ever could.

After a while, more contestants trickled into the back yard.

Sandra came out and sat by Veronica, but zeroed her cool girl eyes in on me. I grew awkward. She raved about Ethan and how she already felt close to him. She pretended not to notice when I almost tipped over on my metal chair sinking into the grass. She did imply several times I had an in with Julian.

Co-conspirators Erin and Serena came outside. They looked at me quite a bit but never came near enough to talk. Past that, I met many of the twenty women shooed outside after their chance to impress Ethan.

"How does Ethan remember all the contestants' names? I know I can't," I asked after an orange woman came by our table, but left after Sandra let her know her spray tan failed.

"I'm sure he's already learned everything, y'all. Those tests and our audition tapes could tell him how to steal our identities," Sandra pointed out.

"I knew I should've looked crazier in those psych evaluations," I said.

47

"You seem just the right amount of crazy to me," Sandra said.

"Don't turn your back on me," I said. She laughed.

"You're right about confusing the names," Sandra said. "I won this modeling contest. I didn't know who anyone was, but they all knew me."

"Yeah, that's exactly what happened to me at this reception I went to after I got my scholarship to Harvard," I countered. Wait, what? Uh, was I competing with her? Veronica gave me a shy but clearly amused smile. I grimaced.

"I'll bet that was a cool reception – I'd like to go to Harvard," Veronica said, lifting her eyes to taunt me. Who was the reality show star now? I laughed, if I could laugh at everyone else, I'd laugh at myself.

"Well I...," Sandra went on and on about being on the cover of a magazine I'd never heard of.

My mind wandered back to the reception at Harvard.

My father's name had been on everyone's lips. In fact, everywhere I went my father's name rang through conversations. So much potential – so much expectation put on my shoulders. Then I started dating Gordon. People called us a power couple. They predicted for us all the glory of well-bred racehorses heading into the Triple Crown.

That died when Gordon did.

Only whispers of my wasted talent followed me onto the reality show about resilient women. I sat with Veronica, a real triumphant person, knowing I couldn't even look my mother in the eyes. These women didn't smell the nasty stench

48

of disappointment I inspired among my father's circles. They never heard whispers of the tragic losses I never got over.

Veronica lightly tapped her foot against mine by accident. I smiled and waved off her apology. Veronica and Sandra didn't know anything about me. They wanted to talk to the funny redhead keeping things light. I liked being this version of myself.

"Sandra, would you like us to call you Miss Georgia," I said interrupting her tirade.

"Your Majesty would be fine," she said.

CHAPTER FIVE

As the sun began to shift to the other side of the sky, Ethan finally stepped out on the terrace, across the lawn from our little group. The fluttering around him became something like the flocking of seagulls to a French fry. Quite a few seagulls forgot to share some important morsel during their interview.

Veronica began to grow nervous again. Ethan glanced at us every time the contestants circling him shifted to create a gap.

"Will you stand up and walk over there with me?" Veronica said pointing to a secluded area of the lawn where she could hide, "We've been sitting here for over an hour. I'm so bloated from all the cheese that waiter kept stuffin' down me. I don't want to be sitting down when I talk to Ethan."

49

"Sure," I agreed, standing up and waving to Sandra who was telling another contestant all about her magazine cover. Cheap buttery cracker crumbs tumbled off the silk skirt of my dress. I bit my lip when I saw the obnoxious dots of grease in my lap. I wasn't sure I could get away with blaming that one on the designer, so I held Addie's very expensive handbag over it.

"I wonder if they meant for us to use the grass as a napkin," I said.

"Right. I don't think consideration is the main goal here," Veronica said. We headed for the textured cement path. It flowed through the emerald green grass like a little creek, rippling its way down toward the ocean. Once on the path, we lingered in the privacy of a tall shrub while Veronica adjusted her dress.

Ethan turned the corner quickly like he was running away and almost ran into me.

"Whoa, there," I said putting my hands out to stop him. He grabbed around my waist to keep from tripping over me. I started to breathe heavily and I couldn't look away from his eyes.

"Okay, last two ladies of the afternoon," the cameraman said walking around the shrub. He was talking to whoever followed Ethan because I heard a few disappointed moans, but no one followed him around the shrub.

"Ladies if you'll put all your personal items out of the camera's sightline."

He eyed my handbag and wrap. I set my handbag next to the shrub and hooked my wrap over an obliging low-lying branch. I self-consciously clamped my arm to my side, hiding the torn place on the dress. I couldn't find any way to hide the grease stains dotting the imported Laos silk.

A woman soon showed up to primp us while the cameraman worked setting up lights. Then he sat us on the bench. Ethan stood over us. That looked awkward. He stood us back up. After pushing us into the bush to find his scene, the cameraman instructed us to look natural.

"Yeah, right," I said. Ethan smiled and nodded in agreement with me.

"Whenever you're ready," he said, uninspired by my humor.

"Now, you're Caroline," Ethan said turning to us, "and you're Vic.... Tur... um... Veronica? Right?"

Veronica looked from Ethan to the camera, frightened.

"Call me Carrie," I said, "only my mom calls me Caroline when I'm in trouble. She called me Caroline when she found out I was coming on this show."

"Yep, my mom called me Ethaline when she found out," Ethan said. I laughed in a stiff manner.

I liked the look of Ethan. I sensed he would appreciate someone like Veronica. Matchmaking wasn't so different from head hunting – it was like getting her a job interview.

Veronica told Ethan in an extremely jumpy manner about her grandparents, who immigrated from Hungry. Her grandfather never learned to speak English and only had a fourth-grade education. He worked in a factory his entire life. Her Grandmother was eight when she immigrated. She started a pantry to feed immigrants with the money she earned doing laundry and other odd jobs. Veronica grew up in extreme poverty, but her whole life her family gave whatever little they could to those who were worse off. She pulled good grades and won a scholarship to college. She works as a computer analyst. She helps run her grandmother's pantry that is now a community outreach program.

Ethan was impressed. I could see his dismissal of her shifting to respect. Her explanation of living in poverty didn't fit with her engineer father knowing architects, but I didn't say anything.

Veronica abruptly stopped talking and looked at me. Okay, my turn.

"Where are you from, Ethan?" I said filling the gap.

"Boston," Ethan answered confused. I was struck and didn't notice the look they gave me. I lost track of everything. My mind flew to Gordon Shaw of the Boston Shaw's. Veronica could tell I'd slipped away. Covering for me she delivered the question I told her to prepare:

"I love Boston. I attended a conference there. It was great – I love that bridge they light up. Do you see it often?" Veronica said this with a break in her sentences – like a child learning to read.

She'd done well. Her question applied perfectly. My throat lodged up. Gordon first kissed me on Bunker Hill overlooking the bridge Veronica mentioned. Change the subject, I ordered. Ethan was saying:

"...sometimes when I jog up –"

"Ethan, what is it that you do for a living?"

Both Veronica and Ethan looked at me puzzled. I realized this information was on his bio. In fact, I knew what he did before he announced he lived in Boston. Everything rational flew out of my head. I didn't care. I nodded at him impatiently. If he said he was an attorney, I made a silent resolve to walk away.

"I'm a pediatrician," Ethan finally said. He looked entertained like he had to figure me out, but he shifted toward me like I was safe because of my defiance.

"You didn't go to medical school in Boston," Veronica said more naturally this time like it just occurred to her. "How'd you wind up there?"

"I visited once," he said. He left something out. I could see it on his face. He continued, "Some of the most advanced pediatric research in the world happens there. I decided to stay."

"That's smart to stay on top of your field like that," I said. Ethan smiled at the compliment.

"What do you ladies do for fun?" Ethan asked.

"I love to read…ah, I swim…and, oh, I scuba dive," Veronica said, after an uncomfortable pause that I refused to talk through.

While she spoke, Ethan gave me a hard look to stop me from acting like a job coach for the chronically unemployed. Unfortunately, that could describe my behavior toward Veronica more often than not.

"And you, Carrie?"

"I run a lot and work a lot," I said.

"I love to run," Ethan said.

"Oh… uh…What do you read?" I asked, turning to Veronica.

"Science fiction," Veronica said, "What do you read, Carrie?"

Oy vey, Ethan, Veronica. You are supposed to ask Ethan.

"I stick to the classics mostly," I said. "I grew up outside of Hartford, and classic literature was kind of shoved down my throat. Our family has a bit of an edge on Nathaniel Hawthorne –"

"I love Kipling's '*Captains Courageous*. Have you ever read it?" Ethan asked.

I nodded, trying not to grin at Ethan, who looked like a young boy on a life-altering adventure of his own.

"Well, Miss Carnegie," Ethan said. "Do you have a deeper appreciation for the book by taking a moment out of your society living to see how the other half live?"

I raised my eyebrows looking from the mansion to the ocean.

"What other half – the architecturally impaired perhaps?"

"Carrie's a design snob, but her dad was a really famous architect so she's allowed," Veronica teased as she had when we were alone. I smiled at her perfect rejoinder. Ethan laughed. Veronica was in.

My work was done. I moved into a get-myself-off-the-show mentality.

I'd have to blow Ethan off somehow. I winked at Veronica and looked over at the waiter wandering around with his tray. I sprinted around the camera to my handbag.

"Oh look! Aged brie! It's so tasty. Excuse me," I said leaving them alone.

I couldn't see Ethan's face, but I could hear disappointment in his voice when he said,

"Bye, then."

To my frustration, Ethan and Veronica only talked for a few moments beyond this. Then Ethan and the cameraman walked around the shrub and up the path. Ethan watched me as he walked. He headed toward me on the terrace where I'd found refuge.

I turned from him trying to find something to look at. Self-consciously I knew Ethan would walk by me. I refused to turn and check to see where he was. Instead, I looked at the knobs on the grill I stood near.

"Do not to make eye contact," I repeated. His eyes held something for me. It was hard not to look at them just out of curiosity. I found amazing eyes extremely attractive. Hadn't I admitted my inclination toward exquisite eyes when Adam taped my audition for the show? I shrugged it off. A lot of women must find Ethan's eyes amazing.

I didn't notice Ethan stop right next to me. I turned. Unprepared for him to be so close, I reared backward.

"Whoa, you okay?" he asked, real concern in his eyes. He put his hand on my shoulder that was bare but for its covering of lace. I couldn't think of anything funny to say. Every fiber of my being went into feeling where his long fingers rubbed oddly against my skin under the lace. I blushed, embarrassed, as his eyes held mine.

I looked away but had to look back. But then I looked away again. He dropped his hand to my arm – touching me barely brushing my skin – as if to stop me from retreating. At his touch, my body gave off a thrilling, confusing jolt like soaring on a swing when it goes too high and jerks weightless.

"You're a hard one to read, Carrie," Ethan said. I forced my darting eyes to look up at him, but they kept shifting to his hand touching my skin.

"Nah, I'm an open book."

"Okay. I saw your face when I mentioned Boston. You hate Boston," Ethan said.

What could I say? I'd been so free living in Cambridge. Even with people watching every move I made, I'd been free. Since Gordon died, Boston changed. Now I only visited to put a rose on his grave with his broken-hearted mother. Ethan watched me so I stammered out:

"You caught me off guard. I have a rocky relationship with Boston. I graduated from Harvard a year ago, but well, my fiancé died there...anyway. I didn't realize you were from there."

"Did you leave because you couldn't be there anymore? Too many memories?" Ethan asked, folding his arms in his black tux. He was relaxed and confident off camera. His features were devastating, unnerving when he relaxed. I never dated boys who were prettier than me.

"I wanted to um... a job opportunity in New York really," I said rubbing the spot where his hand had been.

"I'm confused. Your bio says you're from Hartford. You said New York and you spent the years before New York in Cambridge. So where do you feel you're from?"

"I lived just outside Hartford probably the longest, but living in New York feels right. Well, except public transit. I drive my car everywhere, and pay too much for my apartment because it has parking."

"I like having a car; it's freedom in a way," he said.

56

"Yeah," I said, "I get teased for it. Anyway, I don't really know..."

I noticed the host, Lance a few feet away. He looked reluctant to interrupt. I smiled, encouraging him, instead of stammering on any further.

"Ethan, I'm sorry," Lance said. "We need to get on with the next segment. The show starts in twenty-five minutes."

"'Kay," Ethan said but his stance stiffened and he leaned into me. A little tremor ran through his body.

"You got this," I whispered bumping shoulders with him. He searched my eyes for confirmation.

"Thanks, Carrie," he said.

We all jumped a little as a table scraped the terrace floor. The Vaudeville star leaned forward to set her plate on a flimsy aluminum table.

"Opsy," she said still leaning against the table. Her spaghetti straps worked so hard.

When no one said anything, she said:

"These strawberries are to die for."

Then without looking away from Ethan the woman picked up a strawberry and preceded to French kiss it while we all watched. Seriously, we could not look away.

"Ethan, won't you escort me in the house?" she asked after she let the strawberry down easy.

"Oh, uh," Ethan looked back at me like I could save him. I still had my head cocked staring in disbelief at the Vaudeville star. I quickly straightened it. Ethan caught my eye and raised his eyebrows with an invitation to laugh. The sides of my mouth curved up slightly before I resisted. I pulled my glance away and waved to Veronica climbing the stairs to the terrace.

"Yah, sure Tess. I'd be happy to," Ethan said. He didn't move away from me, but Tess didn't seem embarrassed to have to shuffle across the terrace toward us.

"I guess I'll see you inside, Carrie?"

"For sure," I said, then whispered, "Be careful. That strawberry is never coming back."

I heard him snort as I pushed around him. Veronica waited politely on the steps for us pass. I took Veronica's arm, snagging my silk dress on the brick terrace wall. I pulled her up, forcing Ethan and the Vaudeville star into a deformed line behind us. I could feel his stare hot on my back.

CHAPTER SIX

Julian joined us before the live segment began. He said little. His wavy silver hair was pulled back into a ponytail. Julian's bearded face seemed to bother him as he absent mindedly tugged at his whiskers, like he could pull them off. His large grainy eyes searched me far more often than they did the other contestants. He gave me the creeps.

Lance instructed us with more tedious rules. Like kindergarteners at a choir concert, we were placed on risers. We were placed in order of height, so I should have been on the bottom riser. I managed to slip up a row to stand by Veronica.

Julian pretended not to notice. The gift of being a Carnegie, or perhaps his penetrating eyes, saw how much Veronica needed me. To be honest I did it because I dreaded being on the front row.

Finally, after instructing the cameramen on what angles he needed, Julian handed Ethan a binder and left.

"Doesn't he need to be here?" I asked Lance.

"Nah, he creates the show from his studio," he answered.

I tried not think about what that meant.

Next, Lance did takes into the camera. It sounded like he was talking to us, but we just sat still in the background. Finally, he turned and the camera scanned us while he did his intro.

"Contestants – Ethan – it's time! Of the twenty women here, only half can stay. Ethan, will you please call the ten ladies, based on first impressions, you feel are the most resilient. You will offer them a key to the safety deposit box filled with one million dollars. The lady can accept the key and be in the running for the title of *The Whole Package.* Or the lady may refuse the key and leave the show."

Ethan picked up the first key and turned it over in his hand.

"Cut," Lance called. "You have to look perplexed, like this."

Lance showed him a few facial expressions that felt a little too Roger Rabbit.

"Are you sure?" Ethan asked.

"It'll look fine on camera," Lance said.

Ethan looked embarrassed to use such a dramatic soap opera tension. He glanced at me of all people, looking for reassurance. I grinned so he knew I found it hilarious. He smiled back, and I earned a few glares from the other contestants.

Lance did his intro again. Ethan tried his best to take enough time. He looked at us, then looked at the key, then looked back at us. I gave him big eyes and a slight, "let's move this along, son," head nod. He gave me half a smile.

All of the ladies, determined to be seen, smiled at Ethan, trying to catch his eye, except Veronica who shyly looked down.

"This has been hard," Ethan said.

"Oh, come on," I whispered from behind Veronica's shoulder. She grinned and looked up right as Ethan scanned us. Ethan gave her half a grin, but said:

"Sandra, will you take this key?"

With a cool girl swagger, moving her perfect blonde hair down her back like water out of a faucet, Sandra walked up to him. The lights caught the sparkles in her silver dress. She reached out and took the key. In a soft alluring southern accent, she said, "Of course."

She stepped to the chosen side. After more excruciating looks Ethan said:

"Veronica."

Veronica looked up, surprised. I caught the look on Lance's face out of the corner of my eye. He also looked surprised. I hid my smug satisfaction, but couldn't help being pleased with my efforts.

Veronica moved forward down the thick step-like
riser. She bowled her way through a few contestants anxious
to make it to Ethan before he changed his mind. She tripped a
little over the Persian rug Ethan stood on. Ethan came
forward and took her arm to steady her.

"Will you take this key?" he said.

"Yes, thank you." Her big, frightened eyes looked like
they might cry. Veronica stood too long looking at the key,
uncertain what to do next.

Ethan rubbed her arm in a comforting way as he led her
over the edge of the rug. She stood next to Sandra. Ethan
stepped back to his spot by the keys. Veronica still watched
the floor as if, the instant she looked away, it would sprout
tree roots and trip her.

Ethan picked up the next key, did his cartoon face for a
while, and then said:

"Tess."

The aggressive, Vaudeville-type woman with straight,
wheat-colored bangs cutting across her brow, came
forward. She walked with cool determination. I couldn't
mask my surprise at his choosing her, and I wondered what
she overcame. Or I wondered if it was more a matter of the
other ladies not overcoming.

"Will you accept this key?"

"Hopefully forever," Tess said pulling the key and his
hand up to her bosom. Ethan quickly pulled his hand away
and nodded.

Ethan picked up the next key rubbing it with
uncertainty. Lance said:

"Stay tuned, when we return Ethan will give out the final seven keys to the safety deposit box filled with one million dollars."

We were live with only a few minutes of broadcast delay, so we paused like we went to commercials. Ethan took a binder and flipped through it. He nodded at Lance and then handed him the binder. Lance welcomed everyone back. Ethan picked up the key, turned it over in his hand, and stammered a little like he couldn't decide who got to stay. The points system didn't start until the first competition. If this was based on first impressions, why the binder?

"Carrie," Ethan finally said.

It echoed in my head. Really? I hesitated, locking eyes with him like we were old friends coming to a mutual understanding. Shorter than most of the women, I became wedged between a sweater model with dark hair in a nectarine-colored gown, and the pillar closest to the door. Neither moved. Knowing the pillar was plastic painted to be marble, I was sorely tempted to push it over – I resisted. The woman finally realized everyone looked at her.

"Sorry," she said.

"I was more worried you were going to move than you weren't," I stage whispered. The contestants smiled and snickered a little. This broke up the tension for a moment. Then Lance told us to start that one over. Again, Ethan said:

"Carrie."

This time, the crowd parted for me perfectly. He stood before me too soon. I didn't know what to do.

"Will you accept this key," he asked drilling his eyes in mine.

What did I want?

For one real moment, I considered honestly. I dreaded going home to my self-made prison. Wrapped up in my near-widowed status, I didn't live any kind of a life beyond work. I wanted to stay and be the funny redhead keeping things light because real life ached heavily on my shoulders choking me.

I looked up as if a completely different person. Confidently meeting Ethan's pretty eyes, I started to play the game.

"Yes. I suppose I will. Thank you."

"No – thank you," Ethan said pretending to wipe his brow like I'd made him sweat it out. I laughed and reached out to take the key. He set his hand on mine too long –to prove that jolt in my stomach would come, but this time, it spread through my chest.

I swallowed, pulling my gaze from his, and walked over with the other contestants. I slipped in next to Veronica and gave her a side hug. Veronica edged even closer to me. She really did need me, and it was only a week.

Ethan scanned the other contestants as if he'd already forgotten me.

"Serena," he finally said. The pretty strawberry blonde nurse smiled excitedly at the camera as she walked to accept a key.

The rest of the elimination went along in this tired manner. Finally, ten contestants were cut from the show. Most of the eliminated contestants showed their

63

disappointment in the guarded polite way actors do when they lose an academy award.

Ethan eliminated the tawny-haired cold couch sitter, and to my surprise she sought me out.

"They say your dad was Arthur Carnegie," she asked.

"Yeah," I said, "you know my dad's work?"

"My brother is a huge fan. He wrote his thesis on him; it was actually published in *Places Journal*. It was a pretty big deal for his school."

I stared at her. I'd heard of her brother's article. It first came out after Gordon... or while I devoured my master's program with a determined frenzy. Adam kept trying to get me to read it, but it was too much for me to deal with at the time.

"I heard about that – Hall," I said.

"James Hall," she said.

"MIT, right?"

"Yeah," she said, "He feels the apartment complex your father built in SoHo is every bit as significant as Philip Johnson's contributions to modern architecture."

"I need to read it. When it first came out I ... well my fiancé...."

"Had just died," she said nodding. "I know."

"Yeah, but your brother, he kind of reminded the world of my dad. I really should have... anyway it's a small world," I said, "So, your brother's an architect now?"

"Well, after he graduated this company called LEDS offered him a ton of money to do computer aided drafting," she said.

"Really," I said. That piqued my interest. This was my golden ticket. My firm was looking to recruit a CADD from LEDS with a very specific skill set.

I fished and she openly expounded on his career. Educationally and experience wise, her brother fit my need perfectly, not to mention the notoriety that came with publishing a paper.

"They have pretty impressive non-compete contracts don't they," I asked.

"I don't know, he complains they have a contract for everything. His two-year contract with them expires in two months or so. I keep telling him to quit and he keeps telling me how much longer he's indentured to them," she said.

"I could help him. My firm has a legal team. You know if he's interested. I could contact him. Get him into a better situation," I said.

"He'd love to meet you, even just for your dad's sake," she said.

"Can I get his number?"

She paused. I held my breath. I needed this. This wouldn't be the first time I used my dad's name to get a foot up at work, with my mom's medical expenses overwhelming me, many times I'd swallowed the acidy lump it put in my throat. However, James Hall could very well be the most lucrative break for me. I could work directly with Vantose, a firm competing with LEDS. Just maybe I'd be able to earn enough money to cover my expenses and be comfortable. At the least, I would get a substantial bonus if I recruited James.

"Look, I'll give you his contact information, and tell him you're going to call on one condition."

"What's that?"

"Please, just wait the two months until his contract is up before you call."

"They'll want him to sign another contract before his –"

"He knows, but he's dodged extending his contract. His friend hasn't signed either. Neither gets the bonus, or a new project until they do. James figured he'll have to live on savings while he finds another job, but he won't look while he's supposed to be working there."

"I can help them both before they run out of work," I said.

"They're designing a subdivision together; it's like six months of work that has to be finished before their contracts end."

"That's perfect, I could –"

"He had a bad experience with his last recruiter," she cut me off. "I'll talk to him for you, but please give him the two months. Trust me, he'll call you. Sophie, my sister-in-law, is freaking out about being unemployed. But James does things on his timetable. You can't push him or he won't even talk to you."

"That's fine," I said nodding, hoping I came across as calm while the sweat trickled down my neck.

"All right," she said.

I pulled a pad of paper and a pen out of Addie's handbag. She even gave me his home address. James was mine, as long as I respected her boundary of two months. She reiterated a few times he'd dismiss me as a pushy salesman if I didn't.

"Hey, if he wants to talk sooner, here's my number," I said handing her one of my cards just in case. I wanted to ask

66

about his last recruiter, but just then Lance called to her. Alexis' bus was leaving.

"Thanks, good luck," she said and went to find her luggage. I may have followed her but decided it would make me look as desperate as I felt.

Now the real question was how to keep this from Adam for two months? Even Andrea would try to take over if she found out. I had to take the lead on this account. Something had to change. I was drowning under my financial burden. But then, they were in New York and I was in California on a reality show, competing for a million dollars.

I told myself several times I wasn't a reality star, but the freedom of it all stuck to my ribs. By the end of the night I convinced myself I wouldn't really compete, I'd just have a little vacation.

CHAPTER SEVEN

I hadn't slept well for years. After a short rest, I lay in bed listening to Veronica's soft snores. I couldn't force my body to relax. I crept down the stairs and opened the French doors as quietly as possible. In the identity-crisis garden, I inhaled the salty sea air mingled with magnolias. I bent down to re-tie my shoe and briefly stretch out my back still stiff from the day before.

"Which way did the host say Ethan's secret hideaway was?" I asked myself rubbing the bumps rising on my cold arm.

The previous evening after the elimination, we'd been instructed like children on a field trip – again. The host told us we could only visit Ethan's bungalow if he invited us. Tess cat-called. That's how I knew to avoid Ethan's private hideaway near the beach.

"He left last night by the little road out front, so I should be safe on the little path out back," I said to the gaudy dragon glaring at me.

Flecks of water hit my shins as I cut through the grass toward the cement path. The path moved down the gradual hill and curved away from the house. The grass was greener and better kept immediately around the Manor House. Everything else grew wild. The path I ran from the Manor House wound through what had once been part of a golf course gone to seed. I passed islands of tall weeds and dirty ponds, once sand traps, built in here and there.

68

After about a half a mile the path hit the old worn road that wound from the front of the manor. The road followed the cliffs overlooking the ocean in both directions.

I stopped, unsure which way to go. Finally, I turned and ran uphill, so I didn't end up back at the Manor House. I couldn't tell if I was running toward or away from Ethan's bungalow. If I saw it I'd back away quickly.

After a few feet in this direction, I lost sight of the ocean I'd been running to find. Carroty-colored poppy flowers fought with ivy to carpet the ground. The road wound back into a grove of wispy white oak trees. The branches reached for each other, intertwining to become a tunnel over the road hiding me from the world. The trunks of the trees bunched the branches together tethering them to the ground. The sweet scent of vanilla coccooned me into an unnamed safety. The beauty of the tree tunnel renewed me somehow.

The grove thinned out as the road curved back toward the ocean. A creek in search of the ocean cut through the grove. I slowed on an old wooden bridge that lifted me over the creek. Just off the bridge, a sign boasted a scenic overlook two miles down the road, and I knew how far I'd be running.

Even though I lost sight of the ocean, I liked to listen to the distant pounding of the waves against the shore. It reminded me of something, but I couldn't remember what.

As I ran, my thick ponytail pounded my back past the tips of my shoulder blades. Sometimes, I surmised, if a fly landed on my back, I'd be able to smack it off with my ponytail, like a horse did. My mind was thus occupied when out of nowhere I heard:

"Hey, Carrie!"

It was Ethan. I kept running. My heart pounded. I pretended I hadn't heard him and sped up. Maybe I could out run him? It wasn't a great plan. I had no clue where I was going. Ethan ran faster than me. He caught up to me before I concocted an alternate game plan.

"Hey," Ethan wheezed out with a cocky grin. I used a head nod and lifted eyes as a greeting and kept running. I slowed, unable to keep up the pace.

"You looking for me?" Ethan said keeping pace with me.

"No, just out for a jog," I said trying to catch my breath.

"Yeah, full out sprint more like," Ethan said.

"Uh...."

"It's okay, you told me you like to run last night, remember?" Ethan asked.

"I'm surprised you remember – last night's kind of a blur," I said, winded and having to slow further.

"For me too,"

"I thought you were by the beach," I said, "I ran the cliffs so I wouldn't—so I wouldn't get in your way."

"It's okay, really. This road actually leads to my bungalow in the other direction. I think they did say it's by the beach, didn't they?"

"Yes," I panted.

"Well, it's only a thirty-foot drop straight down; everything's cliffs here," Ethan said.

"Um hum."

"Anyway, if you follow the cliffs in the other direction you'll find it. You'd be welcome anytime you want to drop in."

"Uh…" At a shift in the road, I turned and started to jog away from him quickly.

"I'm not…" Ethan panted catching up to me. "I didn't mean that in a perverted kind of way… I have an Xbox… you'd be welcome to come and play."

He shrugged trying to look innocent like he wasn't really inviting me down to his bungalow. I lifted my eyebrows and gave him a "yeah, right" look.

"I already told them this is going to be a mellower season then in the past."

"Right," I laughed.

"Come on, even a few of the make-up ladies have told me I'm not the usual flavor of Man Candy."

"They called you Man Candy to your face?"

"Oh, that's nothing. I'll try to say something and Julian shushes me – seriously he shushes me. I'm not supposed to speak, just look pretty," he said.

"At least you didn't have to lose the extra ten pounds the camera gives you before the show even started."

"I had to gain twenty pounds of muscle."

"Twenty pounds?" I asked.

"Yep, normally I'm too scrawny."

"You're fine," I said. He flushed.

"Anyway, I haven't really talked to anyone since I got here. Everyone just walks around me like I'm…"

"Λ prop," I asked.

"Yes. Is that how you feel?" he said.

"Well… I think the production crew sees us that way," I said.

71

"Yesterday you and Veronica are the only ones who asked me anything about myself."

"Seriously?"

"I don't even know why they chose me," Ethan said.

"I'm not feeling sorry for you. I mean, seriously, poor you here to judge all these women," I said.

"I don't think … I mean it's flattering, but …."

Ethan looked overwhelmed.

"I don't understand," I said, "How'd you get here then?"

"My office manager, Beth, nominated me. She's about to retire. She's kind of the mother hen type. She wanted to make sure I'm taken care of when she leaves. And somehow her first thought is 'Hey, why not reality TV?'"

"Nice," I said nodding.

"At first, I told her no way. Then after a month of pleading and her assuring me there's no real pressure for the contestants to date on the show –"

"Yeah, right."

"I know, but she's so persuasive. She almost started crying when she told me about some of her favorite contestants."

"Yeah, my little sister did that, too," I said.

"I'd love to see the look on Beth's face if she saw Julian shush me."

"She'd be upset?"

"That's an understatement. When I gave in and let her make a tape of me, she acted like she was saving me. She'd never believe what this really is."

"Well, you're stuck now," I said.

"It all happened so fast. I still can't believe they chose me."

"Whatever…" I was about to say I could see perfectly why he was chosen but realized that may not be the wisest way to get out of this predicament. I finished with, "You're in private practice then?"

Ethan grabbed my hand and stopped jogging. I jerked to a stop, looking around for a dog on a rampage, or at least an angry bee.

"What? What's the matter?" I said. He turned on me, examining my face.

"How did you get here?" he asked.

"Oh…" Right, I was here too.

"You lost a bet, didn't you?" Ethan said not letting me look away. I couldn't breathe. How did he figure that out? Ethan had his hand on my shoulder and the weight of it pulled me toward him somehow while he waited for an answer.

"You're strange," I said. "You're stuck here with all these women vying for your attention. You've already decided we're devious."

"Oh, I know you're all devious," Ethan said moving both his hands to my waist forcing me to look up at him. His silver eyes flashed with mischief. We were playing chicken. My stomach flopped. My pulse rushed.

His hands moved toward my rib cage making me more aware of my midsection than I'd ever been. If I were really trying to win his heart or no, it was a million dollars … right? Either way, this opportunity would be ideal for me. Instinctively, I knew he was messing with me.

I stopped squirming and looked at Ethan's shoulder uncomfortably. For a moment, I saw myself laying my head

73

on it. My head would fit perfectly in his strong-arm joint. I shook my head to remove the image. Ethan took this to mean I was uncomfortable, so he let go of me and took a step back. I took a deep breath trying to slow my pulse rate.

"I'm sorry. I didn't know it'd be like this. You're great, and all these women… well, they're a lot more substance than I thought they'd be. I don't want to offend you. Really, my co-worker, Adam, wouldn't let up making this bet about an account at work. The loser had to see who could get the furthest on a reality TV show. Well, I'm the loser," I said.

"I'm the man candy," Ethan said.

"I didn't mean to make you feel like that."

"You didn't. You making fun of everything yesterday helped me. Seriously, some of those women's lives were so tragic and yet inspiring. I'm the jerk asking them to leave. You being funny reminded me it's all just a show; they have real lives to go home to."

"That has to be a lot of pressure, though," I said refocusing him on himself.

"Yeah, so what bet did you lose?" he said redirecting me.

"It was stupid. Adam bet me he could fill a position before I did. Whoever's candidate was chosen for the job won and got a bonus."

"Winning a bonus wasn't enough?"

"I don't know. It was a huge bonus, which is what started the bet in the first place. Then somehow a reality show came into play. Looking back, I'm not even sure how. When it came down to it, my candidate fell through and the company hired his. I'm not even sure how that happened, my candidate was solid. Adam's didn't seem as qualified."

"Adam, is he your boyfriend?"

"That's what you got from us competing for a bonus?"

"You never know," he said.

"He's my co-worker, and our company has a strict fraternization policy, as in 'Don't do it,'" I said.

"Probably smart," he said.

"Right, not to mention Adam practically bullied me into coming onto *The Whole Package*; I'm still pretty pissed at him. Anyway, he got this account away from me. Then our boss, Karl thought it was funny and said if I mention my firm he'll pay me."

"The bet was you have to show up on a reality show?"

"The bet is I have to try to win a reality show."

"Trying, is that what you'd call your performance?"

"I didn't know what to do. I've never seen this show, sorry."

"I'm not offended," Ethan said. "I didn't get what you're doing here. Losing a bet was the only thing that made sense. You're confident, you know, strong, but you aren't a leech after my blood."

"Was it that bad?"

"Yeah," he said grinning at me.

"Well, thanks for understanding," I said turning away from his warmth, I started jogging again. When he caught up to me I said:

"I guess your first elimination is going to be a pretty easy one? That could be nice huh?"

"Oh, you aren't getting off that easily."

"What?"

"You have to take the key if I offer it?"

I stopped. He stopped. I stammered. I looked at Ethan in complete alarm.

"The way I see it, you're the only guarantee I have. I know you'll take the key every time."

He started running again.

"You aren't serious?" I said, panting after him.

"Yes, I am," Ethan said. "You can be my spy. Maybe together we can really figure out who deserves the million dollars. This'll be fun."

I grabbed his arm and stopped him from running.

"I won't spy on those women for you." Then with the insight that sometimes comes from speaking the truth, I added, "Except to say this one thing. Don't hurt Veronica. She's delicate."

"I don't hurt women," Ethan said.

"You know what I mean."

"Secondly," Ethan said as if uninterrupted, "I was kidding. It's against the rules for me to talk to one contestant about another. Julian's really exacting about the rules. Run with me in the mornings; joke around so I remember this is all a game. I won't ask you about them. Isn't that gentlemanly of me?"

"You know you're on a reality show, right?" I said.

"You're joking about it won't let me forget," he said.

"Right and all you want from me is a nudge in the right direction."

"All joking aside, you spying for me would be a breach of both our contracts. Both Julian and Lance are intense about the contract I signed." Ethan blanched a little. "We'd both be sued if Julian found out; it'd be pretty sleaze-bag of me, anyway."

"Yeah, it would," I said. We were quiet for a few minutes. Then Ethan said;

"Carrie if you really want to go I'll eliminate you."

"Good –"

"But," Ethan said, "You know that wouldn't be honest, either."

"How do you figure?" I asked, trying to read Ethan. I sensed some agenda underlying his trying to be playful. We took a steep hill at a jog and couldn't talk for a minute. All the while, I wondered by what far stretch my leaving the show wouldn't be honest. Ethan seemed to be concocting the best argument for his flimsy rebuttal. Winded at the top of the hill, Ethan said;

"Could you honestly say you did your best to fulfill the bet?"

"I'd sleep like a baby in my own bed," I said, also winded but trotting forward along the cliff.

"But since you're getting paid anyway," Ethan said, "you could stay for a few eliminations. That'd teach your boss to give paid leaves for losing bets –"

"Oh, he only said three days, but I have vacation saved up. I'm sure any more time is coming out of my vacation days," I said. I realized too late that sounded like encouragement.

"Seriously, please stay, I like you; you don't make me feel like a hunk of meat."

"Would beef jerky be considered the man candy of meat?"

"That's me – beef jerky. One of the contestants I eliminated last night kept asking me to make-out with her. She said just once and I'd know she was my soul mate."

"Did you?"

"No! But she promised I'd make it to third base like we were in junior high."

"Oh, was that the woman who bragged about being an actress? Because she wasn't even in her high school stage productions."

"How do you know that?"

"She said she was an actress. I wanted to know what she'd been in."

"You and Lance, he kept telling these cheesy jokes about her burrito commercial. He said something about beans and the house odor. I had to get rid of her so I didn't have to listen to him anymore."

"Lance is the host, right?"

"You've really never seen this show, have you?"

I shook my head in the negative.

"Yes, he's the host."

We were quiet again for a minute and I felt much more comfortable with Ethan. He didn't seem as intimidating when it came right down to it. The morning mist hitting my face kept me comfortably cool while I ran.

"Despite all the pressure on you, this is kinda nice right?"

"What," he asked and I could feel him examining me without even looking over.

"This has to be kind of like a vacation for you, being away from your practice. That's nice, right?"

"I'm bored out of my mind. There is so much down time. This morning I memorized a case study on childhood diabetes. It's lame."

"Childhood diabetes, I agree," I said.

Ethan looked taken back. I laughed – well wheezed with little breath behind it – to show him I understood what he meant. My laugh was contagious, and Ethan couldn't help laughing as well. A huge weight pulled off my shoulders seeing how little Ethan thought of *The Whole Package*. We became comrades, a secret society fighting the silliness together.

Then the opportunity opened up. The dragon grew inside me. Seeing Ethan talk so flippantly about the show I wondered if we couldn't just be friends. He wasn't using the show as an opportunity to take advantage of the contestants like I'd originally assumed.

With two months to kill before I could move on James Hall, I had nothing else to do. I had to somehow keep a secret from Andrea who had a way of weaseling things out of me. The idea of no cell phone reception became palatable.

In short, if Ethan had to play the game, if he had to give away a million dollars, why not give it to me?

I banished the thought, but somewhere in the subconscious of my mind, it became tangible. There is a moment in caged people's lives when they feel the glimmer of freedom. No matter how I dismissed it to myself, something I could not examine insisted fervently that I needed a vacation.

I slowed to a trot to catch my breath. Ethan slowed and turned to make sure I was okay. I flashed my glossy teeth at him.

"Okay, I'll stay as long as you don't expect me to swoon over you. I'll even stay away from joking about dairy products as long as you promise to laugh even if I'm not funny."

"Huh?"

"Lance – cheesy jokes," I said. Ethan smiled, rolling his eyes.

"That was funny; you were to slow to catch it."

"Um hum," Ethan said nodding to indicate he wouldn't courtesy laugh for me; I had to earn his amusement. And oh, how I did.

"Speaking of slow, can we pick up the pace?" Ethan asked.

"You go right ahead." I swept my arm indicating he could run faster. He didn't seem very motivated. He looked worn out. I felt sorry for him. We curved up the hill and the coastline opened up.

Above the crashing waves, a lone twisted ancient tree shaped by the whim of winds stood in the distance clinging to the side of the cliff. The tree's gnarled roots weaved in and out of the cliff. The tree looked so lonely fighting the elements to survive.

"That's a Cypress coming out of the side of the cliff," I said pointing.

"I don't see how it can survive like that," Ethan said.

"It can grow in really bad conditions as long as it's close to the ocean. It feeds off the moisture. It's fighting to stay alive, though."

"I'm suprised it's grown so big off the side of the cliff like that."

80

"I'm sure it didn't know it was on the edge of a cliff when it sprouted roots, time blew the sand away exposing them long after they already took hold."

"Oh, deep down I think it knew," he teased

"You would make that assumption," I countered.

"We'll have to watch it over the next couple weeks, just to decipher," he said.

"Two at the most," I answered, knowing he was asking me how long I'd give him. I would have said two months but didn't want to look greedy, like I expected him to give me the prize money.

"How often do you take a two-week vacation and look at this?" He grinned.

Waves rushed, curled then crashed against the deserted beach below. A misty sky rose from the ocean in the distance. The moist, salty air mingled with musky seaweed. The damp, almost rotting, scent of the ocean smelled like time itself.

After a while, I didn't bother with the small talk. Ethan didn't seem to mind the silence between us. I soaked in the peaceful accompaniment of the waves after the day and a half of noise while waiting for *The Whole Package* to start. We moved in time with the ocean's flow, watching the view from the cliffs as much as the road ahead. The ocean beat time for our feet to lift, extend and then reach back onto the pavement. There was something inside me that mended when our feet hit the pavement together. I usually ran alone.

All at once we took a sharp turn and the road opened to the scenic overlook boasted by the sign. In the distance, the cliffs curved into a cove and dissolved until only a rocky

81

peninsula stood out of the water. An abandoned lighthouse stood at the end of the peninsula. I'd grown up touring lighthouses.

Then I remembered why the ocean was so familiar. It reminded me of a blissful childhood – on a different beach. In a different life, I ran with my father down open descending sand into crashing waves. I grew up with the ocean always whispering near, an old friend guarding my happy childhood.

No, the lonely Cypress didn't know it grew so close to the cliff until the wind blew the dirt away exposing its roots. Only then had it started to grow inward, hanging on for dear life.

CHAPTER EIGHT

We turned around and ran back the way we came in the same silence. When we ran back through the tunnel of trees I left part of myself behind. The closer we ran to the Manor House, something closed over me, like a sandwich bag with all the air being sucked out of it.

I stayed with Ethan on the road instead of heading to the back of the Manor House on the golf course path.

"You want to meet me here tomorrow morning?" Ethan asked when we came to a path that led to his bungalow.

"For sure, but maybe we keep it between us," I asked.

"Yeah, I have a feeling all the other contestants may need a run if they find out," he said.

I waved, then followed the road a half a mile to the front of the Manor House. I stopped on the front walkway and followed what I could see of the road as it meandered through the valley. Eventually the lone road slipped through the hills and lead away from here. How did Julian find this little hamlet out in the middle of nowhere?

I stopped for a minute on the porch to stretch. I wondered what style I'd paint the valley in if I ever picked up a paint brush again. When I opened the door the smell of breakfast hit me. I was half starved. I trotted to the kitchen to investigate. A few of the other contestants, including Veronica, sat at a huge table in the center of the room.

"Hey Veronica, I didn't wake you this morning, did I?" I asked.

83

Her innocent green eyes turned to see who addressed her when she worked so hard not to be noticed. Tess, the Vaudeville star, who stood at the stove answered for her:

"Where've you been all morning?"

"I was out schmoozing Ethan with the smelly athletic look," I said lifting my arms to show her my wet pits.

"Eww," Tess said. She looked different this morning. Her natural features, saggy long sleeve tee shirt and scrub bottoms, made her look more like a person and less like an airbrushed centerfold.

"I didn't hear you," Veronica said after I looked at her waiting, "You were gone for a while. I've already finished my makeup."

"And you look so pretty," I said. She rolled her eyes.

"I meant you've been gone a long time. What time did you wake up?"

"Early," Then talking at Tess as she walked toward me with a plate of food, I said, "I'll be exhausted by tonight. If we're going out with Ethan, I'll leave him to you ladies."

Sandra sat in cool confidence next to Veronica. She ate a banana and read a romance novel with a bare-chested man on the front. She looked up through a curtain of her amazing shiny hair.

"I don't think that'd matter y'all. Tess has this magical power of dominating everything around."

"This is a million-dollar game," Tess sneered at Sandra.

"Let's at least try to get along," I said, "No man wants to see cat fighting; it's not attractive."

"You know so little about men," Tess said.

"Not the kind you're used to," I returned.

84

Tess fiddled with her plate and put a red fingernail to her voluptuous lips. I waited for her to throw the plate at me, or at least gouge one of her fingernails into my eye. That was my idea of reality show stars. To my wonder, she laughed, tolerably amused.

"Sorry, Sandra," Tess said, "It's hard not to get on edge in this situation."

"I totally understand y'all. I find deep breathing and a teensy shot of wine brandy does the trick," Sandra said.

"Uh, right," Tess said. "So, Carrie, right?"

"Yeah, Carrie," I said and plopped next to Veronica, my legs trying to recover from the extra exertion it took to run the rolling cliffs.

"Can I make you breakfast, eh?" Tess asked turning to me still holding the plate unsure what to do with it.

"Are you going to poison it?" I asked taken back by the Vaudeville star's kindness. Tess laughed and set the plate she was holding in front of Veronica. Veronica took a huge whiff ready to eat.

"I release my nervous energy by cookin'," Tess explained, "Eggs and toast then?"

"Sure, thanks," I said, eyeing Veronica's menu-topping meal.

"If you find yourself nervous at lunch time, I enjoy Chinese food. Mostly General Tso Chicken or Dim Sum," I added, to which Tess didn't respond.

"Do I have time for a quick shower?" I asked.

"You'd better, it's getting late and I can smell yah through the bacon." Tess returned to the stove, where she competently stirred a skillet.

85

While I tried to encourage my shaky legs to stand up, Serena, the nurse with new-copper-colored hair, azure eyes, and bright white teeth, walked in.

"Morning everyone, isn't it a beautiful day?" she asked, but then continued before anyone could reply. "I saw a bird chirping right outside my window, and I decided, 'This is going to be the best day ever.'"

"Wow, Serena, really?" Tess said.

"Of course," she said.

"I hope either you or I get cut next because that's too perky for me this early in the morning," Tess said. Though I suspected Serena finally took her Prozac, Tess didn't need to say it aloud. Veronica looked at Tess astonished. Tess glanced back at her and Veronica shifted her nervous eyes back to a book full of crossword puzzles she bought at the airport.

Serena appeared hurt, but in the last year, I'd seen that kind of hurt. I interviewed candidates three or four times a day. I started to notice when some of the candidates used the "feel sorry for me even though I'm not qualified" defense. It was a controlled, looking-for-pity kind of hurt that Serena expertly displayed. I would've been impressed if she didn't rub me the wrong way.

"Don't worry Serena," Sandra said breaking the awkward silence, "from what I've seen, y'all will be here long after she's gone."

Tess walked back over to the table to flick Sandra's hair more enthusiastically. Tess kept doing this because Sandra didn't notice she ate both banana and her luscious smoky blonde hair. This diminished her cool girl status a little because I found it disgusting as well.

86

"I'm not a morning person," Tess said. Then leaning over until Veronica looked at her uneasily she finished, "I see the look you're givin' me; I'll try harder to be a little less sarcastic. I'm not tryin' to be mean, eh."

In my retreat to the shower, I paused, reluctant to leave Veronica alone with Tess. Only it was unnessesary. Tess worried more about Veronica than she did about Sandra or Serena, both of whom could clearly take care of themselves. Wasn't that too perceptive for a Vaudeville star?

Veronica smiled a little tilting her head shyly onto her shoulder in an adorable way. How could I get her to look at Ethan like that? She didn't even want the million dollars; she wanted a boyfriend. Whether he admitted it or not, I couldn't see Ethan letting his paid employee send him on this show if he wasn't interested in finding a nice woman.

His ability to read people would be perfect for him to get to know the child-like Veronica. Both were self-made and gifted. They would get along. Would it be so bad if he fell for Veronica, and I won the million dollars?

Tess handed Sandra an over-easy egg, bacon, hash browns, sourdough toast and a glass of orange juice.

"May I have my egg scrambled?" I asked looking at the runny egg staring up at me.

"Sure. Do you want breakfast, Serena?" Tess asked as if her efforts weren't a big deal. Serena returned a smile that once housed braces. In a sweetly accusatory tone, she replied, "I sent in my dietary needs weeks ago. A protein shake is my breakfast. I won't be losing the gap between my thighs, thanks."

"I'm out," I called before Tess could respond. The promise of another spat inspired me to go shower. Erin came into the kitchen, tucking her now flat, short, pale blonde hair behind her ear.

"I don't know how my suitcase ended up in the kitchen," she said, "but I really need it up in my room. I can't keep running up and down the stairs everytime I need something."

"It could be good exercise, those ten pounds aren't going to keep themselves off," I said. Erin analyzed me for antennas. She looked to her best buddy, Serena for help. Serena avoided her glance. Instead, she looked over Veronica's shoulder to answer one of her crossword clues.

"Here, let me help you up the stairs with that," I said.

Erin looked back to Serena, who worked way too hard at Veronica's crossword and gave no indication she'd help tote the enormous suitcase up the stairs.

"Okay, thanks," she said.

By the time Erin and I lugged her suitcase up the stairs, my legs were burning. I repented of my genius idea. If I saw the makeshift bellhop again, he owed me.

I quickly showered. When I reappeared in the kitchen, Tess pulled my scrambled eggs from the stovetop. I wore a towel wrapped around my head to soak up my thick heavy hair. I put on faded jeans and a different Harvard tee-shirt. My grandmother bought me a million of them after I was accepted into Harvard. She called it a testament to my father. Financially unable to replenish my lounge clothes over suits for work, I looked way too proud of my education most of the time.

I tiptoed across the cold speckled tiled floor with bare feet, as if crossing hot coals. I sat next to Veronica. Tess set my plate in front of me, but waited, needing my reaction. I ate a bite and sighed with hammed up pleasure. She grinned, pleased.

"What did you put in these? Are you a chef?" I asked.

"Nah, financial adviser," Tess said with a dissatisfied tone in her voice that meant she may be ready for a change in jobs.

"You missed your calling," I said.

"Thanks," Tess said, "So what do you do for a living, Red?"

"I'm –" Serena started.

"I meant non-medicated Red. I've never seen so many redheads in my life," Tess interrupted. Serena huffed.

"Headhunter," I called after looking to Veronica who could also answer, but refused point blank. "I'm the youngest recruiter ever at Kimber & Stophers."

"Who are they?" asked Sandra.

"Best recruiting firm in New York, people who contract with her firm will become wealthy," Veronica said because she knew the answer. She heard enough of them the night before, as I spoke highly of my firm to Alexis, the cold couch sitter.

"So, you must be a good headhunter," Tess said.

"Ah, I do all right."

I rarely told people in conversation, even offhandedly, that I work for the top in the business. Most people even considering a new job fawned over me. I didn't like the vain ridiculous sensation that spread through me when I made a point out of it, like I needed the attention. In this case, I did it so Tess wouldn't be as quick to tell me what to do.

89

Tess did show me more deference when she sat next to me chatting about her financial planning company while we ate. Even so, I couldn't prevent an uncomfortable sensation from creeping over me. Especially considering I hated the constant grasping and shoving of corporate headhunting. What did that matter? I was good at it, and it paid the bills.

The more Tess talked, the more I decided I liked her, despite her Vaudeville qualities. Tess was domineering. The control she needed felt like her mask, but underneath it, she was straightforward and unpretentious. Her sarcasm amused me, though not in the refined way I appreciated most.

I preferred her to Serena's pretentiously perfect positivism. I wondered what she did with the Contestant Fourteen persona I'd spoken to in line the day before. It didn't make sense for her to pretend even when Ethan wasn't around.

I spent breakfast trying to talk to Tess. Tess would pause to take a bite and Sandra cut in, showing an overwhelming need to be the center of attention:

"Well, I'm a model, y'all."

"Oh, right. I'm sorry Tess. What were you saying about –"

"My daddy's a doctor. That's why I'll be so good for Ethan," Sandra insisted sounding like she had no doubt she'd win. She didn't even notice her conceit; she must always get whatever she wanted. Serena noticed, and cut in sounding affronted:

"I'm in the healthcare profession."

"At a nursing home," Sandra said trying not to laugh.

"I'm an RN –"

90

"That's great," Sandra said, but the tone of her voice said it wasn't.

"You never said how you got on the show, Sandra," I asked before they could squabble.

"I used to be bulimic," Sandra said. Then after taking a huge bite of the egg at the end of her toast, she said, "But my daddy helped me get healthy. He weighs me most mornings."

"You still live at home?" Serena cut in.

Sandra didn't answer. The way her thin wrists moved the food from her toast to her mouth again concerned me.

"Are you sure you can control it? Do you need a support group or anything?" I asked, looking to Tess and Veronica who also looked worried.

"Don't be silly. I'm all better now," Sandra said.

"I guess that's a good reason to be twenty-five and still living at home," Serena said.

"Right, well, we couldn't all be thrown into the foster care system when we were twelve," Sandra said.

"Oh, what happened?" Veronica asked.

"My parents died in a car wreck," Serena answered. "I became responsible for my little sister. We grew up in a group home. Now we live together in Albuquerque." Serena's tone suggested her story could beat any of ours.

Over the next few days, I would hear that same tone in many of the stories told in the Manor House. Everyone overcame, and most were certain what they overcame trumped what anyone else went through. With the exception of Veronica and Tess. Veronica only saw the gifts in life after growing up in the grips of poverty. Tess didn't seem inclined to expound on how she'd gotten into the Manor House. She was the exception.

Most of the women wanted to talk about all they'd been through as though they needed a group therapy session. It didn't take long for me to feel sorry for them, though, like me, they would never accept pity even while telling their stories. Something hardened and scrappy pulsed through us all. Perhaps I would call this resilience, defined as the ability to make it through Hell still standing.

The similarity among us went only that far.

The differences in us soon became apparent as well. The way we overcame rather than what we overcame linked people together. Some wounds healed better than others. After all, the scars from stitches marred the skin minimally compared to a gash covered only by insufficient Band-Aids.

Some women like Erin and Sandra had therapy and a family support system. Those without healthy advantages found other ways to cope. Serena collected things and people she may need later. She made sure everything was beneath her. A few of the women drizzled alcohol through their veins dulling everything.

The saddest few, like Tess, seemed to use overbearing sexuality as aggressively as an addict would heroin. She acted like the magic of a relationship would save her, and sex was the only asset she had to give. I observed this all analytically, from a distance, unwilling to engage, unless I could do so philosophically. After losing so many of them, I saw emotional connections as weakness.

Sitting at the table the first morning I didn't see the desperate compulsions our broken personalities used to calm nerves. Only over time the patterns would emerge, and, with so much opportunity to observe them, compulsions became obvious.

CHAPTER EIGHT

After I ate, Tess grabbed my plate and stood up to wash the dishes.

"Tess, I'll get those," I said. "You cooked. I'll clean."

"They are all yours, eh," Tess said. "I need to get my hair and makeup done anyway."

Tess left checking her watch to see how long she had before she would see Ethan again. I grabbed the plate Veronica pushed aside to focus on her crossword. There was no dishwasher. In the dishwasher's place sat a fully stocked wine cooler. It was always fully stocked, and, especially at first, well used.

As I finished the dishes, all the other contestants trickled out of the kitchen except Veronica. She closed her book and started to dry the dishes I placed in the strainer.

"We start taping today. You okay?" I asked.

"I think – "

Lance's voice shouted from the other room: "I need everyone to come down to the sitting room right now, please!" Veronica and I exchanged looks of interest. We walked to the elimination room.

The host and Ethan stood there. Ethan smiled at me. I suddenly became very aware I wore a wet towel in my hair. I pulled it out and started running my fingers through my wet hair a little too harshly. I pulled out a knotted chunk of hair my conditioner couldn't smooth.

94

I didn't know what to do with it. I nervously rolled the hair in my fingers as my wet hair soaked through my tee shirt. Ethan looked so put together, his bungalow must have been a lot closer to the path by the road than the Manor House.

Tess walked stately down the stairs with her hair and makeup done. When she neared the bottom of the staircase, she posed for a camera. A man came up to me and started attaching a microphone pack under my tee shirt. I turned and smacked his hands.

"Whoa," he said, handing me the strap like I should be fine with him reaching up my shirt if he wanted to. I pulled the microphone up under my shirt and clipped it near my mouth while he kept telling me to readjust it.

"We need you to keep your microphone on at all times. We'll have cameramen wandering around interviewing you. Before you come down in the morning, put it on. Wear it as discreetly as possible. Get used to it. It's your new best friend, one you are contractually obligated to be close to," Lance instructed. We all fidgeted to adjust our microphones. "There will be recharging portals in your rooms with a fresh battery pack on it at all times, so no excuses."

Here he looked at me. I blinked innocently back. He laughed a little then continued:

"Taping schedules will be posted daily in the design room. We are on a tight deadline. Wake up early enough to eat breakfast and exercise – you have to keep off the ten pounds you lost to get here. By eight-thirty you need to be here in the common area with your microphone on."

We all looked at him exhausted with the same tired instructions he kept giving.

"Are you ready?" Lance said to a few cameramen setting up around the room. One man grimaced. Lance shrugged. I could tell I missed something, but I couldn't think what.

"Okay, we have our first challenge this morning. After which, you'll meet your designers."

"Yes," Serena said.

Even Lance squinted, disbelieving her sincerity.

"Just act naturally," he said then nodded at the cameraman, "Let's go again."

"Being *The Whole Package* means looking out for other people," Lance said. "These ten designers are all top-of-the-class graduates with their careers hanging in the balance. How far you get in the elimination process can launch their careers."

"We wear their designs on the show?" I asked.

"Yes. The longer you stay on the show determines how many original designs your designer creates for you. The winning designer usually gets the most exposure. Last summer's designer is now with Sears so how well you do can launch their career," Lance said. He looked at me intently so I understood some artist's fate was in my hands. That's all I needed, another person depending on me.

"But, before you meet them, we will have our first challenge. Go put on tennis shoes. The bus leaves in exactly ten minutes," Lance announced.

At this, all the contestants made a mad dash for the stairs, a clot of beautiful bodies. The urgency pulsed through me too, but I stopped myself from reacting. Instead, I smiled at Ethan

with big eyes. He coughed a little. I could sense his
amusement. I merged into the back of the line, swinging my
towel like I had all the time in the world.

That moment marked the first noticeable change in
me. I'd lived for years cantering like a whipped pony,
stopping and starting whenever I was supposed to. Showing
Ethan I wouldn't canter, trying to prove I was unconcerned,
changed me. I wondered what would happen if I were not on
the bus in ten minutes. Wasn't I on vacation?

I thought of a few interesting alternatives to getting on
the bus. The most pleasant included having the whole mutt of
a house to myself and taking a dip in the pool. The way Julian
got so worked up about everything infected the personalities
of everyone who worked for him. I doubted I'd get away with
it. Most likely the bus driver would lean on his horn until I
sauntered out the door – I would saunter, not canter.

Why did one person get to rush everyone else until they
looked almost crazy? Julian never looked rushed. Everyone
around him certainly did.

When I finally made it to the room with a bed on each
side that Veronica and I shared, I blow-dried my hair at the
vanity. Then I sat on my bed in a relaxed manner to put on my
shoes. Veronica bounced a little waiting for me.

"I'll save you a place on the bus," Veronica finally said,
cantering out the door nervously as I pulled at my laces.

I shoved my foot back into my sweaty shoe. Then I
grabbed a few elastics and a brush. When I walked down the
stairs brushing through my hair, Lance hurried me. I saw him
clutching his ear. Not Lance, but Julian hurried me. I smiled at
Lance, he smiled back. He didn't care if I delayed the bus a

couple minutes to have dry hair. It wasn't even eight-thirty, our proclaimed start time.

I climbed onto the charter bus. I patted George on the arm as I passed the driver's seat, and he grinned at me. I couldn't understand the hurry – I was on vacation. I sat in the second row next to Veronica and knocked knees with her as I scooted in. Veronica smiled at me nervously.

"Aren't we supposed to show them what we're like in our daily lives?" I asked.

"I don't know," Veronica said.

I noticed Veronica wore a tan button-up blouse. The dull color brought the red out in her hair and made her eyes look like bright emeralds.

"You look so pretty, Veronica," I said. Veronica ticked her head a few times in the negative which didn't make sense to me.

"What's happening?" I asked.

Serena's heart-shaped face answered from across the aisle:

"Haven't you seen this show before?"

"Ahh…"

"This is one of the challenges," Tess cut in so Serena couldn't toy with me, "Two women will be deemed in the running for the title of *The Whole Package*. They get extra points and time to impress Ethan. At least that's how it worked on past shows."

"We'll most likely do something active y'all," Sandra cut in, holding up her tennis shoes in an obvious way. I opened my mouth to say something, but she just kept talking. Veronica said aside to me:

98

"Do you want me to French-braid your hair, Carrie?"

"Please, in fact, can you do one down each side?" I said. Veronica nodded. I leaned into the aisle and, cutting Sandra off, said loudly for the appreciation of anyone who cared to listen, "What happened to the limo? This bus is kind of a sad trade-up. Does anyone else feel like we're on a prison transfer?"

"Oh, you would know, wouldn't, ya, Red," Tess said.

Appreciating Tess's sarcasm, I laughed.

Later, when the episode aired, it showed Serena gasping. The gasp originally occurred on our way home when Serena pretended to be offended at something Tess said to her. Through Julian's own creative editing, Tess looked rude and Serena appalled.

He didn't show my reaction because I laughed, both times. Thankfully I didn't know any of this at the time. Though if I had I wouldn't have encouraged Tess's sarcasm with my laughter—she drank it up.

In all fairness, I could never have imagined Julian's artistic liberties in creating drama.

CHAPTER NINE

The bus dropped us off in a parking lot that had been blocked off. Beach goers ranged from curious to put out that they had to park out on Highway One and carry their surfboards to the ocean. We helped unpack gear. Then tents were set up and we changed into swimsuits. Not the swimsuits we brought with us, no. These were provided.

We all wore different kinds of swimsuits with shorts over them, and our own tennis shoes. Apparently, when we answered questionnaires about what we liked to wear, Tess must have put down a shoe-string bikini. Thankfully, in my amusement, I said I only wore a racing unitard. I was put in a one-piece Speedo.

We were placed in teams of five. Lance evenly spaced us around the playing court while the camera captured shots of us from different angles. Then Lance explained into the camera,

"This is the first challenge. It's a test of the women's sportsmanship and working as a team. The last two women on the winning team will win our first cache of ten points each and an evening out to impress Ethan."

Lance shifted and found another angle as if he talked to us and not the camera. Then he said:

"Remember, if you catch the ball, you can pull someone back into the game. This isn't just about who can play competently, but who you do or do not want spending extra time with Ethan. Plus, there's a twist...."

"And he's going to pause," I whispered to Veronica.

"The last girl standing wins," Lance said while his expressive face curved in anticipation.

"Drum roll please," I said.

Veronica giggled on accident but bit her lip when Ethan looked over at her. He glanced at me with a question. I nodded for him not to worry about it. He mouthed the word "later," to let me know I would be expected to share my aside later. Lance finished with:

"Ten thousand dollars!"

Serena cheered for the camera. The camera panned over to Sandra, who took a wide-legged stance. She'd gotten serious. Tess pulled at her bikini trying to tighten it. I suppose I did feel the ruby-eyed dragon stir within me. One day, one game... winning a game of dodgeball couldn't be construed as embarrassing or even prostituting myself – could it?

"Remember," Lance said as we all started. "The two women who win will debut their designer's fashions before anyone else."

Continuing a long tradition of public humiliation, Lance pulled out a net bag with three brick-red dodge balls in it.

"Give me a minute," one of the stagehands called out. "The cameras aren't transmitting." Lance nodded. He handed Ethan a binder to look at and sat in his chair to write something on his note cards while we stood and shivered.

Serena looked slyly at Veronica and her other teammates and said loudly enough for us all to hear:

"Tess will get out first because she doesn't want to move too quickly. She might fall out of her swimming suit."

There she was. Syrupy sweet Serena reverted back to the contestant I waited in line with the day before.

"Just ignore her," I said, and Sandra who stood with us on our side of the line nodded in agreement. Serena stood across the blacktop from me. A white line spray painted a barrier between us. I wanted the ball. I wanted to pelt her out first; I wanted her to storm and whine in front of the camera.

"All right. We're ready," the cameraman said.

"Here you go Veronica," Lance said tossing her the ball.

Serena did a little dance with her long arms when Veronica pelted Tess surprisingly hard with the first ball. Then, I really wanted the ball. Tess moved carefully to the sidelines, nearly exposed. Ethan looked like he couldn't find a place to keep his eyes when she claimed his arm. He watched the game even more intently, needing both arms to cheer.

Finally, I got a hold of the ball. I hurtled it across the line as hard as I could straight at Serena's shins. It hit her hard and tripped her a little. She made a shocked grunt. It felt good to throw her out. She made no scene.

"Aw well... I did my best," she said, proving her good sportsmanship. I could feel her irritation as she moved to the sidelines to talk to Ethan.

Then the strangest thing happened. As if Julian hit a reset button, Serena and Tess were both put back in and we started over. We were told to replay the same moves. The cameraman positioned us almost exactly where we were before.

The next time I pelted Serena, she kept the same determined smile on her face. I grew more amused. After a few hours of this, the amusement dimmed and we all just wanted it to end.

Half a day of playing dodgeball, and Lance kept putting contestants back in. Then Veronica threw them out again. Turns out she'd played volleyball during the off-season of the swim team in high school and college. She could spike the ball at the other contestants with perfect accuracy. She pelted each woman fifteen to twenty times before Julian let them go to the sideline and be out. She bruised a few of the contestants.

Sandra proved extremely athletic and Veronica's favorite target. Sandra may have outrun her if her bikini didn't leave her worrying about a wardrobe malfunction. Veronica didn't really aim for me at first, so it always came down to me against her. Then a timeout would be called. We'd start over, knowing eventually it would come down to Veronica and me again.

I bounced around with energy; I couldn't sit still. I couldn't throw as hard as Veronica, but I dodged well. My legs burned, but I ignored them, something inside me came alive. Ethan cheered for me after I dodged a particularly fast-moving ball, and I tried harder because of it. Finally, the inevitable had to be acknowledged.

Veronica and I would have to face each other. One of us would have to get the other out. At the beginning of the day, it wouldn't have been a big deal. The way we started over, again and again, it became a huge deal to everyone. Some of the cameramen started making bets. The other contestants became extremely competitive.

Veronica held the ball above her head; her strong silhouette could have decorated a sports drink. She glanced at me. I fidgeted ready to dodge. She pivoted and instead pelted Sandra with the ball for the eleventh time. "It's not fair. Carrie's wearing a workout suit," Sandra fumed.

"Cut," Lance yelled.

"I want a different swimsuit," Sandra complained.

"She has feet like a football player," Lance answered.

"So do I," Sandra said, pulling her swimsuit up for dramatic effect.

"In your profile, you said what kind of swimsuit you prefer," Lance said apologetically.

"Not to play dodgeball in," Sandra said.

"Carrie, Veronica, go get a drink of water and sit down," Lance said holding his ear.

"For how long?" I asked, glancing at Veronica poised across from me. She wouldn't look me in the eye, and I knew she'd resolved to throw me out and win the game making the competitive tension palpable between us.

"I have no idea. Julian needs a few minutes for something," Lance said. Sandra looked like she wanted to continue her discussion. Lance quickly headed over to a cameraman calling over his shoulder, "You two go get your hair fixed."

I walked over and sat in a chair next to Veronica.

"You are playing so well," I said trying to get her to look at me. She may have if Sandra hadn't hollered:

104

"Carrie don't let her psych you out." Sandra won ten points and a trip to the Opera Benefit if I won.

"Veronica, get your drink and come over here to strategize," Serena said, glaring at Sandra.

"Ahh," I stammered.

"Carrie! I'm serious. Don't talk to her," Sandra called again.

"It'll be fine," I said back.

The stylist undid my braids, to redo and tighten them again. I had a headache starting.

"This is fun huh?" I said. Veronica grunted, but couldn't respond much with her head wrenched back so her bangs could be braided into her pony tail.

"Carrie," Sandra said sidling up to me, "Your stance is a little too squatted, it may keep you from moving fast enough. And you just have to get that ball y'all, because you cannot dodge forever. You have to go on the offensive."

"Did they teach you that at the national dodgeball tournament?" I asked.

"No, twelve years of cheerleading and gymnastics," Sandra said.

"What?" I asked.

"I have been to more competitive sports games than you for sure, so would y'all just listen to me," she said.

After a long while Julian finally came out of the white kidnapper van he hid in most of the time when we were location shooting. He looked like he'd gotten dressed in the seventies and forgotten to change. He didn't talk to anyone, or instruct Patrick who instantly went to his side. Instead he locked eyes with me. I looked away, but I could still feel him watch me intently.

As he watched me expectantly, it occurred to me he purposely pit me against Veronica. We were the only ones in reasonable active wear swimsuits. Apparently, women getting along didn't captivate high ratings. He meant to break up our friendship by forcing one of us to get the other out. And to ensure we would, he put ten thousand dollars on the line.

I turned my face away from his sightline.

What did I do? What was right? How did I keep Veronica as a friend? I looked back to be sure I wasn't just imagining Julian's agenda. A grimy unwashed sensation hit me in the chest when Julian caught my eye and smiled at me like he'd given me a gift. He gave me money, and all I had to do was turn a friendship into something catty.

His smug, undiluted, self-importance cracked something inside of me. My chest grew hot until it boiled over with indignation. I hated his nudges, his ridiculous need to control everyone and everything around him. Grown men and woman all cantering for him.

A feeling of overwhelming claustrophobia trapped me inside my own skin. The idea of letting him tell me I couldn't be friends with Veronica infuriated me. My mother hadn't helped me pick my friends for years. No more of that. He didn't get a say. I would throw the game. I would not win and give him power over me.

Why did this bother me so badly?

It wasn't just an annoyance; it was a volcanic eruption of bottled up lava inside me.

Over a dodgeball game?

"Carrie, you okay?" my stylist asked.

"Sure," I mumbled.

"Okay, well you're done," she said eyeing me.

"Thanks," I answered. I forced a grin on my face and turned to Veronica. I had to let her know I would be fine with her getting me out so I said: "Don't bruise me, all right?"

"Whatever," she said relaxing and smiling back at me.

"Places ladies," Lance called to us.

I walked to the spray-painted court. The prop guy threw me the ball, but Lance showed no indication we were starting. On the sidelines Tess made Ethan laugh. It bugged me. A few of the contestants were taking advantage of a cooler filled with light beer.

Two of the women in particular needed to take the edge off. They started drinking while we were primped and continued on pretty strong after they were finally released from playing. I didn't want to butt in, but someone should say something. They were starting to act drunk. I had no doubt Julian filmed it, and one of them owned a private law practice she'd built up from nothing. I left the dodge ball court where I'd been placed and walked over to them. I pulled a water bottle out of the cooler.

"Hey, you guys look like sisters," I gently teased one of the women quietly.

"We don't look anything alike," she answered not bothering to lower her voice.

"You both have that silver can attached to your hand," I said as nonchalantly as possible.

"That's right," said the other woman who was a hostess at a night club. She toasted her friend, "We're the drinking sisters."

"As long as you're not the drunken sisters; especially on film, right?" I asked.

They laughed and laughed, but I can't be sure if it was because they were inebriated or actually found me funny.

"They are the drunken sisters – being a lush isn't attractive girls," Sandra said over their mirth rolling her eyes. She then nudged me back to the dodge ball court talking about really watching the angle of Veronica's arm as she threw the ball.

I regretted my interference. As if encouraged by my comment the drunken sisters spoke louder and tried to joke around, tripping over each other.

"Okay, Carrie you're up," Lance called after talking to the camera a few times.

I had the ball. Julian stayed out of his van to see me pelt Veronica with it. He wanted to give me the ten thousand dollars. I needed the money. I shoved the dragon down. I grinned at Veronica. I raised my arm, stumbled a few times like one of the drunken sisters, thinking maybe if we all acted drunk, they wouldn't look so out of it by comparison. Maybe the viewer would think we were playing dodge ball drunk to see who could hold their liquor the best. I threw the ball off to one side in a goofy way – nowhere near her.

"What was that!" Tess called.

"Yeah, Carrie, what was that?" Sandra called pretending to be amused but clearly put out.

"Did I hit her," I asked one of the drunken sisters with a glassy expression and a Stevie Wonder head nod.

"Nnnnope," said the attorney too loudly, her drink slopping as she pushed Tess out of the way, "Did you see that? She didn't get her."

Julian's carefully planned out game quickly hit a stalemate. Veronica, catching on, staggered a little, and threw the ball way off.

"I guess I shouldn't have had that last one," she said, too quickly to be funny,

We laughed. The women getting sloshed thought we were funnier than anyone else.

I refused to throw Veronica out, and, despite her amazing spike, she couldn't hit me. I tried to run into the ball. Veronica wouldn't pound it anywhere near my path. After a few minutes of this pitiful effort, we were gut-laughing. The competitive edge in the air dissipated some. Ethan, who had no real stake in the game, started cheering us on by taunting us to fail.

"Come on Carrie, she's going left... you can run faster than that... How do you ever expect to get out like that?"

"Yer not gonna get some like that," Tess called after him, slowing down on her innuendo to make sure we all got it.

"Oh, aren't y'all funny," Sandra said through tightly clenched teeth.

"Even I coulda gotten her that time," one of the drunken sisters yelled.

"Yeah, yeah, I coulda gotten her out that time," said a woman I called Pete.

"Yeah, yeah, me too," said her self-proclaimed bestie whom I called Re-Pete.

The musical montage of the game the viewer enjoyed didn't feature footage of a very frustrated Julian calling a time-out. He came in close to me claiming there was something wrong with my microphone. He reached under the lip of my swimsuit. His sausage like fingers fiddled against my skin to adjust my microphone. His hot stinky breath hit my face when he whispered,

"I know you need the money."

"I don't need anything that badly," I said knocking his hand away.

I shook a little. How could he possibly know that? I never wrote it on anything or admitted it in my audition. Did Adam tell him? But why would he? Is that something the Private Eye learned about me? All the contestants seemed to have secrets exposed in some way or another. Perhaps this was mine? Affronted as any well-bred lady would be, I scowled at him.

At this he shifted, trying to sound more congenial like he'd tipped his hand too quickly.

"I didn't mean… I know Ethan's really impressed by you. He isn't showing as much interest in any other girl. And with that kind of assurance, a million dollars isn't an amount to be brushed aside. Try a little harder. That money is yours."

This was harder to dismiss.

Lance started talking into the camera, indicating we'd soon start taping again. I jumped over to pick up the ball before a slight breeze could roll it to Veronica's side of the makeshift court. The ocean swirled in the background as I hugged it tightly in my arms. I glanced over at Ethan. Was I hurting his feelings? Did he think I didn't like him because I wasn't trying?

No! I wouldn't let Julian manipulate me; he wanted me to canter.

Ethan noticed me looking at him and grinned. I smiled back. I wanted the million dollars. It came over me in a way I couldn't ignore. To get it, would I have to canter for Julian? I wouldn't canter for him.

"'Kay, Carrie, whenever you're ready," Lance called after finishing his take.

It wouldn't be hard to peg Veronica. She stood so still waiting for me to throw the ball. I raised my arm higher. Veronica flinched, expecting the ball to hit her.

Would I throw a ball at my friend? Perhaps losing her camaraderie for money – for a night out to impress Ethan? Would I let Julian's smug smile grow? Really?

Before I could think about the money, I took a step and pretended to trip. I lost the ball, and it rolled over to Veronica.

"Oops," I slurred too loudly and Veronica started laughing again.

I turned.

I waited until Julian looked me straight in the eyes.

I smiled my most charming smile.

I shouldn't have. I considered him the comedy relief, and in that moment, he knew it. His face hardened.

Veronica, in turn, mirrored my trip and sent the ball back to me. Julian whispered something at Lance, then stomped toward his van.

111

"Okay, let's start over again, but this time, let's mix up the teams," Lance said.

Everyone groaned.

"Nobody's won yet; everyone has another chance," he said.

Veronica and I were put on the same team. Sandra was left with Serena. She complained gently in her sweet southern drawl that only made her more appealing.

"It's only fair. They have consistently played the best," Lance said but he didn't look her in the eye.

"Seriously Carrie?" Sandra said appealing to me.

"I'm sorry. Sandra," I said. How could she not be frustrated? A horrible guilt dribbled over me as we started over again. I dodged everything thrown at me, which increased considering how I frustrated everyone. By the end of the day, I wasn't sure standing up for myself was the right decision.

Only the viewer was surprised when Veronica and I won the trip to the opera benefit. Julian didn't make them sit through another half a day of agonizing taping to get to the obvious outcome.

The closing shot was of me raising my eyebrows at Veronica like we were our own team and we'd won. Veronica laughed hysterically or maybe frantically, but she managed a laugh. Of course, we'd had this interaction while taunting each other on opposite teams, but it fit better at the end of the game after Lance announced we won. Julian was an artist after all.

112

CHAPTER TEN

That night we met our designers. My designer, a buxom woman named Becky, didn't say much to me. She started pinning the dress she already started for the opera onto my body.

"It's a little short, isn't it?" I asked, coloring.

"You'll for sure have to borrow some different underwear," she said staring at my granny panties hanging out.

"Or you could lengthen it," I said.

"Seriously?" She asked looking up at my face for the first time, realizing I wasn't, in fact, a wire frame.

"Yep, I'm not wearing it like this. It's way too short for me."

She and I quarreled back and forth over my butt hanging out of the side of her slanting dress until it turned heated. Finally, she agreed to fix it, but disgruntled she made me leave before she started. Why did it have to be so hard to have a say in what I wore? I wasn't obligated to show my butt on national television, was I?

The next day she set to work while we went to volunteer at the nearby Veteran's Home. We sat outside waiting for Julian to gain us admittance. Apparently, the last time he'd brought some of his Whole Package contestants, they'd been extremely rude.

Serena, in her element, lectured the group on how to change bed pans in a steady stream of advice. I walked to

113

the furthest bench in a little garden to drown her out, unsure if I could change a bed, let alone a bed pan. Finally, Lance encouraged her to interview with a cameraman. I only looked back up when Ethan sat down next to me.

Sandra walked toward us, like she wanted to share our bench. Before she made it, a stylist claimed her hair fell out, and sat her down to fix it. I didn't mind, I needed the quiet moment of repose, though I did notice the backup cameraman trying to look innocent with his lens trained at us.

"Glad you became a doctor?" I asked.

"You have no idea," he said.

"No bodily fluids for me, thanks," I said.

"Noted," he then continued in a whisper, "I enjoyed our run this morning."

"Me, too, except I think my legs are going to fall off," I said bumping his shoulder.

"You played a pretty mean game of dodge ball yesterday."

"Yeah," I blushed recalling my behavior and shifted asking, "will they let you actually help these people or will you pretend doctor today?"

"I don't know. It's a veteran's home that recognizes a physician's license across state lines."

"So, you can practice," I said.

"If it's the same as working with the Public Health Services, it should be fine. Julian has all my paperwork so we can do Doctors without Borders."

"He says with a gleam in his eye. Are you excited?" I asked.

"I've always wanted to do it," Ethan said.

"Then I'm excited for you," I said.

114

The makeshift bellhop, Julian's assistant, Patrick, came out into the garden where we waited.

"Oh, Patrick, are we ready?" I asked.

"I'll be back for you in a minute," Patrick said, collecting Veronica, Tess, Pete and Re-Pete to go with him.

Ethan and I were undisturbed until all the other contestants trickled out of the garden. Then Patrick took us to the end of a long hallway full of doors. We entered a small room covered in pictures and hospital equipment. The cameraman, already set up in the only free corner, told us we could get started. The nurse in charge introduced us to Harold, a bed-ridden Marine.

"Hey Harold, what's the problem," Ethan said smiling at the old wrinkled man.

"My ankle's bleedin' again," he grunted. Ethan pulled the sheet back. He exposed an oblong open wound just over Harold's ankle with curdling fat and tissue coming out of it. I bit my lip hoping Harold hadn't heard my gasp.

"Do you always lie on this ankle, Harold?" Ethan asked without flinching. I, on the other hand, tried to breathe through my mouth so I couldn't smell his rotting flesh.

"They move me off it, but I can't sleep unless I'm on my right side," Harold complained, "If I can't see the window how will I know if they invadin'?"

"Who's invading?" Ethan asked.

"They comin' for me first. I killed a lot of em—I got a medal," Harold said seriously nodding to a dusty shadow box with what looked like a Purple Heart, along with another medal in it. The room went silent. The nurse rolled her eyes

115

at me. I clenched my jaw. This man lost his luccidity, and thought he was still protecting our country. What could I do?

"I know they comin'," he said to the nurse who ignored him.

"Harold, we scared 'em into hiding," I said taking his hand, "they're too afraid to attack because of you. You can sleep easy."

Ethan and the nurse peered at me.

"That right?" Harold asked.

"Yep, you can sleep on your back. You're safe," I said.

"You always know, LeeAnn," Harold said kissing my hand.

"I do and I need you to sleep on your back from now on. You hear?"

"All right," he said, reaching for me. I gave him my cheek and he kissed it.

Ethan cleaned the wound. I turned my back talking to Harold so I didn't have to watch, until the flesh was covered. Next, Ethan asked the delusional man a lot of questions he couldn't answer. Ethan must have suspected Harold was mistreated. By the time he finished, the frustrated nurse kept insisting Harold refused to sleep on his back.

I liked this Ethan who held other people's lives in his hands. He never hesitated—even when asking the hard questions. As he cared for the aged Marine everything I accomplished in my life shrunk to insignificant.

"Ethan, we need you in room 211," Patrick said coming into the room after a while.

"Oh right. It was a real pleasure to meet you," Ethan said to the aged Marine. He stopped to wash his hands while everyone else filed out. The nurse and the cameraman left talking to Patrick.

"I'll be right back," I told Harold following Ethan into the hall.

"You are amazing," I told Ethan.

"Thanks, Carrie," he said.

I'm not sure what happened. I think he opened his arms to me. Maybe, in my enthusiasm, I threw mine around his neck first. I wanted to be a part of someone who didn't dissolve upon closer examination. Ethan hugged me back lifting my feet from the ground.

"Thank-you for helping him," I said into his ear. Ethan squeezed a little tighter, and then put me down. We left each other without saying anything else. My spontaneous hug embarrassed me. I sat with Harold the rest of the day. He weaved in and out of dementia. I tried my best to relieve his post-traumatic stress, wondering who would do it tomorrow.

CHAPTER ELEVEN

"Ah, here's the limousine again," I whispered.

"We can hardly go to the opera on the bus," Ethan said.

He led Veronica and me to the limo. Veronica fidgeted. Ethan let go of her arm. She looked disappointed. Ethan didn't notice. I dropped his arm so she didn't feel bad.

I wore a much longer gingerbread-colored dress. An ornate rose, the same burnt red as my hair, embroidered in a slant down the bottom half of it. The bottom of the dress swirled around my ankles when I moved just right. I swished all around the opera house.

I tried to thank Becky the next morning, but she didn't say much in return. I hoped our argument at an end. We said little to each other over the rest of the weekend. I barely saw her, except to stay still while she put a piece of thin paper up to my body to create a pattern for my elimination dress. She only came over from her hotel room in town every so often to fit me. She didn't like to work in the back room with the other designers.

On the day of the second round of eliminations, Becky called me back into the room full of mirrors. She handed me my dress, and a puffy slip saying:

"I need to run back to my hotel. I'll be back before the eliminations."

After she left the room, Veronica helped me step into the avocado green satin dress. It dragged the floor. The slip puffed out awkwardly at my shins, but nowhere else. It had an open oval neckline. The straps fanned out into barely

118

sleeves creating a lip of a collar that the bun of curls at my
neck continually snagged. At the high waist, a thick strip
of bright white mesh pulled the dress tightly to my ribs.

Becky definitely made her frustration over our quibble
affect my elimination dress. I wanted to take it off and put my
opera dress back on but felt that would be admitting defeat
somehow. Instead, I stopped looking at myself. I focused on
Veronica whose designer at least tried to make her look good.

"Your dress is... fun," I said.

Veronica swallowed down and nodded. Veronica's dress
bunched in the front pulling the hemline up past her ankle,
where her slip peeked out. It dipped in the back like a train
dragging on the floor. Veronica kept trying to pull on it,
hoping somehow, it'd get longer in the front.

"Don't touch," Suzie, her designer snapped and Veronica
pulled her hands back.

"Do you think one of us is getting booted off tonight?"
Veronica said looking away from her reflection.

"After the VA, it won't be you," I said.

"I hate that... I ...I hope Merle knows I wasn't being nice
to her for... you know, to show off or whatever," Veronica said.

"Oh, you were so sincere and she liked the cameras."

"Stand up straight," Suzie said. Veronica's designer eyed
the foreign looking mesh on my dress, barely watching what
she was doing.

"I'll be downstairs to touch up your make-up in a few
minutes," Suzie instructed taking one last look at the mesh.

"Thanks," Veronica said, watching her leave.

"We'll go down together," I said puckering my pale pink
lips in the mirror. I turned and struck a pose for

Veronica. Veronica lowered her voice and looked out into the hallway to be sure Suzie couldn't hear, then said,

"At least you don't look prego, wearing a maternity gown."

"You're kidding, right? You look perfect – a little punk rock, Tim Burton with your slip coming out like that. I'd blend in with army recruits. Becky doesn't seem to know what to do with the slip they challenged her to use this week. This has to be payback."

"Even if it is, I'm proud of you for making Becky fix your dress. Not that... I mean you have really pretty legs... I didn't mean. It's just if you're uncomfortable, you shouldn't have to show them off."

"My butt was sticking out – seriously," I said.

"At least you can stand up for yourself; it takes guts to throw a tantrum with Becky. I'm wearing the maternity gown – I can't go downstairs in this."

"You look fine, own it, and smile!"

"Right."

"And it wasn't a tantrum," I said.

"I'm not being rude, there's something to be said for being the Diva."

"I'm not the Diva," I said, trying to mask my embarrassment. As far as talent went, Becky was the best designer in the Manor House. All the other designers sucked up to her; instinctively they knew she'd make it. I wouldn't have switched Veronica designers for anything. Still, I couldn't walk around with my butt hanging out either. I couldn't.

"I'm forcing her to become more creative. Very creative," I said fingering the strange-looking mesh at my waist.

"Julian was pissed."

"He's always kind of pissed with me," I said.

"He's kind of weird about you. Have you noticed that?" Veronica asked.

"Yeah, maybe he's a fan of my dad's or something. It seems like he hovers around me sometimes, right?"

"Yeah, stalker-like, crazy," Veronica said. She tugged at her dress.

"Ronnie you're pulling on the seam," I said.

"Oh," she said tucking a stray thread into the fabric.

"Come on girl, let's go," I said.

"I can't," Veronica said looking in the mirror.

"Be bold," I said talking more to myself than her. I steeled my nerves for appearing like this in front of the cameras. It was Becky's career, and if she wanted to pout and ruin her chances, what could I do about it?

After I finally convinced Veronica to leave the back room, we walked down the hall. Veronica stopped before the stairs panicking. Sometimes she needed a minute before we joined the chaos. I looked down below. The house moved with colorfully dressed women who fluttered around like butterflies in a construction zone. Something about it struck me as artistically beautiful, and I wanted to paint it.

The thought startled me; I hadn't painted in almost four years. Not since Gordon would sit and watch me, encouraging me to immortalize these moments. I wondered if this vacation of sorts was good for me. Then I wondered if it was about to end.

That morning, during our jog, Ethan and I hadn't discussed my leaving. Ethan seemed to avoid the subject

121

every time I brought it up. I didn't know if he wanted it to be a surprise or if he feared I'd make a request and get him in trouble. He worried more about upsetting Julian than I did. At times I almost wondered if Julian held something over his head to make him so concerned. Of course, he couldn't say.

Either way, I didn't let it affect me. Instead, I battled with myself for not wanting to leave. I rationalized Veronica needed me. She was doing so well in the competitions, but needed me to help her relax.

Veronica gasped. She popped her seam.

"Veronica, leave it alone, seriously, your figure is flawless. The way the dress bunches in front does not make it look any less flawless. However, if your skirt falls off..." I said.

"Okay," she said, her hand shook. I bumped her a little so she'd walk down the stairs. Veronica started humming a song her grandmother taught her and moved downward.

At the foot of the stairs, I let go of my dress and it billowed around me, creating a bump on my shins where the fabric rested against the slip. Candice, my favorite stylist, threw a bib around my shoulders. Ever since she slipped me morsels of information in the limo, I whispered questions to her. She answered them for me if she could.

"Do you know who's in the lead?" I whispered sliding my thumb over my microphone.

"No, but you and Veronica are popular on the website," she whispered grinning at me. Veronica smiled, shyly blushing.

Ethan saw us and walked over from the elimination room. Veronica disappeared stammering about her makeup.

"Hey, do you need an intervention?" Ethan asked eyeing my avocado green dress. His grin told me Becky was mad.

I couldn't answer. My attention focused on the mascara wand coming toward my face. I grew even more wary when the tip of the wand was inches from my eye and Candice turned to Ethan.

"Do you want me to get yours?" she asked.

"No thanks. Focus on Carrie," Ethan said. When she turned back to me, he finished with, "I was attacked and subdued before I put this tux on."

I couldn't see any trace of makeup on his face except his very moist lips and the sun spots on his left cheek disappeared. I said:

"What boys do to be beautiful for girls!"

"My mama taught me right," Ethan said.

"Yeah, your mama taught you to put on makeup for girls," Pete said laughing.

"Makeup... your mamma taught you," Re-Pete said louder and laughed harder.

"Um-hum," I said. By the week's end, neither Ethan nor I had much patience for photocopied people. Pete and Re-Pete re-teased Ethan like they'd never had an original thought in their lives. Clearly their insecurities never let them say anything not beta tested first, so I tried to be patient. It took an effort to laugh for them after I'd already laughed for who they copied.

"Okay. Everyone over here, please," Lance called, walking briskly into the Manor House. He wore a nice suit tailored to fit him perfectly. Ethan's tux bunched a little in his shoulders, but Lance took the time to tailor his suits. I liked Lance. His hair curled back off his forehead and his face almost forced me to watch him or I'd miss something.

"Hi, Lance. How are ratings?" I asked, pulling off the bib to indicate to Candice I wanted to be done. She nodded and backed off. I turned quickly from her, running into one of the tall, unstable tables that housed eclectic vases of weeds. From out of nowhere, Patrick threw out a thin, bony arm. He stopped the table before it could topple. I grinned at him.

"That still doesn't make us even," I said pointing at him. Over the last week, this was our ongoing joke for my having to pull Erin's suitcase up the stairs. Patrick laughed easily for me. I liked him. He seemed normal and friendly in his Star Wars tee shirts when everything else in the Manor House felt too Hollywood.

"Did you ask me something?" Lance said turning to me after he finished writing something on a note card. His eyes dropped to my dress and I could feel him appraising my look.

"Umm..." I said. I threw my shoulders back determined to pull off the dress, because I had no other choice, "Oh right. How are ratings?"

"Better than last season, actually. Everyone really seems to like... um, Ethan."

"All that make-up is paying off," I said, turning back to Ethan. "Your mama must be so proud."

"Almost as proud as when I graduated from medical school, I'm sure," Ethan said dryly. He stepped toward me to cut off Lance who tried to join our banter.

"Oh please! What's medical school to half the women in America being in love with her son?" I shot back. Lance stepped around him by clapping a hand on his shoulder and laughed. Ethan shrugged his hand off, and I could feel a strange tension between them.

Lance stopped suddenly and grabbed at his ear. I could hear Julian yelling something at him in his earbud. Patrick instantly disappeared with only a slight wave to me. The two contestants I inadvertently nicknamed the drunken sisters sauntered in with glasses almost empty of wine.

I felt bad for labeling them such after Ethan announced he really did think they had a problem. Julian point blank refused to monitor the amount of alcohol coming into the Manor House. Ethan took to scolding them about their livers – proving he was, in fact, a doctor.

"Okay, ladies, line up," Lance said.

"I wonder," I asked, determined to be unaffected by Julian, "if you feel like a dairy farmer at milking time?"

"Ha, ha," Lance said, "by the way, that green looks really pretty on you."

"Oh yeah, totally." Ethan quickly agreed with a smirk stepping in front of Lance again.

"Ah yeah. Thanks, guys," I said trying to keep my head high and my back straight. I would not droop like Veronica simply because of what I wore. To prove this, I walked over to examine the reflection of my skirt flaring a little as I turned in the mirror by the door. I forced as much of a smile as I could manage. For all his teasing, Ethan watched me in a way that made me feel pretty.

"Here," Becky said, walking up to me from out of nowhere. She looked around to make sure no one watched. She produced a thick piece of golden Venetian

Lace that looked like a short table runner. She quickly hooked it into the white mesh at the high waist, covering it completely. Tendrils of tightly weaved golden lace curled and climbed down the dress.

Becky bent over quickly hooking everything together in the back until I couldn't breathe. It pulled the fabric in until it hit the slip, now at my knee. With the dress pulled against the tulle slip, it became a mermaid dress that flattered my figure in a way I'd never seen or imagined possible. The cool green color of the dress looked perfect as a background for the thick gold lace. The whole dress became elegant, complimenting my coloring.

"Wow," I said admiring her work.

"Go get your competition pictures taken quickly," she whispered close to my ear.

"Kay," I said. She looked nervous. I walked back to the cove, where they set up a backdrop and lights. One of the cameramen took my picture to post online for Becky's part in the competition. When I walked back into the elimination room Lance did a double take. Becky tried to look defiant, but she seemed uncomfortable.

"That's really nice," Lance said to Becky and I could see something going unsaid between them.

"Becky, Carrie looks gorgeous," Ethan said, grinning at her. She flushed.

"Did you hand-stitch this?" he asked, coming in for a closer look.

"Nah, I used my embroidery machine back at the hotel," she shrugged and scurried away when this made Lance examine her again.

"Hey Ethan," Tess called from the stairs pulling his attention away from me.

I walked away. I took my place in line, biting my lip. Tess would get Ethan's full attention, so I pretended I gave it to her instead of her taking it. Tess came carefully down the rest of the stairs in a strapless dress that was so low in front it would fall if Tess made any sudden movements. Her designer used the slip to create a skirt comparable to a Bavarian serving wench costume.

"Oh hey, Tess, how are you?" he asked.

"I'm good. I spent the morning making an apple pie crumble from all those apples we got at the fruit stand."

"That's ah, great, Tess," Ethan said.

"Yeah, we should have some later," Tess said. I couldn't be sure what she offered up, considering she leaned over to throw her apples in his face.

"Tess, in line please," Lance said, not at all shy about appreciating what she put out on a platter. She turned and came toward us.

"Carrie, your dress is amazing," Tess said reaching for straps that weren't there.

"That was pretty amazing. You look so pretty," Veronica said coming in to stand next to me without even a trace of resentment.

"Thanks," I said.

"Ron you look retro, your dress is fun," Tess said encouraging her.

Veronica shrugged, but glanced at me looking guiltily. At night, Veronica and I talked a lot about Tess. Veronica often felt guilty for gossiping. I didn't know if trying to understand

127

Tess was gossiping or just trying to know her. I wanted to figure her out, simply as an observer of people. Was that wrong? I would talk to Tess about it if I could, but Tess wouldn't discuss what happened to her. What would make someone like Tess, so fun, compassionate, and smart, act like she had nothing more to offer than her body? Every time a man showed interest in her, it's like she flipped a switch and everything she did or said became suggestive.

Raised in an exceptionally religious household, I didn't understand sex. The whole concept diverged miles away from the mandatory classes I took addressing it in high school.

Julian acted like flippant open sexuality was normal and should be encouraged. In my opinion that mentality only benefited the Julians of the world, who would, of course, love for women to give it up to whoever whenever. But then, didn't that create trails of Tesses?

Was there a line between a degraded porn star and a woman with a healthy sex drive?

This topic had been forefront in my mind the last few days. Tess thought she'd win if she could get Ethan to sleep with her. Veronica believed she would as well. That didn't make sense to me, though.

The rules of *The Whole Package* encourage the impartial judge to be swayed. That's the fun of the game. Lance said this several times:

"The contestants may present themselves to Ethan in any manner they think makes them *The Whole Package*."

This in and of itself suggests a woman could seduce Ethan to win, which is how Julian would like us to play. But

128

then Dr. Corbon put in place the point system. The weight of
the competitions left little sway for whoever Ethan finds most
attractive to win.

If the points were delivered fairly, Veronica would be in
the lead. Both in dodge ball and the Veterans Home, she killed
it. Other points were delivered for attitude and behavioral
considerations but those were vague. The rewarding of those
points was subjected to Ethan's opinion. But what did that
mean, and how many points did he give out?

Dr. Corbon was supposed to help Ethan understand
resiliency. I'd never seen Dr. Corbon. I asked Ethan. He
couldn't tell me what happened behind the curtain but did
admit he'd never met Dr. Corbon, either. Julian made Ethan
read her book a few months before the show started, but
never mentioned it or her again.

Veronica and I figured Julian had total control. Julian
worked hard to keep libidos running high. Romantic movies
and love quiz magazines were all he allowed into the Manor
House. Unrealistic sex muddled around in my head until
nothing made sense. Maybe Tess would win if she slept with
Ethan. But then would it be because she won, or he felt
obligated or guilty? This thought jumbled my ideas even
further.

Would Ethan commit himself to Tess if she could get him
to have sex with her? I really couldn't say. If it were broadcast
on *The Whole Package*, would it be more like a wedge or
glue? Wasn't there supposed to be some level of commitment
before sex? Tess obviously had plenty of sex but didn't seem
to understand it any better than I could.

Gordon hadn't tried to push beyond kissing me. I suspected he wanted to a few times. I never put together sexual desire with time he tried to move the wedding date up. His mother refused to hear of it, and that was the end of it. Looking back, we would have married before he died if she'd given in.

Gordon must have wanted to have sex with me. Did I ever really want to have sex with him? I thought about loving him, but the desire to have sex didn't overwhelm me in any way. Was there something wrong with me?

With Grandmother on one side of the spectrum, while on the opposite side was Tess, who used sex as a lure to hook a man – it all felt wrong.

My mind tended to wander like this during all the waiting we did. I would watch the other women and try to understand why they acted the way they did, based on what happened to them. Sometimes I could see clearly why they behaved like they did. Other times, I didn't understand them at all.

I didn't notice my endless waiting, coupled with exaggerated reality show behaviorisms, started to mold my mind in new ways simply as a way to stave off boredom. Refusing to accept Julian's picture, for the first time in my life, I started to find my own.

CHAPTER TWELVE

I refocused when Ethan gave me a look. I turned to see what was funny. Tess tried to stand by Serena. Serena showed herself to be offended by Tess's appearance. She stepped around her to be in front of Veronica, on the same riser. Veronica almost tripped.

"Oopsy, sorry Veronica. You don't mind if I stand here, do you?" Serena said like a wolf going after the slowest deer.

"Sure," Veronica said, stepping off the riser.

"Of course, you understand why I can't stand by her," Serena said in a loud whisper nodding at Tess.

"Whatever, Serena," Tess said walking over to the end of the row by the door.

I couldn't smile with Ethan.

"Here sweetheart, you stand here," I said. I gave Veronica my spot and caught up to Tess.

"Hey, Tess. You okay?"

"If I don't sweat through my dress I'll be fine," Tess said.

"Yeah, but on the flip side you have to keep the ten pounds off somehow," I said loudly so Lance could hear me mock him. Tess rolled her eyes at me. But she also leaned in a little and smiled at me for real.

"Okay, ladies," Lance said. "We've just gone live."

I raised my hand.

"Cut," Lance yelled, then in a polite tone he asked, "Yes, Carrie?"

"Why do you say that we're live, we're obviously not live? Don't you think that's a little misleading to the public?"

"Anyone can read about how it works on the network's business license. We're on what's called a broadcast delay. We aren't far off, though, so we can claim it."

"A couple hours is considered a broadcast delay?" I said.

"Pretty much." Lance shifted uncomfortably. He said, "We'll be closer to live at the reunion show, nothing between. Carrie, seriously, can we get on with this?"

"Does Ethan have a script he reads from? What are those binders he's always looking at?" Serena asked.

Silence. No one answered.

We'd all been placed and prompted, and repositioned while repeating something we were told to say. Julian expected the show to go a certain direction. We all had roles to play as if we'd been actors cast in a movie. Serena's interest in Ethan's genuine role in the show wasn't unwarranted. I ran every morning with the man, so I didn't doubt his sincerity. Even so, I have no doubt if Ethan had been holding a script in his hand Lance still would've answered:

"No, he does not. He has certain obligations under the contract he signed, just as each of you have."

"Whatever do we have to do, y'all?" Sandra asked. She rustled her super puffy princess dress.

"Like, we can't just leave the show. We have to either be booted off or accept the key on film," I said, remembering Adam told me this.

"Yeah, plus we have to wear microphones all the time. When you're eliminated, Sandra, you'll have to unload your experience on camera in the limo," Tess said.

"Well, some of y'all will have to do that," she said.

"Actually, with the microphone packs we have to –" Pete started.

"'Kay, I got it," Sandra said, proving she never actually needed instruction. She just didn't like a conversation where she wasn't being looked at. This should have cost Sandra's beauty some of its charm. Ethan and Lance stared at Sandra appreciatively. They didn't care what came out of her perfectly shaped lips. This annoyed me.

"Is everyone ready?" Lance said, holding his ear that Julian was absolutely on the other end of. He smiled at me when he caught me watching him. I grinned back.

"Hey, go find your own harem," Ethan said hitting Lance. Harem – really? Ethan used the word harem?

The room exploded in laughter. Everyone laughed at Ethan's joke. The other nine women laughed as if they were at a group job interview and only one person won the job.

The drunken sisters laughed too loudly. Pete and Re-Pete copied them. Sandra fiddled with her necklace and giggled a slight flirty laugh. Tess leaned toward Ethan, giving him a view, as she laughed. Serena forced a laugh like she catered to a child while she watched Erin who smiled with exactly the amount of enthusiasm the joke deserved. Veronica in her sweet pureness smiled coyly and watched everyone else to make sure the joke had been funny.

I didn't laugh. I didn't find his joke funny. I didn't want to be one in Ethan's harem. I couldn't believe my sensitive friend Ethan would imply such a thing. Especially considering how sex-driven Julian taunted us to be. Ethan didn't want a harem, did he? He didn't seem as uncomfortable with all the attention as he had at first. I assessed all this in the extra

133

moment of forced laughter, forced as employees will for a boss.

"All right, everyone," Lance said. "We have just gone live."

He looked expressively at me and everyone started laughing again. The expression on his face looked like he'd been tickled. I smiled at him – I couldn't help it. But I got the impression he'd been trying to make me smile. The cameraman had the lens trained on me. Had Julian informed him I didn't find Ethan's joke funny and I needed to smile? A shiver went up my spine. I felt like I had a peeping Tom. Lance did his intro then nodded to Ethan.

"Veronica, with the full points for last week, you are safe," Ethan called. This turned my mood instantly and I smiled, satisfied. Julian couldn't escape Dr. Corbon's point system no matter how annoying he found Veronica's cowering.

The elimination process was far more drawn out than they showed on TV. Every time Ethan chose a woman Lance gave a blurb about every woman already picked. Then he referred to Ethan as the twenty-nine-year-old pediatrician from the Boston area that had the difficult job of sorting women, like some of us didn't fit anymore and needed to be sent to Goodwill.

At first I thought Ethan would pick me, but then he called woman after woman until there was only one key left. I could feel the camera on my face every time I didn't get picked and I wondered what Andrea would see when she watched Julian's edited version of the show.

I tried to smile and look unconcerned, but the drudgery of watching seven out of ten women receive their keys sucked

134

something out of me that made me droop. After an hour only the drunken sisters and I stood on the risers without one. I felt like a child enduring her punishment for being naughty.

When Lance finally turned it back over to Ethan to give out the last key, I held my breath. I almost passed out while Ethan paused and considered in his Roger Rabbit way.

I wanted a key. I wanted to win. I wanted a million dollars. I wanted to go to Doctors without Borders and see Ethan work again.

"Ethan, who will be the last contestants still in the running for the title of *The Whole Package*," Lance asked. Then he gestured to Ethan.

"Carrie," Ethan called. I let out a deep breath and grinned. I walked to him and he took my hand warmly into his. He dropped the key before I even said, "Okay."

Oh, how I smiled at him.

Anyone who saw me knew, even before I could know, what was happening inside me. The camera watched me the whole time.

"Our final contestant Carrie Carnegie is a twenty-six-year-old recruiter for the prestigious company Kimber and Stophers in New York City," recited Lance. "Her father, famous architect Arthur Carnegie, died when she was fourteen. She worked her way through school to get a scholarship to Harvard in his honor. Little did she know, only ten years later Carrie would again be faced with tragic loss! Her fortune five hundred fiancé died in a tragic accident. Carrie didn't wallow in self-pity, but instead went to work completing her MBA in his honor. Carrie deserves a spot among the resilient, and may even be *The Whole Package*."

By the time Lance finished, I couldn't swallow. I'd never heard my life's devastations summed up so matter-of-factly.

Ethan told the drunken sisters to watch their alcohol intake. He kept chanting if they found they couldn't stop drinking to get help. The attorney tried to keep it together, but kept looking at the camera; she finally realized she'd been exposing herself, and had to go back to reality.

Julian didn't come to the Manor House until Patrick loaded the drunken sisters into the limo. We all changed into comfortable lounge clothes hoping the night was over when Lance called for us to gather. Once in the sitting room, Julian came bouncing in like he had great news.

Julian wore a pirate shirt with a vest over it. His wavy brown hair streaked with gray sat loosely on his shoulders. Oh, the comedic material wasted inside my head. Patrick was Julian's favorite punching bag, so I didn't tease him out loud anymore.

"I just got a call from the head of the network, Mr. Richard Blanchard. Carrie, I believe he's a friend of yours?"

"I don't know him personally," I answered.

"Really?" He said, genuinely surprised. Something flinched behind his eyes before he pushed it away and embraced his excitement again.

"Anyway, our people ratings are so high the network is moving us to the coveted Thursday night slot," Julian said.

"Congratulations," Lance said.

"I'm not sure I understand," Ethan said. Only Lance looked genuinely impressed by this news.

"We have a following," Julian explained, "The network is going to rerun the first two episodes next week, and then

136

premiere the next episode on the following Thursday. If this season goes well enough, we may even get a spot in the fall line up!"

"Wait. We aren't filming next week?" I asked.

"No, we'll still film. We'll have two weeks' worth of footage before we air again, plus Richard, or Mr. Blanchard, added another week at the end, so we don't have to shorten the series."

As Julian said this he looked to me as if I purposely used some unseen power over this man I'd never met to give his show a boost. I'd seen this look before. My boss loved this influence I had over people who wielded commanding positions, but for some reason needed a Carnegie's approval. It wasn't uncommon for people I'd never met to go out of their way to get me scholarships, and boost my career. Julian believed I would share his excitement in using me and my last name to get what he wanted.

Unable to ask him if he'd found his booty, I sat back humiliated. Three weeks. Three weeks on a reality show while Julian learned to use the Carnegie currency. At least my boss, Karl, frankly acknowledged the con, and didn't pretend I should be as excited about it as he was. My desire to win dwindled into nothing, replaced by the same old feeling of being a pawn. Reality set in. I needed to get home to my mom. She was all softness, turning to mush.

CHAPTER THIRTEEN

At first, I couldn't fathom what Julian would use extra footage for, considering he only had forty minutes of show a week. And yet the extra week rushed by faster than I could acknowledge. I ran in the mornings with Ethan. For a few days, we went into San Francisco helping panhandlers find shelter and clean up. Julian made us help specific homeless people, less fortunate who magically wanted help, and wept their thanks to us on camera.

Veronica and Erin gave a few random homeless people hygiene kits while we waited to film. Julian snapped at them not to touch anything unless they received permission first.

Most nights we ate barbecue chicken on the terrace while cameras followed our every move. We wore the same dresses every night. Julian meant for the scene to look like one night. By the third night, for some reason, many of the contestants relaxed. The familiarity of the situation made them let down their guard. The cameramen, who normally badgered us to gush over Ethan or be nasty about the oddities of the other contestants, stayed in the background.

The gap in competitions lulled us all into a false sense of security. By the second week, no one was prepared for the Fourth of July, though it started innocently like every other day, with a run.

Ethan told me about a little girl who nearly died because her mother waited so long to bring her in.

"What did you do?" I wheezed, then sucked in the cool wet air of 6 a.m. on Independence Day.

"My office is next to the hospital. It has saved a few lives, but that one was the closest."

138

Ethan slowed down and huffed.

"Anyway, I was able to get her into emergency surgery before she died."

"Ahhh ... do you have to say it like that?" I said shivering.

"Sorry," Ethan grinned holding his arms out toward me like I should hug him again.

"Knock it off," I said.

"I know how my doctoring makes you swoon," he said. I rolled my eyes at him and he stopped.

"I am really glad you saved her," I said. Ethan turned to me and started to open up his arms again.

"Knock it off," I laughed, and ran faster, making Ethan catch up to me. I couldn't keep up the pace so I slowed causing him to slingshot ahead of me. Ethan ran too slowly for a good workout most days. I couldn't force myself to run any faster. He always kept pace with me no matter how often I encouraged him to run ahead.

I called over the pounding surf to Ethan: "Why did you choose to be a pediatrician? Was medical school more interesting?"

Ethan turned from me and looked out over the beach being swallowed up by the low-lying wispy clouds. He didn't answer at first. He slowed to breathe steadily. I was slightly behind Ethan, so he put out an arm and caught me. Usually, I avoided a subject; Ethan – open about everything – taunted mc to be open as well.

"Sorry," I said, "Is that too personal a question?"

"Uh..."

"You don't have to talk about it," I said, searching for another subject.

139

"No, no, I … well, I became a pediatrician because I had a little brother who died when he was seven. He was improperly diagnosed with severe stomach flu instead of diabetes."

"Oh, Ethan!"

"All it would have taken was a blood test, but the doctor made up his mind. It was tragic."

"Didn't anyone see something more was wrong?" I asked.

"We put too much stock in the doctor's opinion. We thought Zack had the flu. He was thirsty. My mom kept giving him sugary drinks that he would drink down fast. She thought he had grown dehydrated from puking because he kept drinking and eating so much. One morning I went to get my brother out of bed, and he wouldn't move. I still remember my mom screaming."

Ethan stopped, so I stopped next to him. I put my hand slightly up his loose cotton sleeve rubbing his arm to comfort him. He leaned into me and said:

"He died of kidney failure brought on by untreated diabetes. It was an unbearable time."

Before I could say anything else, he told me in a rushed way all about losing his brother. He told about his mother. In her grief, she volunteered with diabetic children, and how he himself ended up letting go of his resentment and getting involved. His older brother hated the doctor and instead of volunteering, lashed out at everyone and ended up using drugs for a while.

"Anyway," Ethan finished, "Helping with the kids – there was never any other profession for me."

I rubbed his arm under the sleeve up to his shoulder and back down to his elbow while he talked, like I could siphon some of his pain. I knew about loss. I knew about the excruciating emptiness in the space where a person should be. I hated that my friend had to experience that devastation. When he finished talking, Ethan pulled me into a hug. His stubbled chin caught my hair. I tilted my head until I could feel his stubble on my sweaty forehead. He lowered his chin so I could feel it on my temple.

Lightning hit inside me. I pulled away.

"I joked about childhood diabetes. I'm so sorry," I said, remembering how Ethan blanched when I'd been so playful about it.

"That's okay, Care, you didn't know," Ethan said, examining me intensely. I wiped my forehead on the gray sleeve of my Harvard sweatshirt unable to look up. My breathing didn't seem to slow, even with resting.

"I never know really, though, my mom always says that kindness is a way of ensuring you don't do further injury, but when I try to be nice I get walked all over."

"Yeah, but at least you're not doing the walking," he said, falling in beside me as we started to jog again.

"I've been kinda mean lately. Julian is like a virus; he makes things so catty."

"He does! I'm not sure I'm holding my own either." Ethan looked away.

"Oh please! You're nice to everyone. I've hurt Tess's feelings a few times; I need to watch my jokes. But then she's usually more hurtful than I am."

"She looks up to you, though."

"Not, uh."

"Yeah, she tries to impress you. There's a responsibility in that. You could influence her to, you know, like herself. She's meanest about herself."

"Do you know what happened to her?"

"Severely bullied is all she really told me, got so bad her mom had to home school her for a few years."

"You can tell she is trying to overcome it. She's fighting her natural reaction to lash out. I think she's doing it for Veronica. Don't you?" I asked.

"Ahh ... actually, I shouldn't say anything."

"Right, your contract ... okay, so not speaking specifically about Tess, let's discuss the way people choose to react. It makes a difference don't you think?" I thought of all the women in the house. Some healed and others simply survived.

"I think if you react with a little bit of class, things turn out for your good. Well, if you let it," he agreed.

"That's doesn't even make sense, Yoda," I said.

"I worked for this children's group in Chicago, but the other doctors wouldn't let me do much. They wouldn't let me build my own clientele. Instead of getting angry, I took it as an opportunity to spend a week in Boston with one of the diabetic kids my mom was close to. He'd been accepted into a study for childhood diabetes, and got all his meds free."

"You left your practice and took him to Boston?"

"Yeah. His single mom couldn't leave her job or her other two kids. I finished my residency doing a lot more research than I had in medical school. I wanted to get into research, especially with childhood diabetes. Going to Boston to see how it all worked made sense to me."

"And you just stayed?" I asked.

"Yep. Doctor Brown, who had three patients in the study, liked me. He took me on as his partner. I dropped everything I owned into it – it was not much, but still he took me on. His practice is ... much more lucrative than working with a group, plus he has privileges at Boston Children's hospital. That alone opened so many doors for me. Last year he retired, leaving me his building, all his patients, and Beth, his RN who takes care of the office. She then got me on this show."

"You just left your practice?"

"Dr. Brown came out of retirement for a few months so I could do the show – Beth's very persuasive."

"I guess."

"Anyway, back to the point, my life has worked out relatively speaking because I didn't react angrily or poorly. I just found another way. Now, I'm here running with you."

"As opposed to?"

"My brother, he still struggles to hold down a job. He competes with me whenever I go home, everything I say he jumps all over just to prove he's better than me. He will never move away from Zack's death. He wears it on him like a badge of honor, or like he loved Zack more because he doesn't have a life. I doubt Zack would have wanted him to ... anyway. We reacted differently."

"Yeah, you did."

"At that crucial time, I forgave and followed my mother's example, and Zack didn't. I am part owner of a highly lucrative pediatric practice; he's in and out of rehab – see?"

143

I couldn't answer. Ethan wanted me to talk. He wanted me to share. I could feel him moving the conversation in that direction.

"I'm glad to be near Children's Hospital. The alumni dump all kinds of money into the hospital for research."

Ethan nudged me, trying to tease me into displaying the dedication I'd shown to my former scholarly institution when he was ragging on it a few days earlier. I grinned to show him that I wasn't going to react.

"Anyway, let's hear it."

He stopped to look at me.

"What?"

"I told you how my reaction to my brother's death differed from my brother's. What ... um ... growth opportunities, let's call it, have come to you since your dad's death?" he asked. For some reason he never probed about my fiancé; he didn't seem to want to know about Gordon.

"I guess I never saw it that way," I said, shutting down to Ethan's question. Was I ungrateful? I didn't really see anything good in my life, just lists in my head of all the bad – all the hard – the unfair.

I decided to tell Ethan something as he told me all about his brother. As soon as I thought this, I almost wanted to tell him, like he might actually understand.

"Well," I said when we slowed down again, "After my dad died, we moved in with my mom's parents. I was promptly put into an intense private school right as my grades started to matter. Grandpa died before I graduated from high school, but he ... he helped me figure a lot out. My grandma used his life insurance to cover what my scholarship didn't. I was able

144

to get a good job and now I support my Mom and little sister. I guess supporting my family is a good thing."

I tried to squash the fear of failing, but it always came when I knew my mom needed more than I could give her.

"You're completely supporting your family in Hartford?" Ethan asked in a cross between impressed and embarrassed he made so many jokes about my being well off.

"Yeah. About six months ago my Grandma's life insurance completely ran out. The upkeep on the old estate is out of control; taxes finished the insurance off nicely. Fortunately, it was after I was able to get a good job," I said.

"Neither your mom nor your sister has a job?"

"My mom has some health issues; my sister's kind of a debutante. Just before she died, my Grandma actually shamed my dad's brother into footing the bill to take her to this big debutant ball."

"They do nothing to support themselves?" Ethan asked again.

"You don't understand what Ladies do and don't do," I teased him.

"Oh, right. The head of the network, Richard Blanchard, he kept saying ladies like the Carnegies don't do reality shows."

"I don't know him."

"He knows you. He told me about it when I was signing my contract. He said it was my pleasure to get to know you."

"Wait." I stopped running. "He knew I was coming on the show when you signed your contract? Wouldn't they have gotten you to commit before looking for your harem?"

"For the millionth time I didn't mean it like that. It's like when people use the word fetish, but they really don't mean fetish," Ethan said.

"When was this?" I asked.

"About six months ago, December sometime," he said.

"And Richard Blanchard, the head of the network, knew I was coming on the show before you even signed your contract?"

"I don't know, but he knew you. He mentioned your family – apparently, the Carnegie's are very exclusive – you don't go anywhere that's beneath you."

"Right – because we can't afford to on my salary. To get into this ball it was $17,000 a table. Not to mention her dress."

"That's what you pay to be with the in crowd?"

"If you can manage to get an invitation—which he probably couldn't," I said.

"No wonder he sounded like he wanted to come on *The Whole Package* to hang out with you. You are the in crowd."

"Yeah, I am. Lucky you."

Ethan laughed derisively.

"Anyway, if he really knew our situation, I doubt he'd want to know me."

"That'd be his loss."

"Thanks," I said.

"Carrie, if I had a choice between struggling to support my family to being a rich kid with roads paved in gold – I'd chose to be struggling."

"I know. That's why I like you." I launched myself up a steep incline.

Men flirt with me thinking I could make them, but Ethan wasn't like that. Like Veronica, he worked for everything he had and respected those who did the same. He didn't realize I wasn't the same; people opened plenty of doors for me. When we reached the top of the incline Ethan said:

"I don't get it. So your sister just doesn't work."

I glared at him.

"It isn't exactly like that. My dad was Arthur Carnegie. People don't expect her to work."

"Your dad must have worked hard," he pointed out.

"He did. He created buildings out of nothing. Once he said he could always see where everything needed to go before he even drafted the blueprints. He never needed a structural engineer like most architects do," I said, redirecting.

"When we get back East you should take me for a tour of all your dad's buildings. I'd like to spend a day looking at his architecture." He paused and looked at me. "It must have been weird to grow up that way."

"I didn't know it was different than other kids. My dad took me everywhere he went, gave me jobs I could do. By the age of twelve, I met some of the most creative – some of the most powerful – people in the world. They'd slap the top of my hard hat like they were anyone you'd meet on the street. I'd do my best to make 'em laugh."

"And your sister didn't respect the work ethic?"

Ugh, couldn't he take a hint?

"She's five years younger than me," I said glaring at him again.

"Yeah, but Carrie, she's an adult now."

147

"Addie was only eight when my dad died. She doesn't remember that life. Grandma put this obligation on her to be a legacy, not a person; she is Arthur Carnegie's daughter. My grandma, she, taught her to...."

"Still –"

"She doesn't know better. My mom has some health problems. My mom's all sweetness, a little too soft for her own good. Grandma took over."

"Your Grandma lets you pay for everything?"

"Grandma died four years ago."

"I'm sorry for your loss," Ethan said.

"I'm glad she's gone." I stopped myself, "Err, I guess that wasn't – "

"It's real. Sometimes you can't help how you feel."

"She ... I didn't mean it like that ... life's easier ... well," I stammered, permeated with guilt. Why couldn't I be sorry she was gone? In a way, though, she never left us. Her mean-spirited criticism sat on my chest telling me when to breathe. I didn't want to think about her.

"All your family passed away, other than your mother and sister?" Ethan asked trying to sound more respectful.

"Pretty much. My Dad's older brother still has the Carnegie estate in Wilton and his portion of the inheritance. His kids get trusts from that line. I received a bunch of jewelry, but other than that, we were cut off when my dad died."

"Wouldn't your uncle help you?"

"No, he's ... very protective of his wealth. Helping us would admit we needed the Carnegie trusts and dilute his fortune. Anyway, he's weird about boundaries and what we

148

should expect from him. Other than really public shows of how he's taking care of his famous little brother's family, like the debutante ball, we can't expect anything out of him."

"It all sounds like a bad movie," he said.

"You would be sick if you really knew the extent the wealthy go to in the name of protecting their wealth. In fact, the lengths my grandmother pretended so we looked like we had wealth to protect."

"Like what?" He asked.

"My mom has a younger brother. He was cut off eight years ago right after Grandpa died."

"Why was he cut off?"

"The real reason, he would have sold the house at auction to get money, then people would have known Grandma strapped us. But my Grandma claimed it was the estrangement between them."

"What happened?"

"It was before I was born. He wanted to be a mediator so he could drop out of law school. He didn't want to bother with my Grandpa's company, Shades, even though it was profitable back then."

"He was disowned?"

"Only after Grandpa died."

"Ouch."

"That's Grandma. He came sniffing for money after my Grandma died. When he found us owing taxes for the house, he left my mom to deal with cleaning up the mess."

"What a jerk. Did you figure it all...."?

"Yeah, we cleaned it up. My dad's oldest friend did, he's in corporate finance. I don't know exactly what he did, but he

149

cleared everything up. Only after my uncle signed something saying he forfeited his right to the estate."

"He just signed that?"

"I never thought about it … Mr. Wilson probably paid him off, I don't really know. I try not to think about it, but if I did, I'd bet he paid the taxes too. He was my dad's best friend."

"The man who isn't even your relative helped you, while both your uncles ditched you?"

"Yeah, forget they both know …." I trailed off. I couldn't force myself to say it. To name it in front of Ethan – who was a doctor and would understand the disease draining the life out of my mother. It was too much.

"Know what?" Ethan asked, swallowing hard with disgust.

"Well, how meager Grandma left us. So anyway, it's just us," I said, back-peddling. I did not want to talk about my life anymore. I couldn't explain Grandma – and what she did to my mother to waste away my father's inheritance after he died. Ethan would never understand the legal measures Uncle Brock took to cut us off before his brother was even cold in his grave. He did it because of Grandmother, that much was clear. That's just what people did to protect their wealth.

I quickly said, "Addie's always joking she's waiting for her Congressman to come along. Funniest thing ever – she started dating Charles Goodrich. His dad is running for the House seat in Connecticut."

"That's what's wrong with this country. All these rich kids who never had to work for anything run our country, writing checks we can't cash."

150

"Oh well...." I didn't know what to say. Ethan's jaw clenched and eyes blazed. Finally, I said, "I bet you have a lot of rich clientele."

"I could tell you stories," he said, "You wouldn't even believe some of the completely unrealistic expectations put on me. I don't have the god complex. They thrust it upon me and then expect a miracle because they paid me their precious money."

"Ah, the dollar rocks the cradle," I said.

"What?"

"You know – I pay the nanny who rocks the cradle so I rule the world."

Ethan laughed. Then he said, "Anyway, sorry. I want to hear about Addie and her Congressman."

"No, I want to hear about your rich clients."

"Carrie, it's your turn to share. That's how friendship works."

I stopped. Is that why I didn't feel bonded to anyone lately? I ... Instead of pushing my mind down this avenue, I said:

"I'm not worried about it, the Congressman's son ... Addie thinks he's a stick-in-the-mud, but it's amusing."

"How old is Addie?" Ethan asked. I could hear the condescension in his voice.

"It's not her fault."

"Come on! How old does she have to be before you force her to be responsible for her own life?"

"She's only twenty-one. She needs to finish her schooling," I finally snapped, exasperated, not trying to keep the defensive tone from my voice now. Didn't he know if I told

Addie to get a job? She wouldn't. She'd been hard-wired to get a husband. She'd marry the stick-in-the-mud Congressman's son she didn't even like. I wouldn't allow that.

I remembered the day Grandmother introduced me to Gordon. I hated to remember my smile, how I'd kissed up. His confidence when he took my hand. I'd been so young.

Addie couldn't know the money was gone – Grandmother planted that burden in her head. That's why I pretended everything was fine. I took her burden. I made it mine. She couldn't know how bad things were.

Ethan eyed me.

"Well aren't you *The Whole Package*," Ethan said, trying to lighten me up.

I tried to nod like I didn't care, but I closed off. We'd slowed to a fast walk while we talked, so I started running again.

"I didn't mean to hurt your feelings," Ethan said pulling up next to me.

"You didn't," I said.

"Yes, I did. Look, tell me about Addie," Ethan said grabbing my arm. I stopped running.

"She doesn't know how bad things are ... I can't ... I can't tell her," I said pulling away.

"Why?"

"You wouldn't understand," I said moving forward.

"Try me," he said.

"You already think she's some spoiled brat. She isn't, she just doesn't understand how to ... it's like people whose parents never held down a job, so they wouldn't even know

152

how to get one. The excessively poor and the excessively rich have more in common than one would think."

"Then tell me about her. What does she do all day if she doesn't work?"

"Duh, she and my mom volunteer in everything. If anything, I wish my mom would slow down a little. Addie's going to school. She has to finish her degree."

"Then she'll work?"

"I don't know." Striving to get the serious tone out of my voice I joked, "Working isn't ladylike. All the other fathers out there protect their daughters from such ugliness."

"So, you aren't a lady?" Ethan said.

I stared at the gnarled tree roots hanging off the cliff in the distance. What had it done to survive after it found itself on the edge of the cliff? My face twisted in concentration on the thought: I was not a lady. I, too, was hanging off a cliff. In a sickening whirl, all the compromises I'd made in the last few years tumbled making my stomach heavy. I started running again. Ethan fell in beside me trying to talk to me, but I couldn't respond with anything but shrugs.

My Grandmother claimed it to be unladylike to work. She told me, because of the way I behaved in public, my only worth was to hire out. With my last name, I'd get a high-paying job but I'd have to drop the status of being a lady. For six months she'd taunted me, reminding me of the other option. There was a young man she knew – he really wanted to meet me. Her voice echoed in my head:

"He's going to be a very successful attorney, like his father. He's expressed interest in revitalizing your

153

grandfather's company. He's sure we can still lay claim to Shades."

"Do I have the authority to hire him?" I returned sarcastically, for the first month at least.

"He's an upperclassman at Harvard. He's gone to some trouble to meet you," she persisted for months.

I could still see the smile on my grandmother's face when Gordon extended his hand to me. I took it. From then on, I worked hard to fall in love with him.

Maybe I wasn't a lady. But I would keep Addie from believing she had to marry young, and as wealthy as possible, to sustain us. Nothing else mattered. She could be the lady. What did I care?

I ran faster than I was capable of. Ethan could tell he hurt my feelings, and kept trying to talk to me, but he didn't understand. He couldn't understand.

"You don't believe you're not a lady – do you?" he asked.

"I don't know. I don't care anymore," I finally said, remembering Grandfather's face. He always insisted I was a lady, especially after Grandmother took to shaming me. But he died. And I learned how to survive without him.

"You're more of a lady than anyone else here," Ethan cut into my thoughts.

"No, Veronica is," I said running with my head turned aloof. Veronica worked hard. She never lost herself for any amount of money. That made her a lady. Earning a living didn't take the status away. The day I'd taken Gordon's very wealthy hand instead of being brave enough to fend for myself, I stopped being a lady.

Then he died, and I lost myself for nothing. I remembered that limo ride best. I left Gordon in the ground. Fear closed in on me, telling me I'd fail. My sister would see my mother's needs that I couldn't fulfill. She would –

"What are you thinking about?" Ethan asked concerned.

"Nothing," I said.

"Come on, you can't worry about being a lady. Who even thinks like that anymore?" Ethan asked.

"My treadmill didn't prepare me for the rolling cliffs of California."

"Come on, Carrie! Don't do that; don't shut me out. I don't know what this is about, but being a lady in my opinion is based on choices and consideration. You are a kind, very considerate person."

"You sound like my Grandpa," I said. I felt worse about my choices.

"What are you really thinking?" he asked, grabbing the back of my shirt so I had to stop.

"I can't believe we have to miss the Fourth of July to tape some competition. That's really unpatriotic," I said.

"That's not what you were thinking," he said. I tried to run but he wouldn't let go of my shirt.

"Fine. I was remembering. Remembering once when I tutored a member of the men's lacrosse team in the mathematics of symmetry. Some of my society friends at Harvard were bothered by it. Especially one friend of mine – he tried to give me the equivalent money to quit."

"That's going too far," Ethan said. "He sounds like a busybody."

155

"Oh, they all are. Everyone watches me, just waiting to pounce on everything I do." I started running again.

Gordon and I dated seriously and then I started to tutor the lacrosse player. I remembered once when the lacrosse player passed us on campus, Gordon cupped my ribcage with his hand and pulled me possessively to his side. He asked me to marry him shortly after the encounter. Was I his? Did I want to be his? Did Gordon need me to fill a certain role for him, as clearly as Julian did?

I couldn't breathe. I needed to run fast and hard. Gordon was dead, and I didn't want to be disrespectful. Gordon didn't deserve that. He didn't place me, not like Julian did.

"Hey wait up. What's wrong?" Ethan asked, catching up to me. I kept moving, but slowed down.

"Have you noticed Julian never lets the camera catch my reactions unless I'm being funny, defensive, or lifting my pinky in good breeding?"

"Yeah, but this is all a game Carrie. You can't take it seriously."

"No! This runs deeper for me. Why can't I show concern or empathy? He doesn't want his audience to see it. Am I preordained to play the stereotypical socialite for the rest of my life?"

"What?"

"I just … I don't want to be anything … Why can't I just be Carrie?"

"I'm not sure I—"

"I don't want to be a character, a role in other people's lives. I'm so sick of being prodded … I just want to … I don't know what I'm saying," I said.

156

"Are you all right?"

"I don't know," I said and pushed my body to run harder.

We came to the end of the trail and stood to look out over the lighthouse. The ocean seemed upset and pounded the rocks, launching huge waves into the air. I tried to stretch out my legs, but they just wanted to be moving.

"What were you thinking? Why did you look so sad just now?" he asked.

I couldn't tell Ethan what he wanted to know. I couldn't tell him what I'd done, why I wasn't a lady. I'd lose the million– but no. No. I was done pretending. I couldn't tell him because it would be like telling Grandfather, who had so much faith in me. He'd lose his faith in me.

"You okay?" Ethan asked.

"I want to be a lady. I can't help it," I said.

"You are," Ethan said.

"No, but I will be."

"What? When you quit your job?"

"No, but I'd like to stop using my last name to get things. I want to work for what I have like my father did."

"That sounds noble – worthy of a million dollars, even."

"Shut up," I said. He grinned. He reached over and took my hand.

"You going to be okay?"

"I think so," I said. I faked a smile for him.

"Don't do that, not to me. Be sad if you're sad but don't play a role for me. Be yourself."

I pulled the hand he held up to my cheek and closed my eyes fighting back a strange pull at the back of my throat to cry.

157

"Thanks," I said.

I opened my eyes. Ethan examined me, so raw and open, and yet he didn't run away. He looked worried about me. My stomach lurched and I wanted to move into him. I quickly dropped his hand.

"It's getting late. I'm always in trouble for taking so long getting dressed," I said. I ran back in the direction we came. I was silent for a long time, thinking.

"You're right about one thing," I finally said.

"What's that?"

"My grandmother has been dead four years, but she still holds so much weight with me."

"What are you going to do?"

"I don't know. How do I stop living her life?"

"You could stop pretending to have money. You don't have to keep up appearances," he said. He watched me like he'd take it back if I didn't like his idea.

"She literally put me in the place of Grandfather – funding her lifestyle."

"Stop then," he said, "Or at least recognize your grandpa was a good person, and so are you."

"Yeah," I said. I didn't say anymore. My grandpa built a business up from the ground. I was on a reality show where the million-dollar prize taunted me daily, reminding me why I had to be so loyal to Gordon's memory. Just in case I couldn't make the bills, if ... no. Not if, but when, I failed, I would keep myself free to find another Gordon. Addie would not. I couldn't be a lady. I needed an insurance policy. I stopped this flow of thoughts. Is that all Gordon was?

I remembered the look on Gordon's face when he'd barged into my dorm room and seen the lacrosse player. It plagued me after he died. At times, I forgot how he looked happy, and just remembered his outraged face when he found me alone with another man. No matter how I explained the innocence of the situation, he hadn't liked the idea of my tutoring. He loved me, obsessively at the end, always checking in on me.

The day he died, he texted me three times during my test to be sure I'd make the second half of his polo match. Had my absence distracted him?

I couldn't think that, I just couldn't.

Grandmother's grating nag came in my head: "Don't examine every bite of your food Carrie. Just swallow. Some things are best unexamined."

I picked up the pace. I ran like something dark and humiliating chased me and if I slowed down, it would catch me. After we'd almost made it back to the little wooden bridge, Ethan said:

"Carrie, can we slow down a little?"

"Yeah," I said slowing to a jog and using the back of my hand to get the sweat out of my eyes. We jogged slowly the rest of the way while Ethan looked at me like I might jump off my proverbial bridge. I tried to escape with just a wave when we came to the split in the road, but he bumped my shoulder and grabbed my arm.

"Carrie, you're too hard on yourself. I don't know all that happened to you, but ... don't let it swallow you. You're a good person, and whatever it was, you've overcome it to become a

159

really good person. You need to focus on that and move forward."

"I'll try," I whispered. I felt strangely comforted.

He smiled down at me. I wanted someone in my life with perfect silver eyes that told me I was a good person.

"Thanks," I said feeling a smile lift up my face. I did not force myself to smile, but it tugged from contentment in my heart, and came easily.

Ethan waved and I moved away from him.

"Happy Fourth of July," Ethan called, but paused like he might say something else. I waited. He said nothing.

"Happy Fourth of July," I called back. I ran forward with a wave.

CHAPTER FOURTEEN

As I did every day, I ran around to the front of the house and stopped to stretch before going in. A Dutch Iris bloomed off the porch. Its bright purple flowers seemed to peep coyily amid the tall, blade-like leaves. As I stretched out my back, Lance trotted up wearing a jungle helmet.

"Let me guess," I said switching legs, "we're going to see who can stick her head in a lion's mouth. The contestants that keeps her head in the longest without getting it snapped off will help Ethan feed zoo animals on Monday?"

"It's a living. I think you're supposed to wear a sundress today?"

"I know, according to Julian, Becky messed up my wardrobe."

"Hurry and get dressed. You have ten minutes." He pulled the door open for me.

"It's only seven-thirty," I said.

"We're starting early this morning," he said.

"Thanks for the warning," I called, walking into the house, "Happy Independence Day."

"Carrie, don't forget to put your microphone on – yet again," he called after me. I did a little back wave.

"Hey, Carrie! Do you want an egg and toast?" Tess called from the kitchen.

"No, Tess. We have ten minutes until Julian's here. We're starting early."

"You've got to be kidding me!" Serena said. She wore an old tee shirt and men's plaid pajama bottoms, her new copper

161

hair in a high ponytail. She madly dashed toward the stairs, about running me over. She smiled at me as she did it, though; that made it okay.

I gave Serena a wide berth then started up the stairs again, though my legs didn't want to support me. With Grandmother in my head, I couldn't help thinking she and Serena had many similar qualities. Complaining until she got pity was one of Grandmother's favorite strategies.

"Hey Tess," I said as she caught up to me halfway up the stairs, "how about you borrow my new red shirt. I got it from Becky yesterday. She wanted me to look patriotic."

"You don't want to look patriotic?" she asked.

"It's not that. Julian informed her I couldn't wear it. Something about my hair, a few shades darker, clashing."

"That's weird. Becky is usually really good about that," she said.

"Yeah, Julian is playing tricks again. Becky gave it to me in front of him and he was all rude about it, then suggested I give it to you, he said ... well, maybe you could afford to cover up some ... maybe they're trying to ... ah ..."

"Keep my chest from getting sunburned."

"Your designer does seem overly proud of how well-endowed you are."

"That doesn't make sense, though. Julian likes me to dress that way."

"I'm sure, but he's a pervert. The show is on a family station. Maybe someone complained or something?"

"Maybe," Tess said looking away and blinking, "But then why wouldn't he give me the shirt directly?"

"I don't know. Becky said it in a rehearsed way like they were trying to manipulate you or me, I can't be sure who. She looked at me and said, 'Well Carrie, you'll just have to wear your sundress then,' in a way that made me laugh."

"They want you to wear a sundress?" she asked.

"Or they're trying to make you wear the red shirt. It's pretty. It wraps around and is really flattering but, I definitely don't have the chest to pull it off."

"Bri seems to think Ethan likes –"

"Your designer failed to notice nobody actually dresses like that in the real world – except at Halloween. What is that?" I asked.

Tess blushed. I shifted my argument and said, "Listen, Tess, Lance is wearing safari gear. They'll probably change our outfits again after they announce what we're doing. Who knows – I'm wearing a sundress. I have nothing else, apparently," I said. I wanted to inspire Tess to join my rebellious movement.

"Diva," Tess said.

"Wouldn't you like to win a challenge instead of trying not to fall out of whatever you're wearing today?" I shot back.

"I'm supposed to wear a sundress, well, actually two strips of fabric attached to a skirt," Tess said.

"Oh, that explains it, they want me to wear my sundress, and you the red shirt," I said.

"I'm not sure. I think I'm supposed to wear the dress," Tess said.

"No, don't wear yours. How embarrassing would that be, if we were twinners? Becky told me to get dressed before we

163

leave this morning. She doesn't have anything else for me to wear."

"Whatever, I guess," Tess said. I pushed again just for good measure:

"If it's wrong, they'll change you before we start filming anyway. They always do." Tess would go indecisively back and forth for the whole ten minutes if I let her.

"Fine, I'll wear it," she agreed and followed me to my room. I handed her the shirt. She ran to her room to put it on. I saw a little trail of manipulation getting me to wear the sundress, but I decoded it, and didn't see any harm in Tess wearing a very cute red shirt.

I showered quickly and put on my fifties-style sundress. I paused looking at myself in the mirror. Gordon bought me the pale yellow sundress more than four years earlier for our honeymoon cruise. I threw it in my suitcase as the nicest piece of clothing I owned.

It seemed silly, but after he died I never wore it out of my room. I put it on every once in a while, but always took it back off, as if it were the wedding dress I never wore. There was some spirit of being bought and paid for in the dress I couldn't shake off. Especially after my run it felt wrong wearing it and I wished I left it home. Now I had no choice. I had nothing else to wear. How did that even happen?

I dried my hair in deep waves, knowing Becky would have a fit if she didn't get to do it. She wanted to try out the perfect hairstyle to go with the dress.

I realized too late Veronica hadn't heard my announcement. She must have been downstairs already. She

164

hated when they filmed her in her pajamas, but usually if she stayed away from Ethan, none of the cameramen bothered.

When I finished it had been more than ten minutes, but I hate being rushed. Grandmother always rushed me here and there. I remember taking my time then as well, just to prove I didn't live my life on her schedule. It always made Grandmother mad, but only because she couldn't control me like she did everyone else. As I put on mascara, Lance called up the stairs, "Carrie, you're the last one, yet again. If you don't have your microphone on, stop and put it on right now."

I applied my lip gloss in a completely relaxed manner. I'd already slipped my microphone on while getting dressed. I picked out earrings with the time I supposed it would have taken. I walked down the stairs wearing my own pale yellow sundress and wicker sandals. Ethan was at the bottom of the stairs talking to Serena but turned from her to see me half way down the stairs. He mouthed, "Wow."

Instead of feeling guilty, I decided I'd be encouraged by the daggers Serena threw with her pretty azure eyes.

Serena, on the other hand, changed her pajamas. Not into real clothes, though. She wore a tank top that almost covered her boy shorts showing off her long thin thighs until they hit black, button-up UGG boots.

She claimed she'd just thrown the shirt on to cover up for breakfast because she slept in her underwear. She appeared genuinely embarrassed while the camera filmed.

I stood next to Veronica who looked like she just jumped out of the pool. She wrapped a towel around her middle, her still-wet hair clung matted to her head. Her friendly green

165

eyes twinkled as we linked arms. She whispered, "You took a long jog this morning – I just barely finished my workout."

"Actually, it was the same as usual. I slept in a little is all," I said. Then I realized Ethan must have waited at the path for me. I moved to say something to him, but Julian walked in from his studio across the driveway. In the unguarded moment, Ethan had a hard, irritated sort of look on his face. Then he forced a fake smile when Julian looked at him.

Julian, as always, gave no entering pleasantries and dove into re-emphasizing the way to act on camera. He often taunted us, like he wanted nothing more than fist fighting over Ethan. He said as if to his kindergarten class,

"Remember you're in this for one million dollars. Think about what you could do with a million dollars."

After he'd actually tried to have us do a "visualize your life with a million dollars" exercise, I raised my hand and pointed out it'd only be half a million after taxes so we should take that into consideration. Julian appraised me wondering if I was joking. As he had no sense of humor, he asked that all comments be contained until the proper time. I noticed the proper time had not yet occurred.

I refocused when Julian came close enough to spit on my face as he said:

"Again, I need the competitions respected. You have signed contracts stating you will compete in these competitions the way they were designed."

"Well, I'm a team player," Serena said smiling at Ethan. Only Serena spoke when Julian was around. The rest of us listened. Even Sandra closed her arms in on herself

166

uncomfortably and fell into silence. Veronica disappeared behind me when he came around.

He leered at us all, but he seemed almost obsessed with me. At times he'd sit near me when we weren't taping, trying to chat like he wanted me to get to know him. Fortunately, this meant he didn't poke at me, or randomly touch me with the excuse of fixing something, as he did with other contestants.

He ended his little pep talk like a monarch examining a feast to be devoured and not people to be respected. After his lecture, directed mostly at me, he walked toward the door, avoiding the front of the camera as usual.

Just as I started to breathe easy Julian paused, he turned and said quietly to me, "You look very pretty, Carrie."

"Becky told me to get dressed, remember," I said.

"Yes, you'll be the only one pleased with today's activity."

I stared at him with my reddish-brown eyes in slits. "Why?"

He didn't answer, and instead walked away, laughing a little. I wondered what we were doing, and why the other contestants wouldn't appreciate it.

All the other contestants wore a hodgepodge of clothes. Erin wore her sports bra and footless tights with a very red face like she'd been dancing and leaping about. I sometimes walked into the empty room and caught her at the end of her workout after my run. I loved to watch her fluid movements.

Only Tess and I were dressed all the way – the red shirt looked too dressy for the cut-off shorts she wore. We all presumed tents would be set up wherever we were filming. At least two hours were blocked out before the

167

competitions. Designers changed us and fiddled with our hair. From what Julian said, I figured that would not happen. I would be the only one dressed. Just then, Lance said, "Okay ladies, your bus awaits."

"Wait, shouldn't these guys shower?" I called.

"Not for today's challenge," Lance said.

I tried to get close enough to tell Tess she should run up and change into her sundress, but there was such a bustle around the door. Tess was the first to walk out followed by Veronica in her towel.

"Quick, go change into a dress or a skirt or something," I whispered to Serena. She stood next to me in her supposed nightwear that could have been on a *Victoria's Secret* ad. She rolled her eyes at me and walked out of the house. I climbed onto the chartered bus, smiled for George, then slid into the high-backed, carpeted seat next to Veronica.

"Didn't you want to shower?" I asked her.

"Lance said not to bother. We must be going to the beach or getting covered in goo or something," she said, as to calm herself.

"'Kay," I said. I didn't really know what was happening. It made me uncomfortable to watch Veronica brush through her wet matted hair with her fingers then put it into a bun with an elastic around her wrist.

What could I tell her? Julian was up to something. She already looked terrified. Nothing could be done, so we fell into a miserable silence.

A fashion hiccup couldn't hurt anyone, right?

Since Ethan publicly denounced the amount of drinking on the show, most of the contestants started to refrain – at least in front of him. This left Julian in need of more inventive ways to create drama. Oh, how I underestimated Julian's ability to manipulate the course of the show.

After an unnecessarily long bus ride, and Veronica scratching her chlorine caked skin through, we walked in late to a small town ticket-only Fourth of July celebration. Everyone aside from Tess and I were in partial stages of getting dressed.

We sat in a pavilion decked out for the holiday in banners of red, white and blue. Our large table sat among smaller tables listening to a quaint little New Orleans style brass band playing patriotic music. The older generation sitting around us wore garden party attire, blouses, skirts, and trousers. They were terribly offended at us – especially at Serena and Erin.

"Oh, don't you look so pretty," an elderly lady said patting me on the shoulder on her way to the bathroom.

"Oh uh ..." I said.

"It's nice to see a member of the rising generation who shows a little respect," the woman said as she glared at Serena.

"I'm sorry," Serena, said looking pitiful.

"Well perhaps you'll make better choices," she said and walked away while Sandra tried to explain they hadn't gotten a chance to get dressed.

A raised podium formed a long line at the top of the pavilion where the dignitaries sat glaring at us. Poor Veronica couldn't look up. Erin did a little better. Serena and Tess did well pretending not to notice anything was even off. In my opinion, this definitely said something about them, but I

169

couldn't be sure what. Maybe they were more fake than the rest of us? Or maybe they really had been through something worse than the rest of us, but no matter what happened to them, they knew how to smile.

No breakfast ever lasted so painfully long. By the end of it, my sundress hampered me just as badly as if I were in my underwear. It sucked me into an awkward hole. When we were all herded back onto the bus, Lance did his stretched-out bits to make sure we were sufficiently in suspense, and then finally said:

"Today's competition winners are Tess and Serena." The cameraman put the camera right in my face. They must have expected to see disappointment. Instead, I gave Tess a thumb up.

My grin faltered when I turned and found Veronica hunched over in the seat next to me, with her hands in her face. I put my arm around her and leaned in, holding my hand up so the cameraman couldn't get a clear shot of her tears. Though I didn't know it at the time, Julian crucified me in this episode. My act of friendship for Veronica was the only thing in the whole episode that redeemed me in the eyes of the viewer.

As soon as the cameramen got off the bus, everyone attacked me.

"Carrie, how did y'all know what the competition was?" Sandra snapped pulling her smiley face Pajama bottoms up to her chest.

"I ... I,"

"I'm the one who showed up in my underwear! You owe us an explanation." Serena knelt up on her seat so I could see her overly dramatic show of anger.

"I swear I didn't. I got an idea from ..." I stammered. On the verge of tears, I couldn't believe I'd been so underhanded. Though I couldn't tell what I'd done wrong either, it must have been something.

"I can't believe you told me not to wear my sundress," Tess said with half a grin and amused eyes like we played a game and I outmaneuvered her.

"Tess, you cannot honestly believe I knew we were going to a pancake breakfast with the mayor. How would I know that?" I asked.

"You're getting pretty cozy with Lance. Maybe he's slipping you information," Serena said. She shrugged her shoulders innocently. Her feigned innocence frustrated me, and I grew even more tongue-tied.

Everyone looked from Serena to me. I ignored Serena.

"Please Tess, you have to believe me. If I could've gone to the bathroom and changed outfits with you, I would've," I said.

"Yeah," Veronica said panicked, but defensively like she had to say something. "She offered to with me...Besides, because Carrie felt bad, she couldn't well ..." Veronica thought for a moment. She strained her whole face, her red-rimmed eyes made her voice sound more congested. "She couldn't ... sparkle like she normally does ... and now you get to go pick up garbage on Saturday."

"Goodie," Tess rolled her eyes.

Serena said, "That's true," like she found the answer to a riddle.

171

And she had.

CHAPTER FIFTEEN

I may have recovered from the sundress incident, as it came to be known, if Serena hadn't leeched herself to me, sucking life out of me. The day before eliminations we went to Six Flags with kids from the foster system. Our trip to the amusement park was the nearest to Hell I'd ever been. Not a good, amusement park kind of Perdition, but Serena's type of inferno. We sat in lines being filmed with underprivileged kids waiting to ride roller coasters. It should have been awesome. People all around us tried to figure out who we were, and the kids acted like rock stars.

Serena, in her element, quickly pushed all the foster kids down. Before we were even in the park, they recognized who was in charge. The kids quickly knew, though I don't know how, I was to be ignored. Serena acted like a martyred saint every time I said anything. I learned not to say anything – just as she wanted. Serena's smile grew more and more sincere every time I excused myself to escape.

I'd only known one other person who delighted in my misery. She died, and I couldn't be sorry for her loss.

I woke up the morning of the eliminations ready to leave. Ethan and I went for our morning run as usual. Though I swore in the beginning I wouldn't interfere, I had to somehow hint I needed to leave. He slowed and turned his silver eyes on me and said:

"You seemed pretty miserable at the amusement park."

"Yeah, waiting in line felt like a tug-of-war for your attention," I said.

"Sorry, I have to give each contestant the same consideration," he said.

175

"I know but, it's all turning a little too contentious for me. I don't want to spend all my vacation fighting with the prom queen," I said. I nodded significantly so he couldn't misunderstand. I wanted to go home.

Ethan nodded like he understood.

Ethan stood with us when Serena mentioned all the things I did wrong. Serena refused to let anyone else in the spotlight. He saw it – he had to know who I meant when I said prom queen and spoke of contention. Everyone else could see it, even Patrick and the stylists.

When we made it to the lighthouse, I made my request clearer.

"You know," I said, "I can't afford to lose my job. It's almost torture waiting around with certain people purposely making life unpleasant."

Ethan nodded. He continued to run quietly. His face took on a pensive scowl when he was really thinking. I hated his face without a smile, but I couldn't endure Serena another week. We stopped near the cliffs, and looked down at the pounding surf.

"That's very peaceful, isn't it?" Ethan said. I barely nodded. I felt too close to tears to speak.

"Days are drawing on like years. I'm never alone. Some of the contestants – well, one woman – gets on my last nerve."

I couldn't be specific, but Ethan knew what I meant. I wanted out!

"The ocean is very placid," Ethan said, looking at me, and not the ocean. With what I took as a nonverbal signal telling me he knew my troubles with Serena he even finished with, "Very serene."

176

"Look how the surf stirs up the sand, just to cause trouble," I replied gratefully.

"It becomes opaque," Ethan commented, looking up at me. "It's impossible to see through the water when it gets like that."

I nodded. He watched me intently, waiting, but for what I couldn't say.

"I'm tired," I said.

He put an arm around me. Sadness washed over me. I had to leave Ethan to leave Serena. I laid my head on his shoulder and my body quaked at the thought, losing a few tears. I closed my eyes and listened to the surf. We stood like that while he stroked my back and I near purred at his touch. I pulled away when I heard a car pulling up, and quickly wiped my face.

Only a few tourists ever bothered to drive out to see the light house, and we'd never seen anyone during our run before. Those who came were always older and not likely to be in the reality show phase of their lives. Even so Julian put a hex on their car with just a look when he saw them drive by.

"Are you going to be okay?" Ethan asked as we started to jog away.

"I think so," I said. Unable to tolerate much conversation, I started running faster. I could run the five miles faster than when we first started. I grew stronger without even noticing.

"So ..." I said when we were almost back to the Manor House.

"Yeah," he turned to me eagerly, slowing down.

"It seems like you and Tess had fun picking up trash," I said.

"Huh?" he asked unsure why I brought that up. I really couldn't be sure myself, except he and Tess really seemed to click over the last few days. Tess and Ethan were friends. Not just the polite strained friendship from before, but real warm friends. While Serena made me a mess, Tess swooped in and took my place as his friend.

"Look Carrie, she needs –"

"I know she needs a friend like you. It's good of you to be there for her," I said looking forward refusing to even give him a sideway glance when I finished, "I'm sure I'll see you later."

He tried to say something, but I sped up and past the path down to his bungalow. The only solace I had left was that Ethan must understand I wanted to leave. Something pulsed, pushing me to run harder with a painful fury when I told myself I was leaving, but it was okay because Tess was taking my place as his friend. Serena tortured me until I wasn't even present. What did it matter if I left?

On elimination days, we endured a long day of primping, and interviews. Us, reviewing why we thought we were in the lead, and what in our performance thus far equated to resilience. The camera men poked until we sounded annoyed, especially with the other contestants.

Julian stomped around raging, interrupting interviews and yelling at his staff members most of the day. We were within an hour of the show airing when he snapped at us:

"Fine! Just get dressed!"

We stood around in the back room where our designers worked. No one moved. He had said this three times and nobody believed for a minute his frenzy abated.

178

"This is the best you guys can do?" He spit out again, mostly looking at Veronica's designer.

"Well," she squeaked, "who decided plaid could be turned into gowns?"

Lance got big eyes and unable to hide his smirk looked down. Julian huffed at him and stomped out of the room saying, "Just get dressed. We film in ten minutes."

We dressed, and it looked like the opening ceremony of the Scottish Highland Games. I looked fine as always, and Sandra looked decent in a black and white plaid, but everyone else looked to be representing a clan. Putting us together on a riser did not help the situation.

It didn't surprise me when Veronica received the first key. The kids all voted her the coolest at the amusement park because, for a big ball of anxiety, she was somehow always willing to ride any ride with them, and she bought them treats at every snack shack. She smiled at me uncertainly because only she doubted her place among the resilient. I smiled back the best I could.

"Tess," Ethan called. He grinned at her. I grit my teeth. Something ugly and hateful sprung from my chest toward Tess when she took her key. The way her body swayed caused her hair to swish so the tips tickled her bare shoulders. It drove me crazy. Tess, in her sweetheart red plaid dress, looked like a Valentine card. She moved in next to Veronica, wearing her pleated school-girl uniform lengthened to look like a gown.

"Serena," Ethan called.

Huh?

179

Serena? This was his last double elimination. For the show to stay a ten-week series with the reunion show at the end, Ethan made two double eliminations. Then it moved to single eliminations. Why did he keep Serena? Did he prefer her to me? Or ... wait .... What had I asked him to do?

Serena in her turquoise plaid baby doll dress moved in and took the key. I swallowed hard multiple times to get the bile out of the back of my throat while Lance did his drawn-out bit.

Why would Ethan eliminate me and keep her?

Ethan gave keys to Sandra and Erin in their turn and left Pete, Re-Pete and me standing on the risers. They wore strange, colorfully plaid bride's maid dresses; sadly, Re-Pete's designer thought bright orange would improve the pattern somehow.

I wore a classy black and purple grey dress that didn't even look plaid accept a few lines moving vertical. The neck scooped, and the dress followed my curves and hit me mid shins. I looked better than anyone else.

A bead of sweat rolled down Pete's face. I thought it almost cruel for Ethan to keep only one of them when Serena needed to go.

"Carrie," Ethan's voice reverberated through me. My head jerked up, startled. It was me or Serena, or not me and Serena. I was supposed to be leaving. I came forward.

"Will you accept this key?" Ethan asked, and then he held his breath.

I opened my mouth, but nothing came out. I don't know what made me. I reached out and took the key more out of confusion than pleasure without saying a word. If I hadn't been angry I may have appreciated Ethan used his last double elimination to let Pete and Re-Pete go together.

I skipped the "I'm still here party" and went to bed early, extremely discouraged.

CHAPTER SIXTEEN

"Carrie, you up?" Serena whispered through the crack she made in my door the next morning.

"Yeah," I said.

"Good. I was afraid I'd miss you," Serena said. She opened the door further and stepped into my room.

"I'm just leaving ... was there something you needed?" I hissed.

"I'm jogging with you this morning. You always go by yourself, and it isn't safe."

"It's good for me. I like a little alone time."

"You don't get it, do you? It's not safe."

Veronica made a noise and rolled over in her bed. I walked quickly out of the room before tying my shoes so we didn't rouse her.

"It is the only alone time I get –"

"Oh, I don't mind going with you. It's the least I can do," Serena said.

"Right," I said. Strangely enough, as I bent down to tie my shoe, I wanted to cry. Not just cry. I wanted to bawl like I hadn't in years. I couldn't even explain the emotional state I found myself in; I just wished I could sit down and cry.

"Let's take your normal route," Serena said.

"If you can't keep up, stay on the main road and I'll run back the same way," I said trotting down the stairs.

"You'd leave me?"

"You haven't been running–"

182

"Still, it's not safe. I'm doing this for you – I can't believe you'd just leave me," she said.

"'Kay, I'll stay with you," I snapped.

"Touchy!" She tried to hide the shadow of her smile that brightened her eyes, but the bounce in her descending steps betrayed the pleasure in her triumph over me.

She couldn't know I met up with Ethan. Truth be known I didn't want anything to do with Ethan who pretended to be so compassionate to my plight, but did nothing to help me. I headed out the front door and Serena followed me. She insisted her speed-walk be our pace.

"You know," she said, winded, catching up to me, "you only have to get your heart rate up. Going so fast will ruin your knees."

"It feels good to me."

"I know what I'm talking about … I'm an RN –"

"Yep, I know," I said trotting forward smelling the damp of the ocean mingling with the sweetness of grass sprouting up among the clusters of succulent plants growing off the side of the road.

"Well, you need to listen to me then," she scolded catching up to me.

"You remind me of my grandma in a way," I said.

"Excuse me?"

"You always have these helpful facts to share – very like my grandma."

I turned and smiled at her. Serena squinted at me trying to decide if she should act offended or not. I moved even faster.

"I'm not an old lady personality," she finally said.

183

I may as well have dug up Grandmother and moved into her coffin with her. I said nothing.

"Well, at least I didn't talk Tess out of wearing the sundress to brunch with the mayor," she said.

"I didn't mean to," I said.

"Oh please –"

"Serena! Let it go!"

"You're so emotional," she said. "I can't see how you don't still feel horrible."

"Considering I tried to warn you and you didn't listen, you don't get to be mad at me."

"Yeah, but Tess –"

"Tess already forgave me; it's time to move on. And I'd appreciate it if you'd stop bringing it up in front of the camera crew."

"You need to learn to compose yourself in front of the cameras," Serena said. She lifted her mouth so smugly that I snapped at her:

"You need to stop making me look stupid in front of the cameras." I pulled my body into a jog.

"Nobody can make you look stupid," she called after me.

Yeah, right. Over the last few days, Serena would act like my best friend on camera. She innocently brought up what made me defensive. I overreacted. Then when I responded she rolled her eyes and made me look like a crazy person.

Sometimes I couldn't even tell what she said to get under my skin, but there she sat like an infected rash. I became so wound-up that my stomach would knot up when Serena walked into the room. Just like with my grandmother.

How was it that Serena and I were still on the show? It didn't make sense. He eliminated harmless Pete and Re-Pete and left me to be tortured.

"Care Bear, you've got to slow down," Serena said trotting up behind me.

Even though we couldn't have gone more than a mile and a half, I said, "Look there's the stairs down to the beach," showing no hint I'd never seen them before. I randomly thought that I'd have to come back some time to investigate. "Well, we better turn around."

She smiled at me relieved. One of her rare smiles that looked genuine with pulled back lips and I could see where her braces once were.

"Serena," I asked slowing down and letting her catch up to me.

"Yes, Care Bear?"

"How did you get braces in the foster system?" I asked. She blanched. I struck a chord. She looked away floundering for words. Why it mattered I couldn't say, but I should have brought it up in front of the cameras. She used my guilt to shame me. She believed it her duty to punish any tenderness as if a weakness. Her idea of cruelly shifting vulnerability to shame latched on to me as if contagious. I wanted to strike out at her; I wanted the cameras to catch her embarrassed.

"My dad got them for me. He said I was pretty as an old-time princess and my teeth should match. He couldn't really ... we didn't ..." Serena stumbled over her sentiment and finished with, "the group home we went to had to keep up on them. Junie didn't get them until last year when I got decent

185

dental insurance. Within the next year, she'll get 'em off. We'll both have straight teeth," Serena said with a real smile.

"You take good care of your sister," I said.

"It's just us," she said looking away.

Who would I have become if both my parents died and my sister and I had no one? What would I have become to protect Addie? Considering what I'd already done, could I really be surprised at Serena?

Serena was like a wounded animal caught in a trap, and, instead of dying, she continually gnawed her metaphoric leg off. Serena scavenged and picked the meat off carcasses to survive. In these moments when she opened up enough that I saw her, I felt sorry for her. Until she thrust her sharp claws in my ribs. Then I stopped feeling sorry for her.

"I don't really remind you of your grandma, do I?" Serena asked.

"She became extremely wealthy at one point in her life, but she didn't start out that way. My Grandpa was wealthy, with a trust fund, a family name and all that, but her parents were upstarts. She helped Grandpa start a business that made them very wealthy."

"Oh, that's cool," she said.

"You know, though, she pushed Grandpa too hard. She pushed everyone past their breaking point. At times she shamed anyone who admitted an ounce of humanity. She made too big of a deal of making mistakes. I'm not sure it was worth it, just so everyone around her could become wealthy. Well, everyone except her only son. She disowned him," I said trying to push my point across.

186

"Oh well. I see what you mean. I am for sure going to make something of myself and Junie," Serena said picking out only what she wanted from my words.

"Okay," I said glancing at her from the side. Serena looked satisfied. What happened to her?

In fact, I started to wonder what happened to my grandma. When her favorite child hadn't become an attorney as she wanted, she cut him off. Granted without a willing family member, Grandfather lost the family business to his partner. At least that's what Grandma said. More than likely he was paid out, and Grandma didn't want to admit what she had wasted the money on.

Instead of admitting she squandered millions of dollars, she cut her son off and acted like their financial problems were his fault. He had the audacity to choose his own path. Did she really think they'd been cheated because of him? Did she really feel it was his duty to pursue a career he disliked to maintain a stronghold in the business because it brought in enough money to keep her credit card paid off? Wasn't that going too far?

"This is a great workout. I should come with you every morning," Serena said after our run ended in silence, me contemplating, and her plotting, or whatever she did when alone with only herself for company.

She opened the front door while I stretched. Any shadow of the real Serena disappeared. I got the feeling she'd been performing long before she came on a reality show.

"Carrie and I are going to run together from now on," Serena exclaimed to Sandra who was walking by to get into the kitchen.

"Yeah, maybe you'll be able to keep up after a while," I said brushing past her and trotted up the stairs.

"Hey Caroline, I'm baking a quiche so about twenty minutes?" Tess called.

"That'd be great," I called back. I stopped on the top stair. Tess knew the nickname Care Bear that Serena persisted in using, humiliated me. In response, she started calling me Caroline.

"Oh, me too," Serena said from right behind me, "Let's eat together, Care Bear!"

Erin, who endured the sting of Serena's torment much longer than the rest of us, stood behind and to the side of her. With the grace of a dancer, she mimed grabbing the back of her head and pulling her down the stairs. I bit my tongue not to laugh – I put my voice into my laugh, and it gave Serena a headache.

I turned and walked swiftly down the hall to my bedroom to shower. I finished my cleansing routine quickly but didn't turn off the water. Instead I sat down and soaked. I couldn't face twenty minutes of Serena while I waited for breakfast. Out of nowhere I started to cry. I hadn't cried in years. I barely cried when Gordon died, but now sitting on the shower floor, the only time I was alone all day, I bawled.

I finished my long shower and dressed.

"You took forever," Serena said meeting me outside my door, "did you put your microphone pack on?"

I walked past her.

"Breakfast is ready," Tess called up from the kitchen. If she didn't offer Serena whatever she cooked, Tess would be

188

withholding food. Even though Serena only drank a shake for breakfast.

"You know if you got me a triangle, it may work better," Tess snapped. Serena ignored her. I moved in next to Veronica and read a few clues to her crossword puzzle. Veronica tried to give me a half smile and I grimaced back. It wasn't just me Serena tortured. She toyed indiscriminately with everyone in the house.

"Is that what you're wearing today, Carrie? Jeans and a tee shirt – you don't want to put on a blouse or something a little nicer?" Serena asked pleasantly.

"I haven't decided yet," I said.

"Let us know when you do, so we can all be dressed up to standard," Serena said as if a pleasantry.

"It may be time you figure out how to dress yourself," I said with too much sarcasm.

Serena put on her hurt face, but I turned to Erin who walked into the kitchen lured by the smell of the quiche.

"Hey, Erin! Do you need help settling into your new room?" I asked.

"Naw, I got it," she said, glancing at Serena. Serena glowered at her. None of us could blame Erin for moving into Pete and Re-Pete's empty room. Tess handed Erin a plate but said nothing.

"Erin, you never told me what you overcame – you know to be *The Whole Package*," I said, trying to refocus the conversation.

"Oh well. I'm a dancer," she said.

"We all know what she overcame. Lance says it all the time," Serena said.

189

"And?" I said toward Erin, who sat and pulled a plate toward her.

"When I was ten I was diagnosed with scoliosis. I wore a brace and kids were … well kids," she said.

"Oh, I'm sorry," I said.

"Because of it, her mom started her in dance classes," Serena supplied.

"And physical therapy," I chimed in, "but how did you work so hard it fixed your back?"

"Well, I spent an extra hour every day building up the muscles around my spinal cord. I'd go to school, go to therapy or dance, then do my homework, eat dinner and before bed I'd build up my back muscles."

"It must have been hard," I said.

"Yeah, but at ten the doctors said I'd have to have multiple surgeries to fuse my back. I worked so hard by sixteen I only had to have one of my disks altered. By nineteen I made it into Barnard University."

"That's Columbia, right?" I said.

"Yeah," she said.

"Impressive," I said.

"Right," Serena said, "but her parents helped her the whole time. In fact, they did everything for her. Really overcoming is doing it all yourself and still making something of yourself."

"You don't know what you're talking about," Erin returned, with such elegant force I could see the fighter in her. I would have to tap into that. Erin needed to be that strong all the time. But then didn't I also need to tap into my strength? I had some somewhere. How did I find it?

190

"Let's try to forget the competition for a minute and pretend we're sitting around eating breakfast, talking," I said.

"You may as well ask Serena to stop breathing," Tess said. Serena put on her most vulnerable wounded face and started to say:

"It's not my fault I handle pressure–"

"Hey, can you get the dishes, Caroline?" Tess cut in.

"Sure Tess," I answered and I got up after swallowing another two bites of flakey crust covered in perfect custard-like egg and sautéed onion mixture, wishing I could eat another piece without Serena commenting on my ten pounds. Erin followed my lead and ate as she walked to the sink.

"You should try to eat more," Serena said, "such a waste to put all that perfectly good food down the disposal." After Tess left the room, she continued, "Not to mention the effort wasted in making it."

"Well, we have to hurry. Lance will be here soon. Maybe you ought to go get dressed since you seem so worried about it," I snapped.

"That was rude; could you be any ruder? I'm just trying to help. You're an emotional mess, Carrie," Serena said. She sat down to help Veronica with her crossword.

"You want me to dry?" Erin asked, handing me her plate.

"Thanks," I said. I moved my lips in an upward fashion trying to smile to boost her up, but it didn't reach my eyes.

We neither of us ever learned how to combat the obviously correct, but oh-so-in-your-face comments that Serena threw at us. Serena was right, we were wrong. She

191

needed to be right as completely as she needed air to breath. Even more, she needed me to be wrong.

I lived that way with Grandmother for years. Why was I still here?

The strangest memory popped in my head while I did the dishes.

We'd been eating in the dining room. Grandmother's stately old neck turned on her shoulders, her icy blue eyes zeroed in on me.

"Caroline" – she always called me Caroline – Carrie offended her – "Caroline," she'd said, "You know my friend Petunia DuPont?"

"Yes Grandmother," – she demanded I answer that way always – "Yes, Grandmother."

"Her grandson will be in town and needs a date to the auction in three weeks," she'd said.

"No, nope Grandmother. I won't do it," I said.

"You will," she said.

"If you try to make me, he will learn things about us you'd rather him not know," I threatened. She glared unhappily at my mother to put me in line.

"Well, she makes up her own mind," Mom said, shaking a little under grandmother's glare, but trying to support my decision.

"Yes, and we'll respect that," Grandfather said. He may as well have been talking to thin air.

For the next three weeks, Grandmother pestered me and contrived. She even tried bribing me to go. In the end, I stayed firm. I never ran a temperature, but Grandmother insisted I not go to school the two days before the event because I had the flu. I'd been strong at sixteen.

What happened to me from the time my father died until I took the hand Gordon offered?

Guilt, never being good enough, always being in the wrong, eventually sank me. That's what happened. I broke. My status as a lady was degraded out of me. It wasn't freely given. Wouldn't anyone trapped in such a situation give in eventually? Didn't Serena drive me to tears?

Why would one person do that to another?

The dubious nature of the reality show, pretending to be real while Julian placed us, and prompted us, forced me to struggle for any sense of control over my situation. My little victories of making Julian wait were small and getting further between. I knew the monotony of this struggle; I fought this fight before. At some point I lost. And if I didn't leave, I would lose again.

I finished the dishes and only half heard Serena say, "You slopped water down your front. If you didn't fill the sink so full, you wouldn't have done that."

I walked away while Serena still talked. Veronica stood up and followed me. Erin left the last dish in the strainer claiming she had some unpacking to do. I would have teased her about her enormous suitcase, but Serena would find a way to turn it nasty.

Eventually people like Serena and my grandmother isolated themselves. Even in a crowded room they ended up alone. But then, how could they stand to be around us humans, so enveloped in our imperfections?

CHAPTER SEVENTEEN

"Hey Ron! You want me to help you with your hair?" I said following her into our room. Out of pure jittery paranoia, we all woke earlier. We dressed and were ready before the morning cast call, no matter how late we'd been up filming the night before. After I helped Veronica with her hair she said:

"Did you notice Becky set out an outfit for you?"

"Oh right, she's been doing that ever since the sundress thing," I said.

"Yeah, she felt bad."

"I know. Strange, but since then, we're working better together," I said. I ran into the bathroom and threw on the outfit. I usually found small ways to alter Becky's outfits just to be myself, but she'd gone to the effort to figure out my style, what she called casual elegance.

It felt almost like I'd won something with her, but I couldn't be sure what. Respect maybe? If Becky respected me, could I find that with everyone in my life, just by standing up for myself? Or was it because she humiliated me, and I didn't hold it against her? What inspired that kind of respect?

"Contestants, I need everyone in the sitting room," Lance called up the stairs.

Veronica ran off, but I sat in front of the vanity brushing through my hair. I couldn't move. I was on the verge of understanding something. Something I'd spent my whole life working toward, but I wasn't quite sure what.

194

How many years did it take for my mother to be left with so little self-preservation that she gave up the fortune my father left us to get Grandma out of debt?

Wasn't I ready to leave this show – in a way giving up a million dollars, because of Serena?

I could no longer be my mother. No. That's not the point. Or was it?

I couldn't be sure, but I would no longer bow down to Serena, just because she taunted me into it.

"Carrie, we need you down here," Lance yelled up the stairs.

Oh, right, how does one retake her life on a show dedicated to Julian's personal brand of reality?

I stood up and walked down into my cage.

My anger toward Ethan may have vanished if I hadn't walked down the stairs to see Serena sucking up to him. Despite all my self-assurances that I shouldn't be annoyed with him, I flared again. My face hardened.

When Ethan saw me, he walked away from Serena mid-sentence. He met me at the bottom of the staircase. He studied my face. His eyes were concerned. He genuinely cared about me. Ethan respected me. What had I done to deserve that?

"You ditched me," he whispered.

"Thanks for the run this morning, Serena," I called.

"Oh," he said. "I understand."

"What? That I wasn't ready to talk to you yet?"

"What? I thought you had another week free – what's the matter?" Ethan whispered back mystified.

"Okay, everyone, fall in," Lance said.

"It's your game, not mine," I whispered as I walked by.

"Carrie, please," Ethan said with total wonder in his voice. Lance took me by the arm to get my attention and asked me to move forward into the elimination room. Ethan looked annoyed with him. Lance nodded his head at Ethan and Ethan walked back into the sitting room.

The cameramen walked in. After the inevitable time waiting for the cameras to set up, Lance stood in front of the main camera. The other two cameras were pointed at us to catch our reactions.

"Today, Ethan is going to take you six ladies shopping. You will each have a thousand dollars to express yourself and your spending habits to Ethan," Lance said in his warm, emotion-wrenching television voice.

"This is my favorite episode," Serena said. Sandra clapped a little, her blonde hair falling over her shoulders in a way that made her elfin, too pretty for the real world. Veronica smiled at me. I couldn't muster any enthusiasm. I kept replaying being combative to Ethan. He'd been kind to me and I snapped at him. Why? At least Serena hadn't noticed.

"We're going to a mall in San Francisco," Lance repeated. No doubt for Julian to splice in after a commercial break somewhere, "and you can buy whatever you want within a thousand-dollar budget. What you buy should in some way reflect who you are, and be worth the money you are spending."

"I'm getting on the bus, I'm getting on the bus," Tess sang a little. I couldn't help it. I laughed slightly.

196

Ethan heard the sound and whipped is head toward me. I turned away.

"Carrie, you're sitting by me aren't you?" Serena asked.

"Nope, I'm sitting by Veronica. Thanks, though," I said in my calmest voice with a very fake smile.

"Are you coming on the bus with us?" Serena asked turning to Ethan.

"No, Julian needed to talk to me about something. I'll be about a half hour behind you in my rental car."

"Oh, my loss," Serena said running her long fingers down Ethan's arm.

I turned from the cameras catching Serena and Ethan's moment and walked out the door. I climbed onto the bus in a weary sort of way. George gave me a smile as I passed the driver's seat. I tried my best to smile back.

"Are you all right, little Miss?" George asked. He searched my face for the storm of emotion he must have seen many times before; he'd been with Julian since the first season.

"Yeah," I said. Pulling all the emotion from my face, I smiled at him.

"Oh, good," George said, pacified. I patted his shoulder and turned to my seat.

"Wow, that's something. Carrie's the first one on the bus?" Lance said.

"Happy birthday," I said.

"Hey, are you all right?" Lance asked. "This last week you've kind of seemed down."

"I don't know," I said. "It's hard, living in a house with little to do but get on everyone's nerves." Then I smiled perfectly like I wasn't too annoyed. I had it perfected.

"You're a good sport, Carrie," Lance said. I almost said more, but Lance turned from me abruptly. He started speaking to George about the route we would take. This wasn't the first time he'd abruptly stopped talking to me. I wondered sometimes if he was trying to keep me from exposing myself somehow. There wasn't a cameraman around. I shrugged it off as my growing paranoia.

I set my purse on the plush seat next to me until Veronica came. Veronica smiled at me and I nodded a little. Now that I understood Serena played mind games to keep me low, I would not stand for it. I had the power now. Ethan and I were good friends – great friends.

I forced a smile on my face. I would fight this ridiculousness.

After the bus loaded we drove through Half Moon Bay, and away from the ocean. We drove past a Chinese restaurant.

"George! Chinese food, stop!" I called out, goading him to stop as I did playfully last week when I saw it.

"It's pretty early in the morning for Chinese food," he responded grinning at me through the mirror above him.

"What is it with you and Chinese food?" Serena snapped, "I swear if Patrick gets us Chinese food for dinner again I'm going to barf."

"That'd be incentive enough for me," Tess popped off.

"You really do like Chinese food," Veronica said quietly enough only I heard.

"It's my stress food," I whispered back. She nodded.

Instead of disregarding my tendencies as nothing, I remembered my grandpa. After my dad died we moved in

198

with my grandparents. Grandpa would smuggle me out of the house to run errands. At least once a week, sometimes more often, we'd sneak out to a Chinese restaurant. He had his favorite, but we frequently tried new ones just to see if we might like them better.

Grandpa never said much on these outings, but I knew he loved me. He commiserated with me over Chinese food about our captivity and I didn't miss my dad so terribly. At times, I would confide to him problems at school. He never told me what to do. He would always tell me I was a lady, and he knew I would make the right decision.

"Just stand up," he would say. "Just stand up and be a lady."

I remembered being miffed when he gave no better answers – forcing me to find my own. Now, though, I saw it as respect. He respected and trusted me enough to make my own decisions. A huge part of who I wanted to be was due to that simple statement.

"Hey, Carrie. You want some licorice?" Erin asked, leaning across the aisle.

"Yeah, thanks," I said. I forced myself to be positive. Outside, rain started falling, and the windows of the bus fogged up, cocooning us inside our moving caterpillar.

"Hey, Erin, did I ever tell you about the time I was invited to a Gala for a stage production of Romeo and Juliet?"

"Uh… no," she said.

"I was only sixteen and I was a little boy crazy. I met this waiter at the Gala. He was cute. My grandma was always trying to introduce me to her friend's grandson. He stood to inherit hundreds of millions, but I ignored him the whole

199

time. I wanted my first kiss to go to this really cute waiter," I said.

"You didn't kiss a guy until sixteen?" Serena said.

"In all fairness, I did go to an all-girls school. I'm kinda glad I waited. He was so cute," I said. I forced myself not to react. Defend without being defensive was one of Lance's tips Veronica wrote down on the first day.

By the time we reached the crowded hilltops of South San Francisco, I animatedly told stories of those years to Veronica and Erin. I wanted Erin to know how I wreaked havoc on my Grandmother's nerves. Back when I had control of my life.

We finally pulled up to a mall in west San Francisco. I could smell the ocean again when the bus doors opened.

"Erin, let me go." Serena pushed, trying to get off the bus in front of Erin who stood in the aisle collecting her stuff.

"Cool it. You are like a yappy little dog. Wait your turn," Erin said. Serena backed off surprised. Erin turned and grinned at me and said:

"Go ahead, Veronica."

"Oh, can I get out too?" Tess said, pulling her bag up from the seat next to her. Erin actually had to back herself and Serena up to let Tess out. We were all ready to laugh by the time everyone climbed off the bus before Serena, who was bright red. All of us except Veronica, who remembered Serena raised herself and her younger sister, and needed compassion.

CHAPTER EIGHTEEN

The rain stopped when the bus did. The parking lot smelled like wet asphalt and soaked pines. The huge russet-colored mall sat on marble pillars like a Grecian temple waiting for its goddesses to arrive.

"Soo ..." Tess said, cuddling up to me in the parking lot. "What's up?"

"How long is this cold shoulder you're throwing Ethan going to last?"

"What?" I asked.

"Oh, come on. We all saw you blow him off and get on the bus. He got all sulky. If you make him happy again we'd all appreciate it. When he's sulky, he's way more judgmental – kinda like you," Tess said shoving an elbow in my ribs.

"I... I wasn't mad at Ethan," I said. I felt a blush crawl up my face.

"We all saw Serena snuggling up to him. Yeah, it's annoying, but he can't help it. It's the game so cut him some slack because I really want this purse without dipping into my savings. I'm planning on spending my entire thousand."

"Okay," I grinned at her.

"Come on guys. It's this way," Serena called so we wouldn't be left behind.

As we walked the mall's marble floor, Serena led us in a single file line toward the food court where the crew set up. I hooked arms with Veronica and walked beside her to break up Serena's perfect line.

"Carrie, you look drunk," Serena called.

I smiled and gave her a thumb up like that was exactly the look I wanted. Just for effect I weaved Veronica and I along the russet marble pattern in the white marble floor.

She moved from the front of the line toward us, a cameraman following her. I pulled Veronica with me to a store window to try and avoid the confrontation that would make me look crazy.

"Isn't that dress fun," I said.

"Hum, it doesn't seem like you," she said looking at the black dress ripped up the bottom in perfect grunge fashion.

"No, but –"

"Carrie, you're holding up the cameras," Serena said. Then, turning to the cameraman, she said to the world, "We ought to call her the Poky Little Care Bear."

"You know Serena, it's great we're still both here together. I just don't know if I could find the film site without you keeping me in line."

While Serena stammered through an, "uh yeah your welcome," unsure if I was joking because she didn't understand sarcasm. I decided I meant it. I wasn't ready to leave the show yet. I was going to face my demon, and vanquish Grandmother at the same time I vanquished Serena. If I won a million dollars along the way, that'd be okay too.

"You know, though, it's not fair to the rest of us, you always slowing everything down," Serena said.

Veronica let her face fall, but I grew defiant. I paused and stared at Serena until the pause grew uncomfortable. The cameraman, who turned toward us like mice waiting for crumbs of contention to drop, quieted. With a delighted look at Serena's startled face, I said:

"We don't all have to skip hand-in-hand at the front of the line with you and your furry woodland creatures. We'll be along in a minute, dearest."

Defend without being defensive. Serena didn't know how to answer. She smiled, of course, but her talented eyes looked confused instead of haughty. I smiled for real, and then I turned from her to look at the dress again. I was done being wrong so she could be right, no matter how much hardship she'd gone through in her life.

Perhaps it wasn't healthy for people to always roll over for her because she'd been hurt. In fact, perhaps, she needed me to stand up to her.

Either way it didn't matter. I was allowed to be myself without her interference, even if she did find me annoying. But then, for my being so annoying, she didn't seem capable of tearing herself away from me. She constantly sought me out. Well, if she chose to be around me, she could take me how I came because I wouldn't suppress myself for her pleasure anymore.

CHAPTER NINETEEN

After the exhausting time it took to set up, Ethan took Tess to buy a Dooney & Bourke crocodile embossed leather handbag, purse, and wallet.

"A purse is going to show Ethan who you are Tess?" Serena asked when they returned and Tess showed us her purchases.

"She's a financial planner," I answered. "You keep your money in your purse, plus the value of those purses can go up so it's an investment really."

"Oh yeah, I never thought of that," Ethan said. He nodded at me, trying to make nice.

Tess paused examining her purse. She looked up to smile at me. Ethan handed her another Nordstrom bag containing matching sunflower colored shoes. Then, I very noticeably pawned Serena's desperate static cling off on to Ethan. He took her to a jeweler. When she got back, she showed us a dainty diamond encrusted bangle on her delicate wrist.

"How does that show who you are?" Tess asked.

"I want to travel to impoverished countries, and help the needy. I know what it's like to be hungry," Serena said with tears in her eyes. "I would start in Bangladesh. The poverty situation there is atrocious. This bangle bracelet is the perfect way to show my person as a human being."

"Seriously," Sandra said.

"You know you have to go back into public after this is over, right?" Tess said.

The weirdest thing happened; Ethan smirked, just slightly, at Tess. That was my smirk, the smirk he did for my jokes.

Serena bounced up to Ethan and said:

"Thank you for this beautiful bangle."

Ethan nodded, but leaned away from her. He seemed ... was he leery of Serena? Serena grew desperate in her attempts to capture Ethan's attention.

"I really am going to make a difference someday," she said getting closer to him.

"I'm sure you will," he said trying to avoid Serena's hand, while he leaned further away from her. Ethan was sick of Serena. Why didn't he eliminate her? She only won a single competition. How many points could she have?

"Can I go next?" Erin asked interrupting my thoughts. Ethan smiled at her with a genuine friendliness, and without my permission. My jaw clenched again.

Ethan took Erin to the Apple store and bought her a tiny laptop, because a person should never stop learning. After that, Ethan and Veronica walked away into the mall, and didn't come back for over an hour. When they made it back, Ethan and Veronica lugged a huge black duffle bag. Ethan set down his side and shifted like he wanted to take me with him next, but I grabbed the bag's cloth handle. Veronica dropped the weight of her side on me and I couldn't get free.

Annoyed that Veronica used me as her personal bellhop more often than I liked, I hefted the heavy bag and asked, "What'd you guys buy? A hit man? And who'd you take out? Serena's still here."

"Jokes, Serena," I said with a huge happy smile on my face as everyone laughed. Ethan smirked at me. I grinned back. And the world was right.

Serena smiled tensely, but the seething in her eyes was obvious. The camera caught her glare. The cameramen tended to ignore Serena's annoying quirks, but not this time. I wondered if the tides were turning for her.

Sandra jumped up and grabbed Ethan's hand. A fire grew inside me, and I turned my back on them.

"Come on, Ethan," she said. "I'm thrilled to show you something that is near and dear to my heart."

"Okay," I strained to hear him say.

"It's called colorology, the study of color and the way it affects your mood," Sandra said. They walked away and I couldn't hear Ethan's reply.

"Where'd you guys go?" I asked turning to Veronica who hadn't stopped playing with her bag. "Tess joked you must have eloped, you know because all you want is to get married. You would've spent the least amount of money so far."

"Well, when we wrote down what we wanted, I put scuba gear. Julian gave Ethan a map where we could buy it out in the city," Veronica said.

"That was nice," I said trying to hide the perturbed tone in my voice.

"Isn't he so sweet to me?" Veronica said. I wanted to ask if she was referring to Ethan or Julian, but instead said:

"He really is."

Veronica sat at a small black table in the generic mall food court. She unzipped the bag to reveal flippers, a wetsuit, snorkeling goggles with a tube attached to it. Beyond that I couldn't see, but Veronica reached in a side pocket and pulled out a watch in a box.

"Well, they didn't have tanks; it was more a boating shop, but look at this watch."

Veronica pulled the huge military-like watch out of the box and strapped it to her wrist.

"It can go down 330 feet, how cool is that?"

"Way cool," I said glancing at Veronica's watch.

"It's pretty much a computer on my wrist. It came with a download kit and a Dive Log memory of up to 24 dives. It tells the depth of the water, so if I go down deep it'll tell me when to stop to decompress as I'm coming up."

"That's really cool," I said more earnestly. I examined the watch while contorting Veronica's arm in an odd sort of way.

"How do you think Sandra is going to show him colorology?" I asked the group. I couldn't focus on Veronica. Occupied by her watch, she didn't notice.

"Colorology is all nonsense anyway," Serena said.

"I've seen some really amazing displays of Colorology in one of my friend's homes," Erin defended.

After what felt like forever, Ethan and Sandra, with Colorology all over her face, walked up to us. Only I was turned toward them. I stopped mid-sip of a smoothie. I looked at Sandra, and then made eye contact with Ethan who gave me a shadow of a smirk—my smirk.

I began coughing up smoothie. Tess grabbed the smoothie and smacked me on the back. After I breathed again, Tess stopped short of asking me if I was okay. She stared at Sandra.

"What did you do?" Tess asked.

"I got makeup," Sandra said holding up four bags with twisted paper handles.

"That's great," Erin said, cutting Tess off with a nod and big shut-your-mouth eyes.

Ethan walked up to me in an uncertain sort of way and put a hand on my back where Tess had been pounding.

"You okay?" he asked.

"I'm better," I said searching his eyes.

Ethan looked back into mine for an explanation.

"It's just the show," I whispered with just the right amount of sarcasm so he knew how annoying his standard answer of late had become.

"Then I will patiently understand and not ask questions I know you can't answer," he murmured back.

"You're a dork," I said grinning. He smiled and held out his arm to me. I took it without hesitation.

I waved to the rest of the contestants and lunged with my free hand to retrieve my smoothie from Tess. I jerked Ethan with me.

Ethan walked with my arm linked to his until we descended the escalator. At the ground floor, I began to turn into the mall. He yanked me back.

"Nah, I found your shop. It's a little drive from here."

"Uh, I wrote down Anne Taylor as my shop," I said, looking confused. "I was going to make you buy me this awesome new suit. There's nothing to me except work."

"You hide behind your work. I don't think it defines who you are."

208

I reared back in surprise. Ethan pushed the door open. I squinted from the sun that managed to drive the blanket of clouds away to the camera, unable to hide my embarrassment.

The cameraman could only follow us to Ethan's rental car. Ethan opened my door for me and I climbed in. I assumed the cameraman would climb in back, but he didn't. The kidnapper van pulled up beside us and the door opened for him.

"We're free," I said covering my microphone.

"Mexico," Ethan said tipping his mouth toward his mic to be sure Julian heard.

I nodded messing with the radio and turning the music up full blast.

As we drove out of the parking lot I started singing, and Ethan smiled trying to watch me and the road at the same time. The image of Julian's kidnapper van never left the rear-view mirror. Still, we were in the real world, alone. When a commercial came on, I leaned against his arm to choose another radio station because we didn't have time to listen to commercials.

Even after we parked, Ethan and I sat listening to the song until it came to an end. The cameraman got my door for me. The show came back from commercial and it was time to perform again.

"See, that's where I took Veronica for her scuba gear," Ethan said. I glanced politely, but the art supply store distracted me like my own version of Disneyland.

"How'd you know I like art? I never told you that, did I?" I said trying to skim over our morning runs to be sure.

"Everywhere we go we're always waiting for you to look at the art. Plus, this last week you've been gloomy and drawing all over everything."

"I haven't been gloomy," I said as we walked in.

"Really?"

"Okay I have, but I'm not doing that anymore," I said. Ethan put an arm around my waist giving me a squeeze. I leaned into him needing his warmth in a way that overwhelmed me.

"Anyway, I asked Julian about it, and he realized your undergraduate was in art." Ethan looked at me. I could tell he wanted to ask me something, but glanced at the camera and instead said: "What medium do you prefer?"

"Oils, but I can do some pretty cool stuff in watercolor," I said. We reached the paints and Ethan started loading the cart with everything in sight.

"I'm sure two canvases are enough," I said walking over to look at the canvases.

"Spending money to enhance your talents is never a waste," Ethan said.

I blocked his way so I could study the canvases he was just tossing into the cart. He reached one arm around my waist to immobilize me. With his other he grabbed another package of four canvases of different dimensions while I elbowed him and giggled. We wrestled for the prime position, and I almost forgot the cameraman was there. I finally gave up and let Ethan throw whatever he wanted into the cart. I only grabbed a primer, and pointed round brush. I didn't bother explaining he'd bought several of the same size fan

210

brushes, but quietly exchanged them for different sizes when his fervor for yellows distracted him.

Finally, the cameraman moved us to the cash register. Behind it, a teenage girl in the acne stage of life eyed Ethan standing shoulder-to-shoulder with me. She rang up our order and handed Ethan the three-foot receipt and his change.

"I hope you win, Carrie," the clerk whispered across the counter.

"Thank you," I whispered back. Ethan grinned.

Ethan slung the easel over his shoulder, the canvases under his arm, and grabbed the bags from the counter. I made to take one of the bags but Ethan said, "I got it. We can leave this stuff in my trunk so you don't have to haul it onto the bus."

I said nothing but felt so content I'm sure it showed on my face because the cameraman kept the lens trained on me. After Ethan stowed everything in his trunk he leaned against the car. I moved in next to him to see the receipt he examined, and he put his arm around my shoulders.

"That leaves us a few hundred dollars for some overalls and rain boots. I'm sure every good artist needs a pair of overalls, right?"

"Of course," I said. My eyes felt alight with excitement.

CHAPTER TWENTY

That night I set up my art supplies and started painting backgrounds onto two of the canvases. We all sat in the living room. Sandra loudly defended herself against Tess's sarcasm about Colorology. Veronica curled up next to me watching me paint a canvas pale yellow. Serena complained of the smell, as if I were coating the wall in a stinky latex base coat. I opened the French doors, but didn't stop painting.

I isolated myself in my task.

I hadn't painted since my undergraduate days in college. I stopped when Gordon died. No, actually I stopped before he died. Gordon would try to tell me what to paint, and what style he liked best. It became grating. Instead of allowing my mind to trickle along in this direction, I cleared it and focused on my work.

I went to sleep satisfied. Today, I fed my soul instead of just my body.

After that night, I couldn't get back to my painting right away because of the tight filming schedule Julian kept us on. Through the magic of television, the viewer missed the long hike of us swatting bugs to get to the perfect rock-climbing cliff. I can't be sure how much was even filmed during the two hours we waited for our belayers to show up, on four wheelers, with our equipment.

However, when Serena bumped Veronica out of the way, so she could get harnessed next to me, the cameraman happened to be right in front of us. In fact, he lined up perfectly to see the look Tess and Sandra gave her. Would Ethan be allowed to eliminate Serena now?

212

"All right ladies," Lance finally said after we learned to use all the equipment, "This week's challenge will be fairly straight forward. We'll be rock climbing, then rappelling back down. This tests your physical endurance. The two contestants who make it to the top of the cliffs and back down first win."

A gunshot rang out. We all started climbing. I never rock climbed before, but caught on quickly. I climbed slowly and methodically up the side of the mountain as my Belayer yelled at me. Veronica and Sandra, who didn't need instruction, slipped up the side of the cliff like scurrying lizards.

Serena barely tried to climb the cliff, calling it a waste of effort. Soon Tess, whose thin arms weren't conducive to pulling her curves up a cliff, stood next to Erin at the bottom of the cliff. Erin had been extremely wary of the challenge and before we even started the cameraman taped her saying that as a professional dancer she'd be ruined if anything happened to her.

Something inside me needed to make it to the top, though I had no chance of winning. The sensation of pulling my body up the side of a cliff, while gravity failed to force me down, made me powerful.

"You lost, Carrie," Serena called. "Why are you still climbing?"

My foot slipped. My outstretched arm grazed a sharp rock. My other forearm caught a slight ledge stopping my body from slipping. My arm started to shake.

"Carrie, there's a foothold, to your left. Your foot is so close," my belayer yelled. I slid my foot around, sure my climb was over. It struck a little piece of rock jutting out from the cliff. I balanced my weight on the foothold, and let out the

213

breath I'd been holding. Then, I reached up with my bleeding arm and found a good handhold from the stone that cut me. I pulled myself up a little further scooting my way up the cliff.

"Veronica is coming down; you lost Carrie," Serena called back up the cliff.

I carefully found my next foothold having to rely on my legs more; my running made them strong. I barely noticed when Sandra rappelled down the cliff a few minutes after Veronica. I continued to climb. I would fight. Serena continued to taunt me to back down, but, determined to finish my climb, I kept going.

I finally pulled myself up over the top of the cliff. Shaky and light headed, I stood and threw my arms into the air with a loud yell of triumph.

"You know you lost, right?" Serena yelled looking to the others to mock me with her.

"I suppose that winning, much like beauty, is in the eye of the beholder, Serena," I yelled back.

Serena started to yell something else. Erin reached over and I saw her smack Serena on the back of the head. They started arguing while the man in charge at the top of the cliff praised my epic climb. I focused on him and turned my back on Serena.

"Do I take a ride down, or free fall like Veronica did?" I asked looking over at the four-wheeler the cameraman used to get to the top of the cliff.

"Rappelling is your reward for climbing," he grinned at me.

214

"Um… okay," I said. He gave me a lot of instructions that I tried to understand but didn't because he used terms I'd never heard before.

I laugh, a terrified laugh, as he lowered me down into the repelling position.

"You have the brakes," he said showing me again how to use them.

"Just walk backwards pushing off the cliff and you'll be fine."

"'Kay," I said.

After many more instructions, I released my hand brake and started down the cliff. I walked slowly until he yelled at me to try bouncing a little. I kicked off. I gave into gravity. My body released into a freefall. I remembered my hand brake. My feet slammed into the side of the cliff.

"Good job!" he yelled so I pushed off again, the terror rose from my stomach to my chest as I raced toward the ground. The rope caught, slowing me. I eased down and stepped onto the ground, and bugs swarmed me. My Belayer threw his arms around me.

"That was awesome, girl!"

"Oh Carrie, you're bleeding," Ethan said grabbing the first aid kit from a supply box. He pulled me away from the man whose shining eyes didn't hide his enthusiasm for me. A decent cut ran down my forearm. He sat me on the back of a truck with the hatch down where they had been sitting.

"You need to really clean that out," Serena instructed from over his shoulder.

"I am a doctor. I can handle this," Ethan said turning from her, "Carrie you –"

215

"Then why aren't you getting out some gauze? Here move, I'll do it," Serena said, pushing Ethan out of the way. The cameramen caught it all. The only thing I couldn't figure out is how Julian got her to show her extremely obnoxious behavior on film? No doubt he did something because he came out of the van to watch her implode. He even nodded at one of the cameramen to move over so he could get the best shot of Ethan looking astounded. After my arm was bandaged, the filming crew packed up. Julian examined me and said:

"You're climb was impressive."

"I lost," I said.

"Did you?" He glanced at Serena. I looked over at her and she stood alone. She looked out at the ocean, and I wondered if she'd ever seen it before, growing up in Iowa Foster Care. I doubted it. I wished I could be more patient with her, like Veronica was. Serena turned toward me, and I thought I saw something glisten in her eyes before she quickly looked away.

"I'm pretty tired," I said to Julian and walked away before he somehow implied how he'd gotten Serena to expose herself to the cameras. Because I knew if he told me how he'd done it, he'd also imply he did it for me.

"It really was a good climb," he said as I walked away and he continued to watch Serena.

Julian must have seen something in me that day because when I watched his version of my climb, I could see the fight in my very posture and the intensity in my eyes when I looked up at the camera to find another handhold. Julian made it look like I barely lost to Sandra, and viewers must have been on the

216

edge of their seats the whole segment. Anyone watching couldn't help but turn on Serena for not supporting me.

The next day Veronica and Sandra helped Ethan at a free clinic. I painted all day; in peace about losing a challenge.

Veronica came home glowing. Sandra talked over Veronica about sick people and wanting a better prize for winning. I couldn't get a full picture of what happened until that night in our room when we were chatting. Veronica assisted Ethan with an eighteen-year-old pregnant woman. She was thirty-two weeks along, but hadn't seen her baby on ultrasound yet.

She told me about the sweet moment when Ethan showed the woman she was having a boy. Veronica's eyes glistened and her cheeks glowed. The woman kissed Veronica goodbye when she left. She thanked her for showing the enthusiasm her boyfriend refused to give. Veronica told me all this in a matter-of-fact way, and didn't even suppose the act impressive. With no brag or elevation to self-importance in her tone, she simply relished her chance to help another human being along the way. Was poverty really such a hardship, such a flaw, if it reared women like Veronica?

CHAPTER TWENTY-ONE

Elimination day dawned the tensest time I'd spent in the house. My not bowing down to her put Serena on the war path. Even Tess started implying we'd all be grateful if he'd boot her, but in the beginning, I told Ethan I only had three weeks. If he didn't kick me off, I'd be on the show for four weeks. Would he get rid of me? At the end of the week they filmed me for more than an hour painting the ocean. On the other hand, the cameraman cut Serena down all week. Did Ethan have any choice in the matter?

How many points did I have? We'd all won competitions except Erin, and so if it really was based on points she'd be next to go, right?

But then why did I have the best designer? Serena's designer was at least as good as Sandra's. Veronica's designer lacked a strong stitch, and her dresses were usually falling apart by the end of the night. What did that mean?

My suspicions were confirmed when Ethan gave out five keys. One by one he gave keys to Veronica, Tess, Erin, Sandra, and then me. Serena did not get a key, all three times.

The first time we taped the keys, Serena nodded politely at Ethan when he said goodbye. Then she responded politely with a parting, but the shake in her voice came through. Lance announced something was wrong with the video feed. He couldn't look at Serena as he said it. He started the whole process over. The second time the keys were shot Serena glared at Ethan the whole time. The third time, Serena

218

walked up to Ethan after she was the only one left and snarled:

"Why are you doing this to me?"

"I ... I'm sorry. I know ... you've been through so much. If I could give all of you the money I would ... I can't keep you on the show if I don't –"

"Forget it, you made a mistake! I am *The Whole Package* and you will regret eliminating me!"

Serena shoved him out of her way, and left. I thought it strange she blamed Ethan. I didn't believe Ethan had any real control over the show. But then did that mean I was slotted to win the reality show?

The next morning on our run Ethan tried to explain why he couldn't eliminate me, but like a government document that had been redacted in many places, it didn't make sense. I couldn't string his explanation together enough to understand. He said something about the points and having to keep things on the level and his contract.

"You don't owe me an explanation," I said because I could see he wanted to give me one and couldn't. We turned back toward the Manor House I said; "I told you I would play the same as everyone else. I'm not going to worry about it. I don't want you to feel guilty for talking to me about Serena."

"Carrie, first of all, after a contestant is off the show, I can talk about her. At the reunion show, they actually want me to ... anyway Serena's gone so now she's free game."

"They want you to bad-mouth us after this is all over?" I asked.

"I don't know. There's more happening here than you know. I really want you to understand the pressure Julian puts on me."

"Pressure?" I said.

"Yes. You don't understand."

Ethan sounded so frantic that I stopped running and looked at him.

"Are you okay?" I said.

"I don't know. I signed this contract; and Julian, he comes and talks to me about really getting to know all the contestants. I can't talk to one contestant about another. I don't know. He asks me who I'd date … that sort of stuff."

"Does he really let you choose?" I asked.

"That's what I'm trying to tell you, I can't just … see, Serena was really popular, up there with Veronica."

"Veronica's popular?" I asked, he nodded and I said, "Awesome."

"Well, from what I understand not as popular as–"

"No, don't tell me anymore. It could get you in trouble, couldn't it?"

Ethan shrugged; annoyed with this barrier between us, he nodded.

"It's better this way. I don't want to be thinking about that stuff next time I'm on camera."

Ethan nodded and looked away.

"I'm sorry for you," I said at his pained expression.

"Yeah, me too. Can I come see your painting?" Ethan said by way of changing the subject.

"I'm not far," I said, "Veronica and I want to swim-slash-paint after lunch while the other ladies are being fitted for ball gowns, so if you come, do so quietly please. Sandra goes slight hysterics when she sees you now."

I threw up my arms and squealed in imitation.

"Are you already fitted?" Ethan asked trying not to laugh.

"Later this morning. Becky doesn't like to work with the other designers – all their designs start to look like hers. Well except Susan, of course. Susan couldn't copy her if she wanted to."

"Yeah," Ethan said. He looked out at the ocean like his mind wandered. He seemed preoccupied. I hoped he wasn't worried he'd said too much about the show. I didn't understand any cryptic thing he said anyway. The show didn't exist on our runs so I plunged into the subject I'd been thinking about for the last few days.

"In January there's a fundraiser for the Special Olympics called the Penguin Plunge. Mr. Wilson, my dad's best friend, found out about it a few years after my dad died. It was in Vermont then, but he's since brought it to Farmington. Anyway, after my dad died, Mr. Wilson tried to make sure Addie and I had… he tried to give us attention. He took us to watch him swim in ice chunks. It was hilarious. I never went back after that year – it wasn't exactly Grandma's type of fundraiser. I always wanted to try it. Will you do it with me this January?"

"Definitely," Ethan said. He looked at me more intently, trying to read me.

"Are you sure? You're kind of distracted today. You did hear the part about the very cold water filled with ice chunks?"

"As long as it means we'll still be hanging out in January."

221

"You didn't think you were going to get rid of me simply by kicking me off a show, did you? I go up to visit … my college friends in Boston all the time."

Ethan turned to look at me, suddenly very alert. He didn't answer and went back to brooding. I blanched and watched him. Did he notice my avoidance? Why hadn't I just discussed Gordon with him at first? We talked about everything except the show. I hated having another subject we had to avoid, but how did I bring it up? It felt like a big deal because we avoided talking about the deceased fiancé from the start.

Ethan didn't notice my distress. His own thoughts disturbed him to the point of distraction. Seeing how preoccupied Ethan looked, I left him alone. The wind picked up and moved clouds overhead. It looked like it may rain on us before the end of our run. After half a mile of hard jogging, Ethan glanced at me. This usually meant he finally wanted to talk again, but didn't know what to say.

"What are you thinking about? Can I know, or is it show-related?" I asked. Ethan nodded to himself for a moment as if making up his mind, and then he focused.

"How did you get to be a head hunter after being an art major?"

"That's what you're worried about?"

"I don't understand."

"I … it's complicated."

"Come on, please."

"Okay, well when I showed up at Harvard, everyone wanted to tell me who to be. Professors fought over me. I … I let a lot of people down when I entered the MBA program. They all acted like my art belonged to them; I

222

always painted what everyone else wanted me to. By the time I graduated, I hated painting."

"That's why you got an MBA?"

"Well, I had to support my family. My ... um. My fiancé just died," I stammered.

Ethan shot a look at me and I tried to sound natural, "I was left with ... I was bitter and my art was ... tainted in a way …. I don't know how to explain it … it doesn't matter anyway. I had to support my family. I couldn't do that painting, or even becoming a curator – especially not at first." Ethan watched me attentively so I continued, "My Career Coach called me into her office and introduced me to Adam – you know, 'let's make a bet' Adam?"

"Yeah."

"He showed me how much I could make recruiting, especially with all my ... uh ... contacts. I didn't even have to do an unpaid internship. He promised they'd pay me from day one and I still received all my college credit."

"That's almost too good to be true," he said.

"It gave me hope. I didn't know how else to support my mom and sister. Depending entirely on my art for a living would've taken years, so I entered the MBA program."

"You left your art behind for the money?"

"I was done with it, anyway," I snapped.

"But even if you were sick of painting, wouldn't you have liked selling art?" he asked.

"Maybe so. I love being around artists." I shrugged.

"That's too bad you can't do what you love," he said.

"Selling art isn't too different than selling a job."

"How do you figure?" Ethan asked, pulling his head in his tee shirt to wipe off the sweat.

"Attractive," I stammered, distracted by Ethan's washboard stomach coming into view. Ethan caught me looking and smiled in a satisfied way. I rolled my eyes at him, but forgot entirely what I was saying.

"Selling art and a job are the same?" he asked.

"Right, in both cases, you must see someone, understand who they are and if they can really fill the position you're trying to hire for. I analyze people and find the best fit. I had an eighty-seven percent retention rate in my first year. That's really amazing for my line of work." I tried to look cocky, but couldn't pull it off.

"Show off," Ethan teased, having lost his preoccupation. He focused entirely on me. I tried not to feel so content about this when he asked:

"Are you sad you left art behind completely?"

"I guess." I shrugged and picked up the pace as I saw the path off the side of the road. Ethan and I always raced to the path when we saw it. I grew disappointed when I easily outstripped Ethan by yards. He never let me win. Usually if I managed to get ahead of him, he would grab me around the waist, and playfully push me behind him. Then I'd worry about Gordon all over again. I stopped at the path up to the Manor House and waited for Ethan to catch up.

"You lost. Bad," I said.

"What about you not using your art as a job?" Ethan asked, almost annoyed I hadn't answered his question. I shrugged, wishing he would drop it. I hated remembering the fear – the stupidity of believing I could make good money painting or looking at art all day. Ethan asked again:

"Aren't you sad you didn't do something with your art?"

"Honestly, if I could be whatever I wanted to, I'd teach high school art. That would never have gone over with anyone at Harvard."

"Who cares? It's your life."

"People saw me as my dad's legacy – even I... I felt I owed it to his memory to become an icon like he was."

"I don't understand that."

"I'm sure it doesn't make sense to you, but you should have seen how amazing he was. Anyway, this guy Gordon ... well, he always said I should collect artists like my dad did architects. He thought I'd be the Emerson of today's art world. I would have but ... anyway an artist can't afford ..."

"To support your mom and sister," he said.

"Right, I had a teacher at Miss Porters, the private school I went to after my dad died, a Ms. Craig."

"A Ms. Craig huh?"

"Yes, I was this cranky, broken-hearted teenage girl, and she took the time to teach me how to refine my skills. She reached out to some people who helped me get a scholarship my senior year, started to show me how to network to get what I needed. I would love to teach. It isn't my lot, though."

I had never told anyone this. I waved goodbye to Ethan, wanting to escape. Out of nowhere, Ethan grabbed my arm and pulled me into a sweaty hug. I waited for him to say something funny, or maybe even comforting. It alarmed me when he said in complete seriousness into my ear,

"I missed you last week."

225

I allowed myself to sink into him. I smelled his newly laundered shirt mixed with his personal musk before I said:

"I missed you, too."

"Then you understand why I could never eliminate you. It would kill me to not give you a key. I never want to disappoint you like that. I need you to try a little harder. You can win this thing and be whatever you want."

Was he serious? I gently pulled away and looked at Ethan.

"No, you're too good," I said, trying to lighten him up. "Besides, Beth is expecting you to find your true love. If I interfere, she'd come find me."

"Who says I haven't found love?" Ethan said quietly surveying me carefully in a sweet and longing sort of way. I stared at him.

"I don't know if you love me back, but you're the best friend I've ever had. I wanted to kick Serena off, but it ...I needed more for you to stay. That's what I was trying to say. We talk about everything. You're amazing. I can't keep doing the show without you. I know you didn't come here to find someone, but I'd be an idiot not to try for you. Think about it, okay?"

Then, in the true manner of a twelve-year-old, Ethan turned and ran away.

CHAPTER TWENTY-TWO

I watched Ethan for five minutes until I realized I couldn't see him anymore. I turned and walked slowly up to the Manor House. Had Ethan just ... what had Ethan just asked me? What did this show lead up to? A million dollars, but ... Did Ethan just choose me to win the money, or did he ... did he want to love me?

I thought hard back to my contract. I wished for the millionth time I'd read it. Ethan picked the most worthy woman for a million dollars. It had nothing to do with love. He said the word love ... Nothing about the show was real – could something real come from the show?

I thought about Ethan's sweaty arms around me. It should have been gross. It wasn't. I could still feel the spot on my arm where he touched me the first night we met. I could feel his bare arms wrapping around my waist, and my back against his chest as he carried me into the ocean when I started a water fight the other day.

In fact, I could recall almost every time he touched me in some random, friendly way. I wanted him to hug me again. Then I saw what he meant. He couldn't kick me off the show. I could never hurt Ethan by rejecting him. It would break me. But what part did the million dollars play into that? Was I forcing myself to like him because he held the key to the safe deposit box?

No – this was wrong. I loved Gordon. How could I ever face Dayna again if I replaced her son in my heart? The life inside me died again. As a shackled woman, I obligated myself to be chained to the sadness. But I could no longer tell if the chains of loss held me down, or if I held to them so I didn't

227

have to let go of the distinction it gave me. I clung to the sad distinction of loss since I was fourteen.

But I didn't want to be sad. I didn't like moping. I didn't like people who made me mope. I wanted to glow like a woman in love. Did I ever glow for Gordon like I did for Ethan?

Wait – I did glow for Ethan. Did I love Ethan?

I couldn't love Ethan, not after only four weeks – I loved the money, and Ethan came with it. Confusion colored my face and I ached again. Sometimes I wondered if I loved my mother and sister anymore. Somewhere within all the deaths I endured, I simply turned off because it hurt too much to feel. Now, without realizing it, someone had come and flipped me back on, but I felt horrible about it. Why did the idea of moving beyond my pain make me feel so guilty?

"You showered," Becky asked when I arrived late to my fitting.

"Yes. You want to smell?"

"As long as I can't is all that matters."

"Where's Veronica?"

"Julian needed Susan for something," Becky said, "She's going to have to fit Veronica later with everyone else."

"Ah, we were going to swim-slash-paint later."

"Julian's the boss."

"Do you think he's doing more funny business?"

"I have no clue," she said looking over her shoulder, "Here, don't pull on the fabric."

" 'Kay," I said stepping into a high waist dark navy dress with gold ribbon interwoven.

"This is kinda like the dress I wore onto the show."

228

"Yeah. See a pattern, my little diva?"

"What?"

She paused looking over her shoulder at the door again then she whispered:

"Julian said not to try and force you to update your wardrobe anymore …. I heard Lance tell a stage hand that's never happened before."

"That's interesting," I said turning and allowing the dress to float around me.

Did Julian respect me? My Grandfather loved me, so he respected me. Julian could not degrade me into a role, a two-dimensional character on his show. Did this earn his respect for me? What did that say about him, the only way to earn his respect was to defy him?

Whatever the case, I believe he delighted in the challenge I presented. And though I was tempted to be flattered by this, I couldn't. I'd known my grandfather's respect. Julian acting like we played chess, forced my movements as any Grandmaster would his queen, so could I really be grateful he no longer viewed me as a pawn?

"I'll tell you what Becks. I like to be covered from here to here," I said. "You are very talented and should get to be as creative as you want, if you can just keep me covered."

"Okay, sounds good to me. Although, just between us, the brown dress you wore to the Opera is still in first place, closely followed by the green."

"Oh congrats," I said.

"Thanks …but I think I can top it … I'm going to get started on your next elimination dress today."

229

She started playing with the material, bunching it differently and I watched her through the mirror. I had no idea what to think anymore. Looking back, I could see how Julian shaped my thoughts. Not just in dressing me like his personal doll, but he pushed me toward the money with a crass vigor even Grandmother would have been ashamed of. How did a person sort through their feelings like that?

It'd been a month since I used the internet, or talked on a phone; Julian disconnected all of us from the world. The concerns in the Manor House smothered me. I couldn't leave the Manor House. I could only be wrapped up in Ethan. Somewhere inside me, I knew making a decision like that was unwise, but it was Ethan.

At times, we sat around having a conversation about home or what we missed most. Lance would just happen to come in. He'd refocus the conversation on Ethan – a conversation they just had or the way he reacted to a certain competition. Often times what Lance said didn't coincide with the Ethan I ran with. Strangely enough what Lance said would often be geared at me, almost like I would prefer the bargain basement Ethan he was selling versus the Ethan I knew. Julian wanted us all in love with Ethan, the Ethan that was a cross between Magnum P.I. and Sheriff Andy Griffith.

Was this feeling I had for Ethan manufactured? Why did Julian need me to love Ethan?

What Julian knew about love, I would learn.

"Okay my little diva, we're done. You can go," Becky said.

"Thanks, I'll see you later," I said. I walked out of the fitting room up the hall to my bedroom. I lay on my bed rubbing my belly where Becky accidentally stabbed me with a straight pin.

"Hey, Lance just told me I get to dance with Ethan first," Veronica said bouncing onto my bed.

"It's probably because you're ahead of us in points."

"I don't even care about that. I know it sounds dumb, but I think he really likes me, Care. At the free clinic he seriously wanted my help; Sandra had a hard time ... well, with the sick people. She just wanted to flirt and let the licensed doctors do everything."

"What do you mean?" I asked.

"Uh, Ethan isn't licensed in California so he could only help. The regular doctor pretty much let him take over after a while, he's so competent."

"No, um ...he told you he likes you?"

"Well, not in so many words. Sandra wasn't helpful at all. He blew her off twice to talk to me, when we were on a break. I'm talking to him like we're friends, like you said. I'm pretty sure he likes me."

"Wait. Why?" I said leaning up on my elbow.

"I just told you, Space Case. He always talks to me about me, you know. And the other night at the barbeque, he put his arm around me."

I nodded and tried to smile, but a new fear started to take over.

"Are you all right?" Veronica asked seeing my face.

"I need a drink of water. After all my non-workouts with Serena last week I ran hard this morning to try and make up for it," I said and pulled my body up off the bed. I walked out

231

of the room and away from Veronica. I didn't like her. I didn't want to be around her.

No, that wasn't fair.

Hadn't I assured her I had no feelings for Ethan? I didn't want a boyfriend.

Had Ethan just said he loved me? Is that what he said?

Did Ethan have feelings for Veronica? She seemed so certain he did, but she barely ever talked to him. Then again, part of me wondered if he was manipulating her – or me. He couldn't really want us both. Could he?

Ethan was two people in a way, my running partner, who I admit I adored, and a he was the judge on a reality show. I wasn't a hundred percent sure about that guy. Where did the two men meet? Did they meet? The way he spoke, he knew he was playing a game, but did the way a man play indicate something about him?

CHAPTER TWENTY-THREE

After lunch Veronica couldn't swim while I painted. As I wasn't very good company anyway, I encouraged her to go to her fitting. I thought it a gift I'd been isolated. I wanted to be alone. We were rarely ever alone in the Manor House.

After Veronica went to the fitting with the other contestants I went out to the gazebo and set up next to the pool to paint. I had a couple hours until the ball room dancing challenge. Because Becky refused to work with the other designers around, I had at least a glorious half hour to be alone. Outside, the rain started pounding, fogging up the windows fogged up. The pool smelled like bleach, so I opened the sliding doors to let the breeze dilute the smell.

The cool draft of air was comfortable in the warm gazebo. I set up my easel and mixed my paint feeling cozy and dry, yet somehow a part of the summer storm. I didn't know what to think about Ethan. I couldn't see what was real anymore. I wondered if Ethan saw himself as two people.

A horrible thought struck me. What if Ethan wasn't two people? What if my running partner just knew how to play the socialite? What if he, like my designer, catered to Julian? What if Julian told Ethan what contestants to romance and when?

I couldn't face these thoughts. After picking out the perfect brush I loaded it with paint and looked critically at the canvas. I already painted a pale image of two intertwining pink roses now in full bloom, from the English-with-a-hint-of-

233

tropical and French-and-Japanese-influenced garden on my yellow canvas.

On my sketch pad, I shaded two copies of the roses when being primped for the eliminations. One copy had the light coming from the top, and the other lit from the side. My brush came close to the canvas, but still I hesitated. I propped up my sketch pad so I could see the roses I'd copied again trying to decide where the light came from. I mixed just a dot of red in my white paint. It turned pearly pink so I could make the roses glisten. Again, I hesitated, studying both my sketches.

Ms. Craig always encouraged me to paint without a sketch, to just feel the shadows contrasting with the light. I did this for my favorite teacher in high school, but in college I went back to my sketch pad. Impulsively I reached out and turned over both my sketches.

I had to learn to trust myself at some point. No back up plans, just me. Succeed or fail – the picture was mine. It bothered me I couldn't see the way the petals layered on the paper. Instead of turning the picture over I wiped some of the paint off my brush and started. I painted and mixed and painted again.

I built the flowers into three dimensions bringing them off the paper. Then I wrapped them in light, pulling my lighter pink through the wet paint. I came back and hid the color in shadow, mixing my richer paints right on the canvas. I lost myself in it. The world became mine to do with as I chose.

"Hey," Ethan said from right behind me.

I jumped a little. Ethan was only two feet away from me. He wasn't touching me, but I could feel him. He must have walked up from his bungalow because his hair was wet.

"Oh, hey," I said setting down my paint brush. I stood up, unsure what to do with my hands. I reached up to brush some raindrops out of his hair and he closed his eyes to my touch. I pulled my hand away nervously. I didn't know what to say, or where to look.

"I like it," Ethan said, nodding at my picture.

I turned from him and looked again. Suddenly I could hear the whisper of Kipling saying "And the first rude sketch the world has seen was joy to his mighty heart, Till the Devil whispered behind the leaves, "It's pretty but is it art?"

Then I saw all the mistakes vividly and wondered why I turned my sketch over. I went to pick up the canvas off the easel, but my fumbling fingers lost it and the canvas fell.

"Hey, be careful!"

"Oh yeah I can fix that, here give it back. I'm not really…. It's been a long time since I painted."

"No, Care, I like it. It looks cool how you magnified the flowers to take up the whole canvas. It looks like they're coming straight out at me."

"The roses are so pretty – I thought I'd have a Georgia O'Keeffe moment," I said, reaching for the canvas he carefully held.

"Do you really like her work?"

"Yeah, I can pretty much copy any of the great artists."

"Which one do you paint the most like?" he asked.

"It depends on who I'm trying to paint like. I can master any of them. It's mostly just stroke work, shadowing. It's all technical if you really know what you're doing," I said.

"When you're just painting like yourself what do you paint like?" he asked.

235

I shrugged. I didn't know what I painted like when I wasn't copying a master. I examined my canvas. After I turned the sketch over my painting took on a life of its own. My flowers looked shiny against wet shadows, departing from O'Keeffe's simple geometric images.

I looked over to get Ethan's opinion, but he gazed into the hot tub, his rippling reflection showed an uncertain disposition. He wore a wet yellow and blue plaid button-up shirt rolled a couple of times at the sleeves; his forearms looked incredible. I craved with a strange urgency for them to be around me. I lost my breath somewhere in my chest as Ethan turned his amazing eyes on me.

"Where's Veronica?"

"Her designer couldn't do her fitting earlier." I said, "Hey, I wanted to talk to you. I'm worried."

"What's up?" Ethan said.

"Veronica really enjoys being on this show," I stammered for something to say, trying to look anywhere but at his strong arms.

"I'm trying my best not to hurt anyone, Care. I'm just the judge – I'm not obligated to be anyone's boyfriend, or father, for that matter. My only job is to get to know each contestant. I gauge how far they've overcome all the hardship in their lives, and give out points." He pulled at a tool loop on my overalls. Again, I couldn't breathe. I started breathing heavily to compensate.

"I don't mean to butt in … I wasn't going to get so involved," I said.

"Carrie," Ethan said. He pulled me toward him slightly by the tool loop on my overalls, "I want you involved. I value your opinion more than anyone's. I seriously ... I know I'm making you uncomfortable, but I can't help it."

I examined him. The only thing that made me uncomfortable was Veronica saying that she thought Ethan liked her. I didn't want Ethan to be falling for her.

"She deserves more – "

"Carrie, it's you. I don't want to talk about Veronica. I want to know how you feel. I can't get you out of my head ... it's only you."

I glanced at Ethan. He waited patiently for me to think, but it looked like I was killing him. I laughed at him a little.

"I know, sorry," he said.

Of course, this sweet Ethan in front of me would never play games. I could feel my stomach swoop as Ethan put a hand on my arm.

"I'm not ...you're my ..." I stammered, "I'm seriously just really awkward. I'm not good at this."

"Yeah?" Ethan said. He slid his hands across my back and under the suspenders on my overalls gradually pulling me in.

"So you're open to the idea of us," Ethan implored. I wrapped my arms around his neck. My whole body curled into his. He leaned down and I closed my eyes and allowed my lips to meet his. He pulled me in with urgency and didn't lose any time coaxing my mouth open, like he'd been waiting forever to do so.

"Wait a minute," I said pulling away, shot through with insecurity.

"What's the matter?" Ethan said leaning his head back so he could see me, but his arms remained intertwined in my overalls.

237

"You aren't kissing all the other contestants, are you?" I said.

"No, Care – of course not," Ethan said. He went in for another take.

"Because, reality show or not, kisses are important to me. I don't let just anyone kiss me," I interrupted.

"Okay, Care," Ethan said.

"Okay then," I said with a pleasant purging joy our mouths met again. Satisfied, and yet unsatisfied I pulled him in closer to me. I lost track of everything.

CHAPTER TWENTY-FOUR

"Carrie if you're out there, we need to get to the dance hall," Lance called.

I pulled away from Ethan, and my face was raw. He put his forehead against mine and breathed like he just finished running a race.

"I'm going to go around ..." He started but then grabbed my head and kissed me again.

"Okay, I'm really going to go," he said. Before I could complain, he walked out of the pool house and moved to the front of the building by the side walkway.

After composing myself I walked around the pool and back into the main part of the house. I couldn't look at anyone. I wanted an hour of quiet nothingness to think about what just happened.

"Let's go. It's just practice today, but you do need the shoes Becky got you. Plus, you may want to put on something more comfortable," Lance said gruffly glancing at my overalls.

"Kay," I said wondering what his problem was. I rushed up the stairs grateful for the excuse to leave.

We danced for hours until my feet killed and everyone had a basic understanding of the waltz. We were each paired up with male dancers who taught us flourishes to the box step. A built blond man with a goatee and major sideburns swung me around the room. I'd been raised in white gloves, etiquette lessons, and dancing. Erin and her partner looked like they could compete professionally. Ethan watched me the whole time, and looked daggers at my partner when he noticed.

The next day we danced until past midnight in the ballroom of a hotel. Our feet were sore and bodies ached from filming what couldn't have been more than a ten-minute segment. The viewing audience only saw what Julian coordinated to the music. Dresses rippling, hands clasped, swaying and turning until the show became living poetry.

No other segment highlighted me so advantageously, almost as if the camera and I were at the start of a new love. I wondered if Julian's obsession of me turned really unhealthy at some point.

For winning the dance competition Julian arranged for Erin and me to take a young man named Jonah, who just went into remission from cancer, parasailing. The sixteen-year-old was bald and positive. I felt close to him, I'd first learned about cancer only a few years younger than he was and we could talk easily. I mostly listened and wished I were as resilient as him.

When we finally got into the boat he and I went up first. He whooped a lot and I laughed. After getting used to the feeling of flying, I lost myself in it.

Sailing through the wind over the bright, blue waves below was unlike anything I'd ever experienced. Did it worry me that I'd confided in Ethan that I wanted to try it sometime? Then it happened to be the reward for a competition I had no chance of losing? Sadly no. If anything, I thought Julian was bending to me, not the other way around.

Erin balked when it was her turn. She didn't feel it a good idea with her back. Ethan told her she didn't have to. Julian

240

settled it by consulting a specialist. The doctor he consulted probably lost most of his business when Marijuana became legal. He didn't hesitate to tell Erin she'd be fine because the boat was in the calmer waters of the bay. Erin believed him, and strapped herself to the back of a boat to impress Ethan.

Ethan watched the boat and the waves the whole time she flew. He yelled at the driver when he went straight into another boat's wake. The cameraman showed Ethan's back turned. The viewing audience took it as Ethan ignoring Erin while the cancer patient tried to keep her calm. I started to wonder if Erin would be the next to be eliminated.

When we went back to the Manor House that night the fight about the competition grew intense.

"It wasn't fair!" Tess said painting her toe nails.

"Erin's a dancer," Sandra said filing hers.

"It was about poise. Erin can't help the competition," I said, "It's like getting mad at someone for being born tall – you can't –"

"Oh seriously! Could you not moralize … I'm going to need some happy pills if I have to hear you moralize one more time!" Tess said.

"It is getting annoying," Veronica said. Everyone stopped. Veronica never sided against me. Tess called her my sidekick. Right or wrong, she always loyally stood by everything I said.

"Oh, a… sorry Veronica, I'll try to cut back," I said. She nodded and left the sitting room. I followed her with my eyes. I couldn't decide why she was mad at me, but she was definitely mad.

241

Despite Veronica's anger, the next few days were pure
bliss for me. I started my morning run with a minty kiss from
Ethan. At times we'd stop at the light house and be so
overcome with each other it would become a make-out
session.

During the days we filmed we would find little ways to
touch. I'd rub an arm against his leg when he passed my
chair. He'd stand behind me to look at something Julian
showed us, and play with the tips of my hair. He always took
any opportunity to be near me, to brush my hand when the
other contestants weren't looking. It was like our secret way
to tell each other that we wished we were alone.

Veronica seemed withdrawn, but I didn't know why. She
had a great segment getting a little fluffy white dog cleaned up
and adopted by a little girl. I congratulated her. She nodded,
but chose to help Erin with her misbehaving Weiner dog. Erin
didn't care for dogs, so I let it go.

By the fourth elimination, the room seemed to grow. The
five of us left stood on one riser, and I couldn't help
remembering the auction block where my grandfather
bought his old restored cars. Then I wondered if I could drive
his old Jaguar convertible. Why not? I loved my grandpa. I
used to love driving around in his car with him. My
Grandmother refused to let us drive it after he died. But why
should his car sit unused in the garage?

"Veronica, will you take this key?" Ethan asked after the
host signaled him to give out his first key. Veronica
paused. She looked like she was seriously considering
whether she wanted a key. She walked slowly over to Ethan.

242

"Yes," she said. Ethan grinned at her, but she searched his face looking for something. It disarmed him and for a moment he became the anxious one and she his judge.

Finally, she took the key and stepped over to the chosen side. Tess and Sandra joined her. When I finally joined her, Veronica wouldn't even look at me. It didn't shock me Erin was eliminated. Erin, however, hadn't seen it coming. She cried. We all hugged her trying to console her.

Erin couldn't seem to pull it together. I walked her out to the limo. She needed help with her enormous suitcase. I always found myself helping her lug it. After we made it out to the limo and I helped George haul the thing into the trunk I asked Erin:

"Are you going to be okay?"

She started to cry again.

"What, what is it?" I asked pulling her into a hug.

"After I flew to California Julian insisted I cut my hair to get on the show. I told him... anyway he insisted. I'm not sure I can get back into my dance company with short hair."

"Oh Erin, I'm so sorry," I said. My heart broke for her, all she overcame to get into her dance company and now she had to start over.

"I wish we'd been friends this whole time. I'm sorry I let Serena in," Erin said.

"She had a gift you can't worry about it,' I said.

Erin laughed through her tears, "She did."

"You ready?" George asked Erin kindly.

"No, but I guess it's time for real life," she said climbing into the limo. I waved to her, but something about the phrase real life taunted me. Didn't I need to get home for some reason? The feeling of having forgotten an appointment spread over me and I couldn't be sure why.

CHAPTER TWENTY-FIVE

"Everything all right Veronica?" I asked what had turned into a revolving question with us.

"Yep," Veronica replied her revolving answer. She curled up tighter in the corner of the leather couch watching the woman on the movie fall in love right on cue.

"Come on. What's up?" I asked.

"We're watching here," Sandra said.

"Let's talk about it later, okay?" Veronica said tearing up. I gave Tess a look and Tess shrugged, also worried. Sandra didn't even notice Veronica's glistening eyes; the movie was at her favorite part.

Veronica announced that morning she would move into Erin's old room. I'd lost my friend, but I didn't know why. Apparently, we shouldn't have to share a room while two sat empty. That wasn't the real reason, but she wouldn't explain.

A week earlier we'd been Gung Ho to keep rooming together despite the empty room so we could continue to talk at night. I came to depend on our nightly talks. It helped us both relax enough to sleep after a tense day filming. Plus, I'd grown fond of her goodness and humble nature. I thought our friendship would last for years after the show ended. Over the last week she just rolled over and went to sleep. No matter what I did or said I couldn't get her to open up to me again.

I could see the romantic movie we watched hurt her, so I asked:

245

"Hey Veronica, you want to go swim while I paint? I'm working on my seascape."

"No, if Lance doesn't come back, I'm going to bed soon."

We all looked at her. Nobody said anything. There hadn't been a competition. It was competition day and nothing happened. We all stayed on edge waiting, but Lance, Julian and even Ethan disappeared after we taped a hot tub scene. We could do nothing except wait for them to come back.

"Carrie, could you please get the popcorn," Sandra said when the microwave beeped and Veronica didn't move. That was Sandra's way of showing compassion.

I walked slowly out of the little cove that held the TV and then through the sitting room toward the kitchen. I savored my walk. I savored any moment I could pull away from the group. I'd daydream about Ethan.

I put the popcorn Veronica popped into a bowl. I couldn't bear to watch the nauseatingly romantic movie again. It made Sandra feisty like she lived as the heroine grasping her way to a boyfriend in a romantic movie. She forgot we were competing for the title of Whole Package, and the show was just another generic dating reality show. I left the popcorn with Sandra and walked out on the terrace with my sketch pad.

My roses turned out beautifully. It didn't keep me from practicing layering waves on my sketch pad. I wanted to get the complicated seascape I'd been painting perfect. In a cool corner of the terrace, I did another quick outline of the ocean's frothy texture. I turned back to my lighthouse and shaded it. It didn't fit into the Monet-like seascape I kept

246

trying. I pulled out my oil pencils and turned back to the waves. All the Impressionistic colors felt wrong. Everything felt wrong.

I didn't want an impression, a sight, a perception that could only stand the scrutiny of a glance. I didn't want anyone to believe Ethan was in love with Tess or Sandra. I didn't want to feel suffocated when Ethan feigned interest in the other contestants. I hated it.

I wanted realism.

I started another sketch.

The picture in my head had to be real. I put the lighthouse in the middle of the picture. When I finished it would look like a photograph. This felt better.

Ethan wanted me to be his girlfriend when this was all over. He promised we'd come back in October and stroll hand in hand at the Half Moon Bay Pumpkin festival. That was a boyfriend thing to do. I asked him to take a weekend this fall to plant tulip bulbs around the path leading up to the house, like Grandpa had every fall. Ethan became even more insistent I take him on a tour of every building my father ever built. In realism, we went on dates and everyone knew he loved me.

As the sun set I walked thoughtfully back into the house. Sandra and Tess sat playing cards at the dining room table. Veronica already headed for bed. I followed her, trying not to draw attention to myself as I walked through the sitting room.

"It's for blondes only," Sandra insisted about her very expensive shampoo. I passed as quietly as I could.

"Carrie!"

"Yeah"

"Are you going to bed?"

"Yeah, Sandra"

"Really – just like that – without saying good night?"

"Good night Sandra – Tess."

The confinement of the Manor House was wearing on us all, but Sandra was having a much harder time hiding her crazy than the rest of us. Sandra glared at me. She wanted me to do something. I didn't know what, but if I didn't figure it out she'd be offended.

"Did you need something else?" I asked.

"You could take the popcorn bowl ya'll got out back to the kitchen."

"Right," I'd noticed the bowl still sitting on the couch in the cove where she'd been watching her movie when I walked by. Trying to stay calm, I walked back and grabbed the bowl and walked into the kitchen.

I, too, tired of the Manor House. The daily grind of primping for cameras and trying to be patient with people who touched my last nerve drove me stir crazy. Having Serena out of the house helped. Still, I had been alone most of the last year and I craved the privacy of my studio apartment.

The more comfortable Tess became, the more perverted and grating her sarcasm became. Sandra's need to be the center of attention brought my hand into slap position – and heaven help us if we laughed without her. She'd attack us, certain we were laughing at her. Even Veronica soaking in her insecurities all the time made me want to scream "buck up little camper."

248

I did better at keeping my crazy on the inside, but Tess's stale joke to find some valium to take me down a notch became old. Apparently, nobody's funny stays amusing in such large doses, not even mine. They were just as sick of me as I was of them. After I put the popcorn bowl in the kitchen I headed directly for the stairs.

"Carrie," Sandra called again. I counted to ten.

"Yeah," I said.

"I just... I've been... Well, I didn't appreciate the way you made fun of me this afternoon. It's not fair, ridiculing me in front of Ethan."

"I... Sandra, I didn't make fun of you."

"I know you're trying to sabotage me," Sandra said close to tears, "You need to back off and play fair."

"What?" I asked looking to Tess who rolled her eyes and made a crazy sign by her ear. Sandra saw this and so it began all over again. Tess actively engaged Sandra's behavior with her sarcasm. They argued a lot more than the rest of us.

Even without trying, though, Sandra found ways to be huffy with me. And she made sure I knew when she was mad. I just never knew why. As I stood there waiting for them to argue I started going back over all our conversations. What did I say? Of course, Sandra wouldn't just tell me. Oh no. I had to guess at how I'd offended her.

Sandra almost drunk fixated on Tess. She'd forgotten me. She'd remember eventually, but I didn't want to deal with it. I saw my window and quietly shifted toward the stairs again.

It'd been a rough day. Friday was usually either challenge day, or prep for the Saturday challenge. Nothing happened. We waited all day but nothing came. After lunch, we were all on edge, and then the cameras were brought in.

Instead of a challenge we were stuck in swimsuits and put in the hot tub with Ethan. The lights were blocked out. Lance told us to pretend to shiver in the night air. The afternoon had been warm and the gazebo had been too warm and the hot tub uncomfortable. Even night sounds like crickets were played in the background.

Tess and Sandra were all over Ethan. With his perfectly sculpted body shoved in my face I couldn't look away, but I couldn't watch either. I started making fun of myself until everyone played along. I told about the elderly water aerobics class my mom goes to.

I acted out what I looked like trying to keep up with these fifty- to eighty-year-old women. It helped release some of the added tension that tended to magnify all our irritating quirks while we tried to perform.

It was short lived. I used a Southern accent when pretending to be one of the older ladies telling me about her broken hip while she out-maneuvered me in the water. Oh, the Southern accent. That must be why Sandra launched a wall of water at my face.

Her playful tended to be aggressive, so I thought we were just messing around. I hadn't been being rude – had I? I didn't compare her to an eighty-year-old with a hip replacement. The woman really did have an accent.

Sandra was exhausting.

Julian, who decided to wear an assortment of ball caps truck-driver style on the top of his head over the last week, was a master jabber. All this resulted in good television, I'm sure. Oh, I just had to go to bed. I turned from Sandra toward the stairs again.

"You going to bed then, Carrie?" Sandra called, affronted I'd go again without telling her, despite I'd already said good night.

"Yep – good night," I replied, wishing just once I could backhand her – just once.

"I can't believe you...." She started to cry. Oh great. My compassion worked its way through the annoyance and frustration. I walked down to Sandra and gave her a hug while she rested her head on my shoulder sobbing.

"We aren't competing to date Ethan, remember? The hot tub had nothing to do with the competition, it's just Julian messing with our minds."

"It's so hard to focus," she said almost falling asleep on my shoulder.

She was so exhausted.

"Look, I'm sorry if I hurt your feelings."

"I know, I don't mean to be like this..."

"How about I help you to bed?" I said.

"No, not yet, one more game of Pinochle. Tess you'll play with me – won't you?"

"Sure, Sandra you already owe me over thirty million dollars," Tess said.

"You're cheatin'," she said.

"I've got to go to bed," I said. Knowing the peace made would be short lived I almost sprinted for the stairs.

CHAPTER TWENTY-SIX

My room was the middle door along the upstairs hall with two doors on each side. The hall led to the back room filled with mirrors where our designers worked. I stopped in front of the door to our room to listen for Veronica's snore, but instead heard sobs.

I walked in concerned. The sobbing stopped. I closed the door quietly so the other contestants thought Veronica asleep and I didn't want to disturb her. I dropped my sketch pad on our vanity and turned on the lamp by my bed. I quietly knelt by Veronica's bed.

"Ron, what's the matter?"

"I saw you," Veronica said sitting up abruptly. She looked angry, poised in my face. I backed up quickly.

"What?"

"I saw you kissing Ethan, when we were all being fitted for our dresses. Susan got a call from Julian after she started working on my dress. He needed her for something so I came down to swim and saw you kissing him."

"Oh," I stammered.

"You're a liar," she said.

My perfect first kiss crumbled to ashes. Julian finally destroyed my friendship with Veronica, and he used my warmest, happiest moment to do it.

"You acted like you didn't want him. You were so angelic about giving everyone a chance at him… You're a complete sham, and I fell for it."

252

"I didn't mean to like him; we get along so well. I'm so sorry."

I never thought sweet, anxious Veronica would turn on me in such a manner. I backed up to sit on my bed across the room.

My startled reaction softened Veronica. She thought I'd be more exultant than hurt. She threw herself back onto her pillow. I sat watching her cast into shadows by the sideway light. I liked to paint interesting light angles.

"Look, I've been thinking over the last few days," Veronica finally said. "If Tess kissed him I would a just been like, whatever, and figured it was physical and still gone after him. But you're my friend."

I walked back over to Veronica and said distressed, "Sweetie –"

Veronica threw me a look that told Sweetie, or any other affectionate nickname off limits. I continued with, "That's the whole problem with this show. Love's not a competition. It's compatibility. It's a willingness to work through life's sucky crap together. Love's not about saying the right thing at the right moonlit moment and then the prince kisses you. Or in this case he gives you a million dollars and finally you're at happily ever after. Ethan and I connect, abnormally so."

Veronica turned to the wall and huffed. I hadn't meant to hurt her feelings even more. I sat on the bed next to her feet and patted them uncomfortably. At first Veronica resisted, but then she grew indifferent to my making peace. I kept patting. Her considerate heart would easily be my friend again. Wasn't she *The Whole Package*?

"Look, I've never been a romantic like you," I said.

253

"I want to be in love – that's not a sin," she said.

"You want to be in love in a movie, not in real life. Veronica, please listen to me, I'm not an expert, but I've been a part of a good solid love before." Yes, I cited my relationship with Gordon, "From what you've told me about your parents, I'm not really sure if you've even seen it. It isn't like some musical montage and then you're in love. Love is built."

"Just leave me alone," Veronica said. However, she didn't pull away or make any attempt to get me to move my hand that I'd rested on her foot.

"You know that I never meant to hurt you. I would never kiss someone to be mean to one of my favorite people ever," I pleaded. Veronica half shrugged, half sobbed so I continued, "I just want to explain what happened."

"I know what happened." Veronica said, "I've thought about that day a lot. I remember the look on your face when I said I thought he liked me. You know, before I saw you kissing him."

Veronica turned her huge bloodshot green eyes on me, her face blotchy, to see if I remembered. I nodded, so Veronica continued, "You looked like I'd slapped you. Then after I saw you kissing him, it all sort of clicked, why you were so worried about me. I know I don't really have a right to be mad. We're on a reality show fighting each other for a guy or a million dollars … you're not just doing this for the money, are you?"

"No … I really like him. Remember the money isn't tied to Ethan. You're doing so well at all the competitions, better than I am. You could still win," I lied, "I just like him."

"I know – I see the way you look at him."

"Do I look at him?"

"Yeah, anyway I can't really be mad. I keep telling myself you came on this show to win. Like we all did. I just feel crummy."

"Of course, you do. Julian wants us fixated on Ethan until we can't see anything else. It makes us fight, and he has good television. Sandra just reamed me out for embarrassing her in front of Ethan, and I didn't know I had."

"Yeah, the accent in the hot tub," Veronica confirmed.

"I wouldn't do that on purpose. You know I'd never want you to feel bad? I never meant to fall for him," I said. "Not like this."

"That's just it, I never got why you came on the show. You never seemed interested like the rest of us... you know... in finding the right guy."

"Oh Veronica, I came for the money," I admitted. And it was true. I let Adam persuade me into doing a reality show, because I needed the money. I played along for weeks, because it was a fat check. After taxes it would all go into savings. I'd have a pillow. I couldn't manage to save anything living from pay check to paycheck with all my bills. To have over five hundred thousand dollars in savings, that was security. I hated that tacky dragon, but I needed it.

"You came for the money?" Veronica said astonished unable to even comprehend such a stance.

"This show's supposed to be about a million dollars, not love, Sweetie. No one here is as interested in finding the right guy as you. I know you deserve him. I just can't help how I feel."

"Yeah, but you never played the game like you wanted the money."

"I didn't play. I escaped from a life I can't handle. I saw winning that money as my freedom. And then Ethan just snuck up on me … I didn't mean to hurt you."

"I don't want you to have to go back to your life," Veronica said.

"I don't want you to be hurt," I said.

"I can't help being hurt; I'm tired of being alone."

"I'm sorry," I said filled with fear. She deserved to win. She deserved the million dollars for being so pure about it, but I couldn't stand to lose Ethan. Then I found I didn't even care about the money anymore. The dragon lost all control over me. I loved him. I needed him. I hated that he came with the money; it confused me, because I needed it, too.

Still, I had become pure in a way. Money or not, I loved Ethan. I would recruit forever if it meant I could be with Ethan. Though from all he said, his practice had to be bringing in quite a bit… err, no, it didn't matter. All that mattered was Ethan. To prove my love for him, I'd give up the million dollars – I'd hint that Veronica should have it.

Maybe I did deserve him.

"But why wasn't it Ethan and me?" Veronica asked interrupting my thoughts. I got back on my soap box a little too enthusiastically. Ethan was mine. I could get Veronica to bow out – for her own good of course.

"I can't explain how I click with him. I just do," I said.

"I know," Veronica said. "Serena used to tell me I'd have to break you and Ethan apart if I wanted a chance with him."

256

"We just need to find someone for you to click with," I said.

"How?" she asked.

"How did you meet boys in the past?" I asked

"I've had a few boyfriends... In college I dated a bit," Veronica said, "I met a guy online."

"You aren't really shocked when the twenty-five-year-old model from New York ends up being a fifteen-year-old with acne and a buzzed head?"

"But he wore a leather jacket that was pretty cool."

"Funny," I said.

"Look, I've been set up a few times. When my cousin started dating her boyfriend she forced him to hook me up with one of his friends. That was all kinds of humiliating because I don't think he wanted to."

"Blind dates aren't your thing. This show has been going four weeks and you're still not comfortable talking to Ethan. Waving from afar isn't going to get you there."

To my relief Veronica laughed.

"Do you go to computer conventions?" I probed in my most Emma Woodhouse way, hoping to ease Veronica into someone else and away from Ethan.

Veronica shook her head no. I sat looking at the ceiling. How could I fix this for her?

"Who was your first boyfriend?" I said.

"That was in high school, Rod Pard. Oh, was that awful!"

"Come on, let's hear." I said. Veronica turned and leaned against the wall. I scooted in next to her.

"I was on the swim team and in computer club in high school. Need I say I was not popular? This guy, Rod, he was

257

the pitcher on the baseball team. He started showing interest in me. I was so excited. He was a cool kid. I thought that by his going out with me, I'd become a cool kid. Anyway, he was like two different people. When just around me, or talking to me on the phone, he was fun and we talked about everything. Around his friends I didn't even exist."

"That does not bode well for this story, Veronica," I said.

"Oh, just wait for it; it gets worse. So anyway, after a while he would call me his best girl, or tell me things, like he loved me. He would always make excuses why he couldn't see me in the halls or eat lunch with me. He finally takes me out, to this place across town. I didn't realize then that it was probably so we didn't run into anyone he knew. I was just so excited we were finally going out. After we ate dinner he tells me that he knows this place up on a hill where we can look at the stars."

"Oh Veronica! You didn't go, please say you didn't go."

"Yah, I went. I went – all the way, if you know what I mean. I thought it would mean we were together – I just wanted to be loved. It was awful though. The whole relationship was all about him. I didn't feel loved, I felt used. If I hadn't known from that, I'd have known on Monday at school when he wouldn't even look at me," Veronica said. She blinked hard trying to keep her tears in her eyes.

"Oh Ron, you totally got landed with a creepy. I'm sorry."

"I've had worse. Well, in college, I didn't understand... in college this guy... Mom tried to tell me...." Veronica said discomfited. She was trying to tell me something. Something had burrowed its way inside her, bruising her soul and it still hurt.

Veronica needed someone to confide in. I did not stop to let her. I shifted because I had to convince Veronica she should love someone besides Ethan. Whatever she had to say stayed bottled up inside her. I glossed over her pain to refocus by moralizing at her. I was never less of *The Whole Package* than in that moment.

"You should never rush into a physical relationship with a guy, especially when something feels off about it. When he wouldn't acknowledge your relationship in public – you should have known."

Aw, but wasn't I throwing stones in my glass house? Ethan split himself between four women when we were all together. That was different, right?

"Anyway, I know some really nice millionaires," I said. "I'll introduce you when this is all over."

Veronica, scrambling to hide the bruise on her soul, did not respond.

That was the moment, ignoring the need of my friend to keep her from Ethan, I started to sink. I would go lower. And within days I would understand why Julian needed us, all of us, to be in love with Ethan.

"You really like him, don't you?" Veronica asked.

"I think I'm falling in love," I said choking over the words.

"Does he..."

"He loves me, Veronica it's kinder for me to tell you he's in love with me, isn't it?" I asked.

"I have no chance," she asked.

"I'm sorry," I said.

Veronica nodded silently, but not an angry silence, a thoughtful silence.

259

"Will you still room with me?" I said.

"Yah, I'm really glad I stayed. I would've felt bad if we hadn't made things right. Losing a guy sucks, but losing a friend like you would've been worse."

Something like tar settled in my chest. Veronica's simple goodness made her more of a lady than my lofty self-assurance made me. I resolved to be her friend for the rest of my life. She made me a better person.

"I've felt so crummy all week, but now that we've talked about it, I feel better."

"Let's talk about something else. I can't stomach this anymore," I said.

"Okay, you can tell me about your first time, now that you've heard all the gory details of mine."

I stopped. I'd learned over the years that I'd become one of a dying breed. I hated the look I got when admitting the truth.

"I went to an all-girls school, then I was engaged a year after graduation to a very religious man," I said.

"You're a virgin?" she asked.

"I just didn't ever want to until I was married – there's nothing wrong with that," I said.

"You're a virgin," she said nodding like that made sense.

"Yes, I'm a virgin. But you know what? Even if I kiss a guy too much, I get so emotionally involved it makes it hard to see what's really happening."

"It's okay, looking back, there are a few times I wish I'd refrained," Veronica said.

"Specialists say that for women – if they have sex, they'll fall in love with the guy before they even know if he's nice or not. It's like you said – when you go diving, you don't want to murky up the water before you have a chance to see where you're going."

"It's whatever, Carrie calm down. You can find a way to moralize anything, can't you?" Veronica said with a smile playing around her lips.

"Oh, don't say that," I said letting it go. I preferred teasing to a lot of the other responses I'd come across. When I start out defensive, people tend to grow defensive with me. But then am I the one attacking instead of defending? Maybe I was. Veronica didn't seem to care. Maybe no one else did either unless I was goading them to. That'd be something to think about in my next bout of waiting.

CHAPTER TWENTY-SEVEN

The next morning, I had to get up and run, but the late night with Veronica left my eyes uncooperative. I remembered Ethan would be waiting. I jumped quickly from bed. Thankfully Veronica slept through me stumbling into her headboard to get into my workout clothes. By the time I arrived where the path met the road, I could see Ethan waiting for me. He ran to meet me.

I loved this part of my day. Ethan always hugged me so hard that he picked me up off the ground and swung me around.

"Are you still going to do that after we go back to reality?" I asked.

"Do you want me to?"

"Yes!"

"Then I'll never stop," Ethan leaned in to kiss me.

His minty kiss ran through my entire body. There was a burning tingle in my heart urging me toward more. It scared me. I pulled away while Ethan still reached for me. Grabbing his hand, I took off running. The sun already fought the hazy weak cloud cover, warming the morning up. I ran in silence enjoying the warmth on my face. After fifteen minutes Ethan asked, "You've finally acclimatized to California time then?"

"What?"

"You were late. I can only assume that's because you slept really well again."

I laughed. Ethan took responsibility for my sleeping better than I had in years. He seemed to think of my sleep as his accomplishment.

"Actually, I was up late with Veronica."

"Did you figure out what her problem is?"

"Yeah."

"What?"

"She's tired of the show."

"Did I hurt her feelings?"

I just shrugged. I didn't know what to say – what I was even allowed to say. Before I could articulate anything, Ethan said:

"I don't know what to do. This show is like a double-edged sword for me. I'm always hurting someone. I feel horrible about Erin. She wanted to dance with that company since she was a little girl. Now she won't be able to get back in."

"You didn't do that. Julian did. Just because we don't see him, doesn't mean he isn't behind the camera."

"I know but he doesn't care. I do. Now I hurt Veronica after you asked me not to."

"What?"

"You know, you asked me not to hurt Veronica, the first time we ran," he said.

"Oh, right."

I couldn't believe Ethan remembered this little detail from the first time we talked.

"No, Ethan it was us that hurt her feelings. Out by the pool? Julian sent her to find us – she did."

"Oh," he said.

"You can't feel so bad. It isn't fair. They both chose to come on the show. Veronica's going to be okay. I'm sure Erin will land on her feet."

"Us?" Ethan said again, "Out by the pool?"

263

I nodded. It relieved me that Veronica knew, but Ethan looked really worried about this. I didn't explain Julian or the phone call leaving Veronica free to come catch us. I didn't ask him what he worried over. He couldn't tell me. I hated having an embargo on what we could say to each other, but I'd given up trying to get past it.

I forgot completely about hinting Veronica should get the money. In the light of day, I needed it. Instead the temptation to tell Ethan Veronica should be his next elimination grew overpowering. I didn't. I couldn't interfere. Thankfully I did nothing; in some cases, nothing is better than something.

Instead I shifted the subject by saying, "Do you know why there wasn't a challenge yesterday?"

"I'm not sure. I have kind of a leery feeling about it, don't you?"

"Yeah, it's all we talked about at dinner. Where did you go after the hot tub yesterday?"

"Julian took me out... or.... What was the consensus at dinner?"

"Whatever's coming, it's probably big, but what's bigger than putting us up in Time Square and a dinner cruise with our friends?" I jogged into Ethan on purpose; he swerved off the trail into a patch of golden wispy weeds.

"I don't know, but I already have questions written down for Andrea."

"What kind of questions?"

"Wouldn't you like to know?"

"Yes, that's why I asked," I said, making to push Ethan off the road again, but he swerved and I almost stepped into a shrub. Ethan grabbed my waist and pulled me back toward him laughing.

"You'll just have to wait and see. I'm sure Andrea will tell you what I ask," Ethan said. He pulled me tighter into him and gave me a quick peck before he released me and we started running again.

"I'm sure she will. I wondered how Andrea reacted when they called her to set it up?"

"She must've agreed because Lance said everyone was on board."

"She always raves about the dinner cruises she and Phil take around the Statue of Liberty. I'm not sure this is going to be quite the same, with cameras in your face."

"Her husband Phil's the school teacher – your ideal man, right?" Ethan said.

"He teaches fifth grade. He's seriously one of the nicest men you will ever meet. I wish he could come, too. He's comfortable to be around, you know. One of those people who are so good, it oozes out of them."

"Oozes huh?"

"Yes, oozes."

"Do I ooze?"

"No," I laughed a little too hard, then when I caught my breath finished with, "you're amazing, but you don't exactly ooze goodness."

"You like me better for it, right?" Ethan looked at me with an impish smile.

"It makes you a little more interesting," I agreed. Ethan grabbed me mid-stride and kissed me again. I purred at his kiss. Ethan's kiss became greedier. I pulled away, alarmed by the intense feelings coming to life inside me. Ethan grinned at me. I smiled back, caught in his eyes. I could see love and desire gleaming silver and bright there as I'd never witnessed before. I didn't know what to say to him.

"Sorry. Did I…"

"I just …. It's a … I haven't known you very long. I don't understand how I already feel like this."

Ethan smiled, looking cocky so I kicked the back of his knee joint so perfectly his leg gave a little and he lurched forward. I turned and started running again. Ethan fell in beside me. He didn't speak though. I thought at first revenge was pending, but after a few minutes he looked thoughtful, maybe even disturbed.

I didn't allow this to bother me. Over the last week Ethan had a tendency to look like this. Whenever I asked him what he was thinking he would mutter something about the stupid show. I didn't even bother asking this time I just ran along and became quiet and reflective myself.

We ran quietly and parted in our own thoughts after I reached up absently mindedly kissing his cheek. Distracted, he hardly noticed me leaving. I started running up the path, but I'd only gone a few steps when Ethan called, "Carrie!"

I stopped and turned startled at the sudden urgency in his voice.

"You okay," I asked.

"No matter what, I love you," he responded

"Me, too," I called back happily with a wave.

Then I turned and ran toward the Manor House. After my run, I showered. Then I dressed in my painting tee-shirt and overalls hoping I'd get a chance to paint before we started filming for the day. I went down to see what Tess made for breakfast.

CHAPTER TWENTY-EIGHT

"Where's Sandra and Tess?" I asked Veronica, who sat at the table eating a yogurt.

"I don't know. I slept in late. I've been down here for like a half an hour and haven't seen them."

"Oh, I bet the next challenge is here. I was hoping for a two-day break. I'm going to change."

Veronica nodded and pulled the yogurt off her spoon with her lips. She looked so relaxed I knew she conceded Ethan to me. Maybe Ethan would notice and stop feeling so guilty about her. I rationalized it would be kindest if Ethan eliminated her. The cruelest thing he could do is give her false hope. Her vulnerable personality would lap up the attention he had to give each contestant as affection.

While I changed, I started wondering if I couldn't do the same for Tess and Sandra. Reconcile them to loosing Ethan. Not Sandra, but Tess may listen. She and Ethan got along well, a little too well. Maybe she, like Veronica thought he was falling in love with her. I thought about how I could get Tess alone, and what I could say to her that would inspire her to bow out.

"Veronica, how do I look?" I called from the top of the stairs. I changed into an open neck shirt and a jean skirt, making sure to put on an undershirt so the battery pack of my microphone wouldn't rub against my skin. I already had a rash forming on my back. When Veronica didn't answer I got the chills.

I couldn't help feeling something was wrong – not just on the show, but something was really wrong. I tried to tease

268

myself out of it by surmising the next challenge must be the chainsaw massacre re-enactment.

"Veronica where are you?" I said walking into the kitchen. Instead of Veronica I found Lance, Julian, Ethan and a cameraman scurrying to get set up. I smiled at Ethan, but he looked at me concerned. My face dropped.

"What? What's going on?" I asked startled.

"Carrie," Ethan said, but Julian cut in and said, "I have unfortunate news for you."

I froze in horror.

"Your mother's in the hospital. She was in car accident. She's been diagnosed with relapsing Multiple Sclerosis. She had some vision problems and her brakes weren't working quite right," Julian said. I couldn't see beyond his feminine leather jacket coming toward me like he could comfort me.

The fire in me erupted. He would not make a show out of this. His slow-motion hug reached me. I swatted him away. Julian looked hurt I didn't want his comfort.

"Is my mom okay?" I asked.

"Your sister's on the phone," Lance said, holding a satellite phone out to me. I hadn't had access to a phone in almost a month and a half. I just stared at it. Then as the truth sank in, I ducked Julian's second attempt at a hug, and lunged for the phone. Heading out the kitchen door I said:

"Addie, Addie, what's going on?"

"Carrie, I'm at the hospital. Mom was in a car wreck yesterday morning. Her brakes were soft even though I swear I got 'em changed three months ago like you asked, I even found the –"

269

"Addie, I believe you, this isn't your fault. Is she okay?"

"She hit her head. She's cut up pretty bad. Her arm is broken," Addie said.

"Is she gonna to be all right?"

"I don't know. I think so," Addie said.

"What happened with the other car? Was anyone else hurt?" I said.

"No, Mom hit a tree. She didn't see a sharp turn. Her vision kind of blurred and with soft brakes she..." Addie sobbed a little.

"Did you call Andrea? Are you there all alone?"

"Charles is here. I couldn't get a hold of Andrea. Adam is here, though, he called to check up on us yesterday morning an hour or so after it happened. He spent most of yesterday on the phone trying to reach the producer of your show."

Oh, thank goodness for Adam. He always did come through for me.

"Thanks Addie. Wait…. Charles – that guy you don't really like is there?"

"Oh no, I like him… a lot."

I turned to find everyone, including the cameraman followed me into the living room. I couldn't concentrate. I turned and walked up the stairs.

"They said Mom has relapsing MS – does that mean it's progressing?" I asked, grasping for details in my scattered thoughts.

"No, the doctor said that's probably the kind she's always had… but she's… she can't move very well. The doctor put her on steroids and said she'll recover… um… movement, but not a hundred percent," Addie said.

I took the stairs two at a time toward my room. So did the cameraman, with Ethan right behind him. I stopped. I tried to close the door to my room. The cameraman followed me. Anger bubbled up inside me. I turned to get mad.

"LEAVE HER ALONE," Ethan yelled pushing the camera man out of my face.

I was in confusion.

"Carrie, Carrie, what's wrong?" Addie asked. Ethan didn't get mad. My mom didn't know Ethan. He was yelling. Ethan got in between me and the camera. It looked for a moment as if the man didn't back up he was going down the stairs – rubber soles up.

I'd never seen Ethan more than frustrated before. Ethan made to close the door to give me privacy.

"Ethan, come in and lock it, will you?" I called turning back to the phone, "Sorry Addie everything is fine, is Mom okay?"

"I think so."

"Are you okay?"

"I don't know, Carrie," my little sister whispered into the phone. "I'm scared... it's just, I... I have a weird feeling. I swear I just got the car fixed."

"I know. I remember seeing it come through on a statement," I said.

"There have been a lot of people around, you know since you went on the show."

"Do you think someone did this?" I asked, my stomach sinking.

"I... it feels really paranoid, doesn't it?" she wondered.

"Don't worry sweetie. I'll be there as soon as possible." I sat on my bed. Then I stood. I began pacing back and forth. What did I do? Was my sister in danger? My mom needed me and I was thousands of miles away. Why was I still on a reality show? How had I dropped every responsibility in my life so completely? I lost track of reality entirely.

I went into big sister mode.

"Look. Tell the hospital your suspicions. File a police report, even if just to have the car looked at."

"I already told the police at the scene. They thought I was just being paranoid. Mom said her vision blurred, and they... they implied I must have been to a faulty mechanic."

"Grandpa's guy?"

"Yeah and when I told him we trusted him – anyway they think I'm just some pampered little girl who –"

"Addie, you don't need to worry. I'll take care of everything. Just stay with Mom, okay?"

"'Kay."

"All the insurance stuff is on file. I have three thousand dollars tucked into the ceramic dog in my bedroom at the house if you need a little extra money."

"How much?" Addie asked like she'd just started listening.

"Don't give anyone your credit card numbers or anything like that. You shouldn't have to pay for a thing. Just tell them to bill you when anyone with a hospital badge asks for money. If anyone makes you feel uneasy or weird inside, Addie, you just tell them they're going to have to talk to your sister. Make sure Adam stays close, he's really sharp."

"I don't know, I'd rather Charles –"

"Addie," I said grasping the phone to my ear, still pacing the small bedroom Veronica and I shared, "the cash is only for this emergency." I turned my back on Ethan not wanting him to hear. Then I continued, before Addie could respond with the normal defense on her spending habits, "Is the car totaled?"

"Yeah, the car's way scarier looking than Mom," Addie said. All of the sudden I grew calm. Nothing changed except Ethan stood next to me with his hand on my back.

"At least no one else was hurt. We can officially take her keys, though."

"Good luck." Addie said. "You can tell her that."

"Is she there?"

"Yeah, I'm just in the hall with Adam; the producer said you could only talk to a family member."

"Can I talk to her for a sec?"

"'Kay, just a minute let me see if she's awake," Addie said quietly.

"Here I'll talk. Your mom's asleep," Adam said to Addie.

I pulled away from Ethan at the sound of Adam's voice. For some reason a slow syrupy guilt dribble through my chest. He took this to mean I needed some space and backed up.

"My mother would want me to wake her up. She wants to talk to Carrie," Addie snapped in her most grandmother-like way. It always grated on my last nerve when Addie talked to people like that, especially people who were only trying to help her.

"Hey Carrie, are you all right?" Adam said into the phone.

273

"Hey Adam. Thanks for being at the hospital with Addie," I said glancing at Ethan. My voice sounded too... sweet... is that the tone I always used with Adam, or was I just embarrassed by the way Addie treated him?

"I promised. I keep my promises. Look Carrie I... I need to apologize,"

"For what?"

"I've learned some things about *The Whole Package*. It seemed like this family friendly show that recognized amazing women. I mean prime time television and all. I thought it would be... classier but I found out..." He stammered.

"What is it Adam?" I asked.

"I found this lawsuit; it makes the show sound a lot sketchier than I..."

"Yeah, it isn't wholesome by any means." I said.

"I'm sorry I... I'm sorry I took the bet too far," he said.

"It's okay –"

"I know you're getting ... close with Ethan –"

"I... uh, Adam, look I –"

"I understand he's this good-looking guy and you have nothing else to focus on besides him—"

"It's not just –"

"Carrie, be careful. Don't let him too far under your skin."

"What?"

"He's being paid almost five hundred thousand dollars to judge the show. That makes him a paid actor, you know that, right?" Adam asked. I looked over at Ethan. He was sitting on Veronica's bed watching me. I didn't know what to think. Adam didn't know Ethan.

Was Adam jealous? He sounded jealous.

"Look Adam."

"Carrie, I'm not trying to hurt your feelings. I only… you've got to see this show for what it is."

"I do, better than you could."

"No, you've been isolated. Your perspective can get warped."

"I know that," I said.

"You're really popular, I mean fan club popular, people following you around popular. We can use that to our advantage once you get off the show."

Of course, every time I thought he was interested in me, he always proved to be thinking in terms of work. I relaxed.

"I can't help any of that Adam. They don't tell us who's in the lead or anything," I said.

"Just keep it together. Don't let them embarrass you; it seems to correlate with contestants being kicked off."

"I've noticed that too but – "

"You can win the million dollars, Carrie," Adam said.

"I don't care about the money," I said.

"Yeah, because your head's in the clouds. You've got to refocus. You are an actress; Ethan is an actor. It's all a game. That's what I'm trying to tell you. None of it is real. You're isolated and focused on him and if you don't see that you'll get hurt. I just don't want to see you hurt."

My heart dropped in my chest. Adam didn't know what he was talking about. I wasn't acting. Ethan couldn't be acting. He loved me. Adam sounded like he was trying just as hard to convince himself as me. Maybe he was jealous.

275

"Give me the phone," Addie interrupted, "my mom is up and wants to talk to her. You can wait in the hall."

I heard a little scuffle and then I heard a very heavy door slam shut.

My nerves twitched. I tried to sit on the bed next to Ethan, but quickly got up and paced from one side of the room to the other. After chewing the loose skin on my finger next to my nail until it bled, I heard my mom say weakly:

"Carrie, is that you?"

"Hey Mom! Are you all right?" I said, hit with an overwhelming realization of how much I missed her. I hadn't really seen her for years.

"Of course, Honey. I'm just a little beat up," she said.

I started crying again, softer this time. Ethan came up beside me and I laid my head on his shoulder. I stopped moving again so he put his arms around me. The calm came back.

"Mom, I'm coming home as soon as I can, okay?" I said. My mother perked up at this statement.

"Oh, no you don't. I'm fine, Carrie. For the last time, I'm the adult. You're still my child. You look like you're having fun. That Ethan looks really nice."

Ethan smiled – indicating he could hear through the phone.

"He is Mom, but...."

"Is he there?"

"Yeah, Mom,"

"Let me talk to him." Ethan took the phone before I could say no.

"Hello, Mrs. Carnegie. I'm so sorry about your accident."

I reached up on my toes and put my ear close to the phone. I heard my mother answer,

"Please call me Irene. Now Ethan, I insist Carrie stay right where she is. Can you manage that?"

"I'll do my best, Irene."

I bristled like a shocked cat.

"Carrie has to do what her conscience tells her. God's will be done."

"Too true, let me speak to Carrie again please."

I grabbed the phone.

"Mom...."

"Well, I like him."

"That's great Mom, but I'm not staying here while you're in the hospital."

"You only have a week until you're filming in New York. They're keeping me in the hospital until Monday, I'm sure you can come and take me home then. If not, the show only has three weeks left. You go ahead and stay."

"No, Mom. I'm coming home as soon as I can."

"Carrie, for the first time in your life you're living for yourself. I'm not sure how Andrea got you on that show. It's been so good for you. You're painting again, and I've seen a look in your eyes that I haven't seen since you'd go out with your father on work errands."

"What are you talking about?" I said, eyeing Ethan to see if he could still hear my mother.

"You looked so happy, rock climbing – the parasailing nearly gave me a heart attack. But still, Carrie, you never tried new things with Gordon. It was always the same old stuff. You're getting back into life. I would feel awful if you gave that up for me."

"Mom, I'm not going to stay here in this unfortunate example of modern architecture while you're in the hospital."

"I'm sure they'll let you come see me when you're in New York next week. We can work things out at that point. We'll manage until then. It's not even a week," she pointed out again.

"Mom, those are seriously the drugs talking."

"Carrie, stop joking around for once in your life. I know what you give up to take care of us. Please just take this next week to yourself. That way if you give up the rest of your life taking care of your sick mother, at least I'll know I was able to give you another week."

"Mom, come on. I love you. I miss you."

"I miss you, too, but I really want this."

After more persuading, I finally conceded I didn't want to leave. I didn't tell her I wasn't really having fun. How could I tell my mother I couldn't leave Ethan alone with the other contestants? I promised I'd talk to the producer. Finally, I told my mother I missed her again, and pestered her about Addie dating Charles Goodrich enough that he was at the hospital with her, we said goodbye.

I hung up the phone. Ethan's arms were around me and I couldn't help sobbing into his shoulder. I never let myself cry in front of anyone over my mother's illness. I didn't want to hurt her feelings so I pretended it wasn't a big deal, just another part of life. I let go of all the pain the illness caused while Ethan stroked my hair. I told Ethan all about

Grandmother and the pressure she heaped on my back when we found out about the MS.

CHAPTER TWENTY-NINE

After a while Ethan asked, "Carrie, why didn't you tell me your mom has MS?"

"I said she has health issues."

"MS isn't health issues."

I thought for a moment. Why hadn't I told him? Then I remembered, way back as if in another life:

"I told Gordon." How Gordon had recoiled from me. As if I had it. As if it was somehow contagious.

"Right. Gordon from Harvard."

"We were engaged when I told him."

"Gordon was the fiancé who died in a tragic accident," Ethan asked.

"He ... he didn't take it well. He didn't call me for a week. When he finally did, he apologized, but he always overreacted when I got sick. He made me go to the doctor and get blood work done when I got the same cold everyone else had." The sting of it still made me feel hideous and diseased.

"Why didn't you dump him?"

"Gordon died. Healthy as anything and he died of a collapsed lung after his horse threw him in a polo match. The horse clipped his chest. I wasn't even there. I was in class. His mom... I'm jinxed – and I mean jinxed."

"No, you're not," Ethan said squeezing me tighter.

"Yes, I am," I said.

"Fine, I'll take you jinxed and all then," he laughed.

280

I clung to Ethan feeling so close to him. I'd grow old and die in his strong arms if I could. A need I ignored for a long time pulsed through me as aggressively as my heart beat. Adam didn't know what he was talking about. I loved Ethan. I loved him as if he'd become a part of me. I needed to love him like that – he made me whole. I would do whatever it took to keep Ethan's love. I slid my hand over his chest and up his neck into his hair.

He felt this change come over me. His embrace changed. It grew intense. His chin followed my cheek. His mouth reached for mine. He kissed me – hard and differently than he ever had before. A hunger – a desire grew inside of me building on this love and need I couldn't resist.

I became consumed with the place his mouth met mine, where his hands curled into my shirt holding me to him. I would never have let go. We drank each other in, desperately trying to quench this unnamed thirst. Finally, Ethan pulled from me, but his fingers stayed wound in my shirt like he couldn't let go. Winded, I rested my head in his arm joint.

There was a knock at the door.

"Carrie, we need to talk," Lance said through the door.

"I'm… um coming," I called after stammering incoherently a few times. Wiping my face, I said to Ethan "Can we talk later?"

"Sure," Ethan said. Then as if he remembered something, he reached over and covered my microphone. He whispered urgently, "Wait, Carrie! Listen before we go out, I can't be too affectionate… well, I'm –"

281

"What?" I asked trying to figure out what he was doing with his hand. I couldn't breathe with him pulling on the lip of my shirt.

"Last night when Julian took me out to dinner, he knew your mom was hurt, but he didn't tell me. He just, well, it's hard to explain…. You know I want to be with you through this." Ethan turned looking with fear at the door. He turned back like he didn't know what to say. He finished, very perplexed, "They're getting hard-nosed about the contract I signed."

I didn't understand the words coming out of his mouth. I still tasted his minty kiss. I could tell he was trying to say something to me, without actually saying it, but I couldn't stop staring at his mouth. I nodded, trying to understand. For all the connection I had with Ethan, I still couldn't read his mind.

He reluctantly backed further away from me when Lance knocked again. Ethan walked into the bathroom soaking up water into his mouth.

"Carrie," Lance said again.

I couldn't say anything. Ethan walked slowly to open the door.

Both men looked at me waiting. I still couldn't move. What happened to me? I would have called Ethan four times that day if I could have. I would have stayed by his side and clawed at any woman getting too friendly with him. I wanted him, crazy, passionately, over the top crazy wanted him. I never wanted a man like that before.

Ethan waited in the doorway, but I turned and went to my bathroom. I splashed water on my face, trying to calm my body. I finally moved forward in a daze. Talking to my sister

282

threw me, but Ethan coming on so strong disoriented me. Or had I come on strong? It felt mutual.

We went down the stairs. I plopped myself down on the couch still trying to figure out what happened with Ethan.

"Carrie, I'll get you a drink," Ethan said moving toward the kitchen.

"Is everything all right with your mom?" Julian asked.

"Yes, thank you," I said, snapping out of the daze Ethan threw me in. Julian looked at me with no pity in his eyes. He looked angry with me. I locked eyes with him. Was this because I ducked his hugs? My mom's accident was supposed to be his moment of fame broadcast to the world? Finally, he looked away saying:

"We missed a challenge yesterday, so we're going to have to do it tomorrow.

"It's Sunday," I said, "I thought we had Sundays off due to religious and personal preferences. You know Sandra will lose it."

"You'll have to smooth things over with her. We won't be able to splice everything together for Thursday night if we don't get it done. The contract states that if any extenuating circumstances come up we can make accommodations. This is part of life, Carrie. When something goes wrong, we accommodate."

"Oh well! I'm sorry my sick mother got in your way. I'll go home and then it won't be an issue."

"No, no, that's not necessary," Julian said.

The satisfaction in his eyes and his half smile told me he won. Everything clicked into place.

"You wouldn't let me go, would you?"

"If necessary we could take legal measures to make sure you either get kicked off the show, or decline the key. Those are the rules."

I stared at his gloating face. I finally understood. I had no control. I'd given my life to Julian the moment I agreed to be a prisoner in his day spa.

"If she died, you'd still make me finish the show, wouldn't you?"

"Oh, a funeral scene," Julian said snidely, "I don't know why you're complaining. Your mother so graciously asked you to stay."

"You listened into my phone call?" I said.

"It came into the house; I have a right to anything that happens in this house. I won't air it if you tell the other contestants what happened and that your mother insisted you stay. We don't have a lot of extra time anyway, just enough to show you panicked on the phone. I'll show Ethan almost throwing the cameraman down the stairs. Then you tell the other contestants about the accident. That should do it."

"How, in front of the camera?" I looked around wildly. "The cameraman is gone."

"Carrie, you naïve little one. You should've read your contract more carefully. I assure you we'll get it on tape."

The room closed in on me. Cameras I couldn't see stared at me.

"You tape everything?"

"We can't have a camera in your bedrooms or the bathrooms. The network didn't want the show to get too trashy. We don't even have a camera in the Bungalow

284

Bedroom– that way the show comes across as inspirational to audiences," Lance said.

"Mission accomplished," I threw back sarcastically, "why do you bother bringing in the cameramen?"

"The mounted cameras are limited. We've found they serve for a moving vantage point," Julian glanced unconsciously up at the china hutch in the dining room while taking off his lady leather jacket.

"In other words, you want us to believe we aren't being watched when they leave," I snapped back as I glanced around, revolted. Of course, Julian was everywhere. He knew everything. Of course, other cameras saw everything.

I started calculating what must have been caught on tape. I saw the "back drop" decorating style and grasped the reason for it. Every area must have a camera. Julian must even have heard whatever sounds came over my microphone when I'd kissed Ethan in my bedroom. Even that kiss wasn't mine. It became Julian's.

"You're a vulture," I said.

"No dear, I'm a very talented producer, and I've been hired to produce a show. That's what I intend to do," Julian said, "It's only another week until we're in New York. You can go see your mom at the hospital before the dinner cruise if you allow the camera to follow you. Ethan will go with you, of course. By then you two will need some alone time. Adam was right about one thing. You will get the million dollars. Easiest million dollars you'll ever earn."

I laughed a little in disbelief and then I grew really light-headed. I teetered ready to fall. Lance ran to me. He grabbed my arm to steady me. He sat me on the cold leather couch.

"You can get the other contestants when you're ready, Lance," Julian said heading for the door.

He won. I'd never been in control. He'd given me morsels to make me believe I was, but I wasn't.

"I'll... tell...." I said trying to stop him from leaving, "I'll tell the other contestants about the car wreck if you don't show anything about the MS. My mom hasn't told her friends about it. I'm sure she doesn't want it announced on national television."

"That'll be fine. Ethan mentioned God during the phone call, so it'd be hard to edit around anyway."

"I'll have to thank him,"

"Ethan was sucking up."

"It wasn't him I was planning on thanking."

"I'll find a way to edit around it, if I have to show how insistent your mother was that you stay so you better sell it. In fact, play down the accident. We'll show Ethan being your knight – the female audience will eat it up – he is more popular than any of my other men."

"Yeah, he isn't your usual flavor of man candy."

"We don't want you to look heartless for not leaving. Try to keep your emotions toned down when you tell the contestants," Julian said. He wasn't talking to me. He talked to himself. "People love your sweetness. I thought with the whole socialite background you'd go another direction, but Sandra is filling that hole. Crusading has become the perfect pull for you. If you play your part well enough, I won't have to waste air time showing any of it, really. We have every minute planned this episode."

"Hey Julian, how do you plan reality down to every minute?" I said.

"It's a gift."

Julian nodded to me. I stared at Lance and then looked at Julian. Ethan came back into the room as I stared at Julian in disgust.

"What? What did you say to her?" Ethan said sloshing my water down the front of him.

"Don't worry about it, Romeo. Go get her another drink. She's feeling faint, and I need her to perform for the cameras." Julian opened the door. Then, as he moved out, he said, "Oh, by the way Carrie, I subcontracted the Manor House with a special kind of architect. It may not answer your tastes, but it serves my purposes perfectly."

I started. Julian really had caught everything on film. A peeper had been caught looking through my windows while I changed, and I signed a contract saying he could. I shuddered as the door closed behind his retreating body. Ethan came back with my water before I even knew he'd gone. I quickly drained it. Then he headed back to the kitchen to refill my cup.

"Vulture was too nice, Carrie," Lance said. He shoved his fists into his jean pockets, "Now that you've seen him in action, he'll use this to lord over you. In the next few weeks, you'll find a stronger word for him. At least you only have a few weeks left on your contract."

Lance's eyes blazed. Before I could ask about it, Ethan reappeared and offered me a quickly thrown together ham and cheese sandwich. My stomach still churned.

287

"I can't eat that. What am I going to say to everyone so Julian won't air my mother's conversation?"

"This hasn't come up much, but I'm a doctor. You ran hard this morning. You need to eat, Care."

"Twenty-nine-year-old pediatrician from the Boston area – I heard that somewhere," I said. Lance and Ethan laughed half-heartedly.

"Patrick took the other contestants into town to the fruit market. The walkie doesn't reach that far. Do you mind if I go get them?" Lance asked.

"Ah, Patrick," I said, finally understanding why my makeshift bell hop always looked haggard, and exhausted. How much was Patrick paid to work with someone like Julian?

"Carrie – the other women," Lance said trying to get me to focus.

"Oh right, please go get them," I said.

"Ethan, you better come with me. You know it's for the best," Lance said. Ethan stared hard at Lance.

I begged Ethan to stay with my eyes. I needed him. He didn't see anything beyond the Styrofoam vase of weeds he stared through.

"Sure, Lance. The car's out front?" Ethan asked. Lance nodded and Ethan turned to me.

"Care, you get some rest. You can perform for the cameras, or whatever you have to do, after you've had a nap, okay?"

I deflated. Ethan left. I was alone. Often in the last few weeks I craved to be alone. There were always people around; contestants, the production crew, designers,

stylist. They must have cleared the house for me. Silence
deafened me.

CHAPTER THIRTY

While I waited for Ethan to return, I searched the house. I went first to where Julian glanced. I climbed up on a chair until I found a little round lens sticking out of the wall, hidden above the dining room hutch inside a fake plant. Julian wired it into the house like an intricate stereo system.

I walked into the kitchen and found another tube as round as lipstick in the corner of a high placed picture. From far away it looked like part of an intricate pattern on the frame. Someone knew what they were doing.

I wondered if Ethan knew we were always being filmed. He hadn't asked how I'd perform for the cameras, and the cameraman left, so he must. I'd been laughed at several times for coming on a show I'd never seen. Now it occurred to me Sandra and Tess performed for cameras – all the time.

I wondered if Julian taped me kissing Ethan. If he sent Veronica to catch us, he must have. Is that what Adam was trying to tell me? Was that what Ethan was trying to tell me? But then if he worried about being seen, why did Ethan wait to kiss me for the first time by the pool? Why not in the privacy of our runs? Did Ethan want it filmed? What did Adam mean, Ethan was an actor?

No, Adam wanted to come between us. Julian wanted to come between us. That's what Ethan kept trying to tell me. I couldn't let them. Oh, of course, cameras taped our every move – stupidity didn't begin to cover my humiliation.

I cringed. I'd been half naked a couple of times being fitted – or getting my hair and makeup done in the back

290

room. Was the back room full of mirrors and stage equipment off limits as well?

Did Julian know Ethan and I ran together every morning? I remembered Lance setting me up with the sundress as I stretched on the porch. Julian seemed to know everything, so he must know Ethan met me where the road met the path every morning.

Then another thought entered my head and took my breath.

What if Julian sent Ethan to catch up with me that first morning we went running? What if Ethan forced himself to love me? No, Ethan loved me. I couldn't believe anything else. I simply couldn't.

I dreaded the other women coming. They were going to feel sorry for me. I would tell them my mom was fine. I would lie. I would say everything was fine. Mom was not fine. She had MS. I had to be fine. I would protect her. I would not have my mother's conversation aired to America. Julian was right. I could play this part. I'd been playing it for years.

I paced around the room. I tried to pick up a book, but couldn't concentrate. I opened the cupboard that hid the entertainment center in the little cove. The nauseatingly romantic movies sat neatly in a row. I wanted to throw all the DVDs into the pool.

Finally, I heard the purr of Ethan's rental car pull up outside the house. Then the chattering of women intermingled with Ethan's voice. I stood in the cove off to the side of the house. I couldn't see the front door, but heard it open. I listened for a minute to Sandra's happy prattle, and

291

Tess's low sensual coos. I took a deep breath before stepping around into the main part of the house.

A concerned Veronica started toward me as soon as I made my presence known. Ethan didn't see me. His arms were around the waists of Sandra and Tess. I hated the sight of Ethan with other contestants.

"Carrie, is everything all right?" Veronica threw her arms around me.

Ethan started, surprised. He looked guilty. I'd seen him grinning like a dip at Tess and Sandra. He backed off when he noticed me. He thought I'd be taking a nap like he instructed. He obviously felt free to lay on the charm for Sandra and Tess. Neither noticed him shift backward because they readjusted and remained attached to him. Veronica stared at me waiting for an answer.

"My mom's been in a car accident. It wasn't too bad, though. She's going to be okay," I answered nervously – just the right amount of nervous; I knew how to act – how to lie. I played the part of socialite like I had so many times for Grandmother, and then Gordon. I would earn my million dollars. If Ethan was really going to give it to me, or no. Not Ethan, Julian, right? It was Julian who finally figured out the key to breaking me. Every time, I'd bow down to protect my sick mother, every time.

Ethan must have seen this because he stopped trying as hard with me. He winked at me but did nothing to detach himself from Tess and Sandra. I knew my part – I played my role. I needed my mother safe. I would earn my million dollars.

Who needed to be a lady? That idea, like my grandfather, was dead. I'd finish playing the role I'd been pushed into after my father died – acting for the pleasure of everyone else – never for myself. Pulling at a strand of my hair, I edged my way toward the stairs.

"Did anyone else get hurt?" Veronica asked.

"Oh no, it was only a minor accident; she's fine – everyone's fine."

"Are you leaving?" Sandra asked.

"No, my mom insisted I stay. She freaked out when I mentioned I'd leave the show for her," I offered with half a laugh. That was true. How had I gotten myself in a position where I had to lie? I was a liar. I was no lady. I was Julian's puppet – as I had been Grandmother's.

"Good, I'd hate to be here without you," Veronica said.

"Look, I got some fresh artichokes; I'll make some tasty Chinese food tonight, eh?" Tess said.

I tried to show her my gratitude, but nothing came because Ethan squeezed her waist to acknowledge her kindness. He wasn't just two Ethan's. He was my Ethan, and Tess's Ethan, Veronica's Ethan, and Sandra's Ethan; he played a role for all of us. Which one was he?

"I don't feel well. It kinda shocked me to talk to my mom and my sister. I'm drained." I said.

"Go take a nap," Ethan instructed. I'd been ready to do this, but then as soon as he told me to, I didn't want to. Anger surged inside me, taunting me to yell at him. I glanced up at one of the lipstick cameras perfectly hidden in another picture frame. Adam was right, as soon as I embarrassed myself, I was eliminated.

"Are you sure you're okay with all this?" Veronica said.

"By next week, if I make it through the next eliminations or not, we'll be back East anyway," I said. "One week, ladies, and we are all going home, after the dinner cruise, anyway."

"Hallelujah," Veronica said.

"But I'm going to miss you so bad," Sandra said to Ethan. I rolled my eyes.

"One week," Veronica said grinning at me. Though we'd said this many time in the last few days, after talking to my mom it became real. Only one week left, and yet the week held its space in time like a pillow over my face. Could I live through another one week? I couldn't return to work because of the show. I'd stay with my mom in Hartford instead of going back to New York. Vindictively, I was glad I could educate Julian on what a well-crafted home looked like.

This thought calmed me down more than anything. Five days and I would be home with my mother, no matter what. It would be intrusive, but I would move in with my mom for the last three weeks of the show. I would move out of the Manor House in five days, and yet each of those days spread before me like a year's worth of a prison sentence.

"Is your mom home now?" Veronica asked.

"No, she'll be in the hospital for a few days. She bumped her head so they want to monitor her for a while. My sister has a direct line to Julian if anything goes wrong. They're sure she's going to be fine. Anyway, she insisted I stay. I couldn't refuse her." I finished trying to sound less worried than I was. I must have accomplished this because Veronica looked relieved for me.

How easily I skewed things. How vulnerable civilization is with technology becoming her truth. I told Veronica and the viewers at home whatever Julian wanted them to hear. They would feel what Julian wanted them to feel. They would see what Julian wanted them to see. They would be relieved for me, though I was terrified out of my mind, they would believe the lie I sold. How many newscasters or television personalities read off press releases moving their mouths, while the Julian's of the world shoved his hand up their backs?

"I'd love to meet your mom," Veronica said. She tried to get me to focus.

"I'm sure she'd like that."

With my usual energy sapped Sandra and Tess did not lose the opportunity to be all over Ethan. I had no joke left in me, nothing to distract me. And I saw Ethan. He flirted effortlessly with the other contestants. Whether he wanted it or not, he had his own personal harem.

I hoped I said enough to leave the conversation between my mother and me off the air.

"Oh yeah, we're having the next competition tomorrow night," I said flatly.

"On a Sunday?" Sandra exclaimed.

"I don't think there's any other option. Julian had to push it back so he could make sure my mom's okay. There's nothing else we can do. Sorry about that," I said.

"I suppose if there's nothing we can do about it, there's nothing we can do," Sandra said. How easily I mollified her. I was staff now. I submitted. I helped the show along until it ended. My dry throat choked me. I didn't know how much longer I could hold onto my act.

I made my way to the stairs looking for an escape. A lens fitted into the side of a fire detector by the door couldn't be more obvious. The red light on the thing winked at me. I ran up the stairs two at a time to the safety of my room. I thought I heard Ethan call to me. I didn't stop until I bolted my bathroom door, while climbing into the safety of a hot shower. Ethan didn't love me. Not as much as I loved him.

CHAPTER THIRTY-ONE

On Sunday we made up table settings for the next competition. It was a quiet activity and I wondered how Julian would make it look interesting. Making up place settings for four at the Ritz-Carlton overlooking the ocean felt too convenient. I had no chance of losing this competition. Raised at dinner parties and cotillion classes, I could have used the measuring stick to perfection, but they didn't bring one out.

I put my salad fork in the wrong place. I did it because I noticed Tess setting her table to perfection. She told me about the etiquette lessons her father had insisted on before she could take over his financial planning firm. I could see Julian watching me, and I pretended not to notice.

"You know, whoever wins this competition gets to go to the gala," Julian said, "fine dining and dancing. It will be the most romantic reward yet."

"Oh, I'm on it," Tess said winking at Julian. I couldn't help it. I put my fork back in the right place. I saw it, the twitch in Julian's mouth, the way his beard curved upward when he examined my table again. I hated him for it. I hated him because as hard as I tried to ignore Ethan's friendship with Tess, Julian found ways to throw it in my face. I lived in morning runs and real life.

After my mom's accident, I forgot I entered TV-land as soon as I walked into the Manor House. On our jogs, Ethan could always defend his friendship with Tess as the show. I loved him so fiercely. I let it be explained away, or even worse, I'd get mad at Tess. Tess who hadn't forgotten she was supposed to seduce Ethan for a million dollars. I would get mad at her. And Julian saw it all.

I concentrated so hard on my décor from that point on, I barely noticed the change in Veronica. She calmed down. When the chef brought out an appetizer he wanted to add to his menu, she sat and shared it with Ethan, forgetting about her table entirely. They chatted and she even made Ethan laugh. It felt like I had an ally, someone to keep Ethan occupied while I dealt with the competition.

Eventually, the manager announced he needed to prepare for his lunch crowd so we had to be done. He easily awarded Tess and I the winner, after Veronica gave little effort and Sandra gave a little too much effort.

That night when Becky tried a cocktail dress on me for the gala I told her to go a little short and just a smidge lower on the neckline. I wanted to look sexy. I barely recognized myself. I flattered myself into believing that my sexy made Tess look slutty. I was pretty angry by that point while trying not to acknowledge the loss in battleground I made with Julian.

Tess, Ethan and I were let into a swanky Thai Restaurant in San Francisco. We attended a fundraiser for immunization awareness month. I doubt the viewing audience could tell it was anything but a loud, nightclub-type atmosphere.

Tess was all over Ethan. She used her body to keep his attention and my efforts to prove he could look at my body too proved insignificant. Tess played this game better than I ever could. Tess demeaned women everywhere – for a million dollars. I couldn't judge. I'd done the same – twice. And Ethan, my Ethan, did not try to stop Tess.

Ethan encouraged Tess to fall in love with him just as he had encouraged me to. He let her put her hands all over him. She kissed his neck – that was my neck, the neck of my other half. How dare she leave traces of her lipstick on it? I couldn't help myself. I charged at Tess and pushed her off him. I turned to Ethan with fury. Tess grabbed my hair and pulled me away from Ethan.

"Carrie," Ethan said his eye brows knit at me. At me!

"Seriously?" I asked, "You're putting this on me, seriously?"

"Carrie, please, it's just one night," he whispered in my ear as he took me back to the table and made me sit down. Then he left to dance with Tess again.

I watched them. He looked to be charming Tess into a better mood. Didn't he see her pull my hair? Wasn't he supposed to defend me? Did he want Tess, a woman who took her button-down, giving him whatever he wanted? What did he want with a woman who knew she wasn't ready and pulled back? Did I have to lose any sense of self-respect to be with him? I sat at the table fuming. Did I know what I'd become? No! I couldn't see clearly – I'd mucked up the water.

Tess dipped down then brushed her whole body against Ethan as they danced. I sat in the background watching. Finally, a man started talking to them and Ethan backed off so the man could have a turn with Tess. Then Ethan finally came back over, he extended his hand to me like nothing had just happened.

"No thanks," I said. I pretended to be into the conversation about the need for pet health insurance happening at our table.

"Carrie, come on," Ethan said squatting down in front of me. I tried to be cold and standoffish to him. He took my hand under the protective shield of the table and started running his fingers across my arm.

"Let's just dance," Ethan said, "I want to dance with you."

"Apparently," I snapped, but couldn't help the little smile playing at the edge of my mouth. He saw me thawing and pulled me up and nuzzled into my neck saying:

"You are adorable jealous."

I tried not to grin, I did. I couldn't help it. I loved him with so much of myself, I couldn't control the grin when he came in close. We didn't move to the center of the floor like he had with Tess. Instead, he pulled me off to a little corner where the camera couldn't get a great angle of us.

"Carrie, I know this is hard on you," Ethan said.

"Do you?" I asked.

"Look for the next couple weeks we are actors. Off screen, you are my girlfriend. You know I am loyal to you in everything I do –"

"So, on screen, you're the cheating creep and I'm your psycho stocker?"

He laughed – like I was kidding.

"Can you do it for me? Just pretend I'm still trying to decide who wins a million dollars?"

"This isn't about the money, Ethan," I snapped.

"I know, I didn't mean it like that, but for the next four weeks until after the reunion show, I have to do this. It's my job."

"Okay, I'll try," I said and Ethan pulled me close. Then nothing else mattered except his warm breath on my cheek. I tried meeting his mouth to mine, but he turned his cheek.

"Care, you can't do that. You know I can't resist you," Ethan said.

"Tess can act like a cat in heat, but I can't kiss you?" I asked.

"Only four weeks," Ethan pleaded with me.

"Whatever," I said looking away to watch people around us dance.

The next two days were ridiculous. I'd grow consumed with jealousy – overcome with this fear I was losing him. He reassured me he loved me while we were running, but he said we had to pretend. He actually encouraged me to disconnect from any emotional bond we had, but just for now.

I became standoffish. I pulled away. I tried to disconnect. Then he acted scared. He turned on me, he made me special, he gave me a taste of his undying love until I came

back, needing to be his girlfriend. After he securely placed me
like a trophy on his girlfriend mantle, dismissed me,
and tried harder to focus on all the other contestants. I
couldn't handle it, and looking over the edge, I fell off his
girlfriend mantle. I hit the ground from a greater height every
time. And instead of letting me lie there broken on the
ground, he mercilessly picked me up again.

CHAPTER THIRTY-TWO

That week we helped in an at-risk youth center. Sandra mentored a young woman with self-image issues. She was really cute teaching her to be a little cocky. She said a little cocky would get her further than insecure any day. I tried to throw my shoulders back, keep my chin forward a little more.

Tess helped another young woman with her math homework, proving for the first time to the viewers she was smart. I painted with a young woman who had no interest in art. Eventually we joined Veronica and played volleyball with some young women who got a little moodier every time Lance announced they needed positive role models. I started giving them my Grandmother's eye roll every time he did his bit into the camera and one of them even laughed for me. I enjoyed being with the teenage girls and it made me wonder if I really could become an art teacher.

That night we played a board game and ate barbecue. Sandra made this amazing Southern dish with pork and coleslaw. Ethan helped her, and they laughed a lot. After dinner she kissed his cheek with long lingering lips. I grew desperate.

Frantically, I began wondering how I could make Ethan love me as much as I loved him. On the day before the eliminations, Julian stopped by the house early in the morning. All the designers trailed in his wake. I was just leaving to meet Ethan for our run when he stopped me.

302

"No, no," Julian said tapping his face, "we can't get away with it. It's so hot in New York, the contestants will sweat all over those gowns."

"What are you talking about?" I asked looking to Becky for some explanation. She tapped her foot and let out a deep exasperated breath.

"Oh, we're all going to have to start over. We can't dress formally on the cruise – Carrie, can you go wake up all the other contestants and ask them to meet back in the design room."

"Oh, okay," I said.

"If we are all getting stuffed into that back room tell 'em to shower and get ready first," Susan said.

"'Kay," I said trying to hide my disappointment. I needed to be with Ethan. I needed to breathe the air he breathed and be a part of him alone so I could disregard Tess and Sandra.

Instead, I had to wake the other contestants. Tess threw a brush at my head for the trouble. Ethan noticeably didn't come around that morning. Instead, we were all shoved into the back room like lobsters in a pot with nowhere to go except over the top of each other.

"Ethan really likes me in red," Sandra said.

"He said that to me. Just because you heard him doesn't mean he likes you in red too," Tess said.

"He told me last night when we were alone," Sandra barked.

I dropped my arms on Becky. Did Ethan find a way to be alone with us all? Sandra said she went into town to get a broken nail fixed, but had been so smug afterward.

303

"My dress is already red so you have to find another color," Tess said.

"You know with you wearing so little of the dress, I doubt anyone will notice," Sandra said.

"Oh, Ethan will notice. He always notices me," Tess said.

I sucked in air. Ethan didn't seem to mind Tess's outfits as much as he had in the past. In fact – he seemed to warm up to everything about Tess. I didn't like the soft wispy lavender dress Becky was making. I wanted to look sexy, not soft.

The morning went on pushing me further and further into a bitter jealousy. The banter became so harsh that even the cameras must have stared at us. Tess and Sandra stood around in their underwear most of the time, and Tess's dress did not require a bra. I don't know if they filmed it or not – the viewer never saw because something had to be cut out after my mom's accident.

After lunch, Lance called me away from Becky's newest creation.

"Hey Lance, what's up?" I asked.

"Can you take the golf cart to get Ethan," he said.

"Sure. Everything okay?"

He looked out the back window and exhaled. He looked miserable.

"Are you all right?" I asked again.

"Yeah, I guess we need more footage for the barbecue scene. I need to finish memorizing some cards. You and Tess are the only ones done with your dresses, and Tess disappeared. Do you mind going to get Ethan?"

"I'm on it," I said and hurried toward the door. He didn't have to ask me twice. I needed to see Ethan.

"He's waiting for you – just walk in," Lance called after me. I gave a slight wave but hurried before Lance could tell me to put on my microphone.

CHAPTER THIRTY-THREE

Ethan had a car. Lance could've used the walkie-talkie. I knew why I was being sent. I didn't even pause. I knew what happened in the bungalow. I went anyway. I wanted to win. I wanted Ethan to show the whole world he loved me – me, not Tess, not Sandra, but me. I drove the golf cart past Julian's studio and wound around the meandering broken road down to Ethan's bungalow. I parked the golf cart next to his rental car and headed for the door.

I was trying to force myself not to think. I was steeling my nerves for what I had to do. I didn't notice all the little things that were off. I walked right past the cameraman who would make sure the world knew Ethan chose me.

"Hey, Eth…" I called but got no further. Tess lay on top of Ethan and they were making out. He looked up startled. His shirt was off, and hers was halfway unbuttoned.

"Carrie," he called, trying to free himself from Tess. He'd never kissed me like that. He'd chosen her. In front of the whole world, he'd chosen her.

I made a strangled moan. I turned. Ethan started yelling after me frantically. He was tangled under Tess because I heard him say: "Tess, move."

I ran past the cameraman who was catching Ethan's reaction.

"Come on, Ethan, she should know you're kissing everyone. It's the only way you can know who you really like."

306

"What?" Ethan said. I slammed the door in the cameraman's face so I couldn't hear anymore.

I managed to run down the crumbling road and hid at the edge of the cliff before the door opened. Ethan and the cameraman struggled at the door each trying to get out. I slid further down to the edge until I couldn't see them, so they wouldn't see me. My legs dangled off the rock I sat on. I heard Ethan shouting my name. I held my breath. He didn't come any closer. He couldn't seem to figure out where I went.

Now the morning made sense. Julian was setting me up. I couldn't make a scene. That's what Julian wanted – my breakdown – my scene. A strange thought flickered across my mind, was this because I wouldn't hug him? Was it because in that moment I didn't give him his scene? Did he need to prove he'd finally broken me? My face was wet and I kept retching. He had broken me. But he'd never film it.

Instead of going back up to the road, I sat on the very edge of the cliff. The cliff dropped down to the ocean. There were some places where rocks curved out of the dirt. I could probably make it down them. Serena and I had discovered a set of old stairs going down to the beach at the other end of the Valley on one of our fast walks. If I could somehow....

Without even considering the danger of scaling a twenty-foot cliff, or if the stairs were even passable, I started to crawl down. I did well until about seven feet from the ground. There, the clumped dirt of the cliff smoothed out and I couldn't find anywhere for my foot to go. I swallowed hard and dropped down to the soft sand.

I sat on the sand listening to the ocean drowning out Ethan calling for me. I didn't call back. Instead, I faced what

I'd been ignoring. He played me. Ethan didn't love me. He couldn't kiss Tess like that, and love me. With my head on my knees, I wept. My sobbing only slowed to retch as the image of him wrestling with Tess plagued me.

After Ethan's voice on the wind quieted, I grabbed my wicker sandals I'd thrown to the beach during my climb. I moved northward. Even through my horrible pain, I knew nothing lay south of the Manor House until Santa Cruz. Either I called back to Ethan for his help or trekked north, hoping to find the rickety stairs passable.

The beach segmented like a curving sliver of a new moon, coming to a point. When I came to the tip of the beach that Ethan's bungalow overlooked, I ran out of sand. I climbed along rocks covered in thick blackish-brown kelp to get to the next sliver of beach. The closer to the water I climbed, the less the warm, smooth rocks were covered in sharp barnacles.

Every time the ocean crashed against the rocks mist hit my face, trying to calm me – throwing Julian's face into my head. My own voice reminded me Julian did pull the strings. And yet, Ethan let him. I didn't want to be rational – I wanted to be pissed.

Piles of kelp and seaweed clumped all over the beach when I finally made it to another sandy shore. I walked above the water line where the sand packed firmly together. It took too much effort to move up near the cliffs on grainy, damp sand that gave way as soon as I stepped on it. The ocean crashed higher on the beach the later it grew. The ocean seemed to comfort me by begging me to remember. It greeted me like an old friend. I ignored it. My mind was not merciful to me as I moved.

I forced myself to look back on everything through Julian's eyes. I was in my own comedy. From the beginning, he needed a romance. Again, I wondered if Julian had seen me leave the Manor House on that first-morning run, and called Ethan to come find me. I wouldn't allow my mind to disregard the idea this time. The idea grew.

Had Ethan been prompted to offer me the million dollars for my kiss? Julian offered me the million dollars during the dodgeball game in almost the same manner – stating how much Ethan liked me. Looking back the two conversations were almost identical. Ethan simply presented it in a much more handsome package with his arms around me.

Where did Ethan's loyalties lie? Was he, like our designers, working for Julian? Did he love me? Could he love me? After considering it, I decided Julian pushed Ethan to love me the way Grandmother pushed me to love Gordon. I learned to love Gordon – sort of. I'd forced myself to love him; I was no lady. And Ethan forcing himself to love me – he was no gentleman. He didn't love me; not enough.

I hadn't loved Gordon enough. If Gordon had lived would I have broken his heart they way Ethan broke mine? When would I have realized I didn't love him enough? Maybe I would have figured it out before we married. After Grandmother died, Gordon and I cooled some, especially after he found out about the MS. Maybe I wouldn't have married him after all.

Most inconveniently my mind brought forth the moment I saw the sun dress. Gordon traveled to New York for a meeting with his dad, who was grooming him to become a partner at his firm as soon as he graduated. Gordon sent the sundress to my dorm room. I suspected his mother actually picked it out for me. She always went to New York with her husband to shop, and considering it fit me perfectly, it had to be her. The note read:

"Carrie, saw this and thought it would be fun for our honeymoon. Though if you want to wear it to that garden party next week I think you'd look gorgeous! Love always, Gordon."

My Grandma died six months earlier and we started to feel the pinch for money. I tried on the sundress and it fit perfectly. I relaxed. Gordon would be my husband soon and I wouldn't ever have to worry about what to wear again. He bought me with a designer sundress he never even saw me in. His obsession with Polo led him to play a pickup game in a poorly maintained field. He died there only days before the garden party.

Was I glad he died, like Grandmother? No, no, he was kind to me. He believed in me, passionately. I remember that limo ride the best, trying to soothe the broken mother who longed for her little boy. No, I wished Gordon were still with his mother. Didn't I feel so obligated to have dinner with the woman every few months to soothe her ache? Didn't I let her talk obsessively of Gordon as we each put a rose on his grave? Of course, I'd give her back her child if I could, but I felt sorrier for her than myself.

I hadn't loved him enough.

Ethan didn't love me enough. He couldn't have kissed Tess like that and loved me the way I loved him. Maybe he shouldn't love me. Karma was satisfied.

Gordon had loved me obsessively, and I'd only forced myself to love him.

A foamy wave swept in high, covering my feet; the cold shocked me. Julian knew how to force me to perform; he knew how to make Ethan perform. Out of nowhere, I remembered Ethan making me earn his laughs—at first. Now he copied Julian's strange chortle for anyone these days.

He kissed Tess.

Was it not a talisman of foreboding when a limo carried me to be presented to Ethan? Nothing good ever came from a limo ride. I'd been warned. In fact, I warned! I remembered my conversation with Veronica.

I could barely force myself to keep walking. I wanted to sit on the sand and rot with the seaweed. To keep my mind sane, I let it continue its ebb and flow about Ethan and his relationships.

I talked Veronica out of Ethan, in the defense that Ethan loved me. But she thought he loved her. She had been so sure he was into her. I was the one to assure her he wasn't, not him. If anything since her withdrawal, Ethan tried harder with Veronica.

Hadn't I told Veronica not to trust the boy who said he was her boyfriend, but wouldn't acknowledge her as such in public? Oh, how silly I'd become! I owed Veronica an apology. Oh, and I'd shoved Tess – in a public place – for throwing herself at Ethan. She didn't know I was kissing him. Ethan never discouraged her from nibbling his neck. I clinched my jaw, I wanted to hate her. I wouldn't let myself. Instead I remembered that night.

311

The condescending look on Ethan's face stung me. How he'd looked at me when he thought I was the one being unreasonable – me! As penitence, I told my broken heart I would apologize to Tess. I would keep a straight face when I did it too – no tears – not even a grimace would be allowed. I would be the lady Grandfather always said I was.

I crawled over a cluster of rocks and felt a surge of relief when I saw the old abandoned set of stairs that climbed the cliff. Moving off the packed sand at the waterline, I walked toward the stairs. The loose, grainy sand seemed to mock me, making me fight for every step I took. I had two choices. I could sit down and give up. Or I could fight. I focused intently on those steps, putting one foot in front of the other. I would fight.

What was I doing? Back alley cat fighting for a man – really?

I hardened –forcing myself to take every last trudge through the sand. I finally made it to the stairs. They were more like wooden planks dug into the side of the cliff. Despite not wanting to touch the rickety old railing, I forced myself up them with only a slight pause. Oh, how my legs burned walking up the stairs. Determined, I took every one of them.

At the top of the cliff, I found my meandering road. I stood at the mouth of the valley only a mile and a half or so from the Manor House. A very shiny BMW drove by. Tourists who must have driven down to the lighthouse gawked at me. They looked down on me – Caroline Carnegie who never had a nose turned up at her in her life. Oh, how I hated Ethan. Because of him, I didn't get to be her anymore. She would never have become a reality TV star. My tormented pride insisted on the title. My last name, my master's degree from Harvard, even my role of sister and daughter were gone – I became the reality TV star.

I refused to meander with the old road, and cut through the red-tipped succulent plants to shorten my walk.

CHAPTER THIRTY-FOUR

When I walked through the Manor House door Julian had his back to me. An angry monster grew inside me at the sight of him. He did this to me.

No. I stopped the anger before it could take hold.

Anger gave him power over me.

He was no longer responsible for any part of me, not even my misery. I handed him my life. I did that. And now I would take it back. I would choose who I wanted to be from this point forward in my life. I chose to make Julian insignificant, not the puppet master over my anger.

"Carrie! Where have you been!" Julian stammered, realizing I was there.

"Out. Is something wrong?" I asked politely. It was a bad bluff; my legs were scratched up and I was a mess. But I held my head high and sold it.

"Are you all right?" Patrick asked, coming down the stairs, his face full of concern.

"I'm fine thank you," I said pushing the perfect sound of diplomacy in my voice.

"Go find Ethan and Lance," Julian said, glaring at Patrick.

"Okay – Carrie I'm glad you're all right."

"I'm fine. We'll talk later," I said. I needed Patrick's help.

Julian started damage controlling. Like I do when a graduate says something stupid in a job interview, and I have to spin it to make it look like the interviewer took it out of context.

"There was some error. You shouldn't have been sent down to the bungalow already occupied by Tess –"

"I'm staff now, remember? You don't have to lie to me. I'll earn my million dollars."

"Even so, you can't disappear like that. You don't even have your microphone on. How many ...."

I walked away. Julian called after me:

"All right. Fine. We need to move on. Ethan and Lance are out looking for you."

"I'm going to shower," I said.

"That's fine. We're going out to dinner."

"Don't you need more footage for the barbeque scene? That's why I went down to get... him in the first place," I faltered. He would at least have the courtesy not to pretend I had some measure of control.

"We didn't have time to set the grill up after you failed to bring Ethan back, and you disappeared."

"Yep, my fault. Sorry I didn't fight Tess and caveman drag Ethan back to the Manor House with me. Really?"

"Well, either way, you didn't bring him back in time for the barbeque scene."

"Yep."

That's all I was doing – getting Ethan for a barbecue. Nothing else would have happened. Julian appeared convinced as I turned from him and stomped away. He didn't think me capable of doing what he knew Tess would do down at the bungalow. Who knows what might have happened if he suspected the true reason I went so enthusiastically to get Ethan. In that moment, he thought more highly of my ability to take a stand than I did.

To the viewers at home, I disappeared from the bungalow and reappeared after the commercials at dinner. No one saw my run down the beach. No one ever knows what happens when the television blips to commercial – the curtain is closed. By the time the commercial ended I reappeared with the other contestants and Ethan at a round table covered with a white tablecloth and fresh-cut flowers in the center.

Painted on the wall of the restaurant above the table, minstrels looked down, laughing at us. I remember laughing at the reality show, too. This wasn't funny anymore. Now I had to analyze everything. Julian kept us in public, so I couldn't react – yet. No doubt he meant to force me into a scene where I reacted. Little did he know I wouldn't give it to him. I was still a human being with a choice of my own. And so, I put on my interview face and set out to see whose will was greater.

Tess – despite her contract – told everyone I walked in on her and Ethan making out. Sandra seemed to take this as a personal insult and doubled her efforts with him.

"I just love this pasta, the carbs are killing me, but fresh pasta mmm, you want to taste?" Sandra asked holding her fork out to Ethan.

"Nah, I'm good," he said, "Carrie –"

"Sandra, did you get something on your dress there," Tess said pointing over Ethan. Ethan quickly pulled away from her like he'd been shocked. Tess's face fell.

"Tess, can I use your oil and vinegar mixture? Mine is gone," I said.

316

Tess paused. She glanced at me, barely looking at me for the first time since I walked in on her. She looked unsure how to respond. Her eyes were confused. Isn't this the part where I hate her forever?

"You know, Tess, I'm not afraid to shove you," I said playfully when she didn't answer right away. She grinned at me, turning her body toward me so it wasn't so obvious Ethan didn't want to be sitting by her.

"I defend myself," she said.

"I know it hurt," I said, "I deserved it though. I'm sorry for shoving you. I can't believe I did that."

"Yeah, me neither," she said, "and earlier when you –"

"Water under the bridge," I said laughing, "Seriously what are the security guards for if they can't handle crowd control, anyway?"

Everyone laughed, except poor Veronica who still fumed for me.

I saw Ethan relax; he must have thought I really didn't care. Tess handed me her oil and vinegar.

"Hey Sandra, can you hand me the pepper grinder?" I asked. Ethan lunged across Sandra to get it so he could pass it to me. Veronica briskly took it from him because he was getting up to walk it around so I'd have to look at him. Veronica didn't have an interview face.

I kept mine planted on, and though I didn't know it at the time, the posts on the show's website were out of control noticing, that, like Isabel Archer in Portrait of a Lady – I would never crawl.

I forced myself to laugh at everything Tess said like we were best friends. Oh, how Ethan relaxed when I showed

317

myself acting like it was all one big joke. I'd done what he asked. I disconnected. Only I disconnected by pushing him out of my circle of sarcasm; he wasn't inside the joke anymore.

He didn't seem worried about the barrier I put between us. We'd have another morning run. How many times had he smoothed things over with me? Even after everything, my heart begged me, as a child would, to let him make it better.

But how did I know? How did I know if Ethan was as much a puppet to Julian as me? What could I do but disconnect from them both?

A spat broke out at the table.

"You're being a brat," Sandra fumed.

"You're just jealous," Tess countered calmly glancing at me to be sure that's how she should react. I smiled, encouraging her.

Sandra's face turned so red it looked like she might erupt.

"I'll tell you what," Sandra said turning and caressing Ethan's chest, "you will enjoy my visit to the bungalow much more. Tess is like a cheap parlor trick, which is amusing I understand, but nothing compared to real magic."

Okay, how long had she been practicing that line in her head?

Ethan's eyes turned to me, but whether it was to enjoy the joke or his concern, I didn't know. I couldn't have been more interested in the dry creek bed out my window.

"Carrie," Ethan asked, speaking right through the women still taunting each other.

"Yes?" I answered.

"Where did you run today?" He searched my face. He wanted to know what happened to me.

"Same place as always, up the road," then I turned to Veronica and asked, "Do you really think this is homemade pasta?"

After that Sandra demanded Ethan's attention by telling him about her daddy, the doctor, now looking to be a college football recruiter. Sandra made something of a spectacle of herself, and I noticed the cameraman focused on her as she did it. I wondered if that meant Sandra was Julian's next elimination.

CHAPTER THIRTY-FIVE

After dinner, they flooded a beach volleyball court with lights. Lance instructed the production crew to set up like the idea anything would come out usable was insane. One cameraman swore he couldn't even see figures in his lens.

Did that mean Julian wanted my breakdown for himself? He didn't want to show the world?

I could feel Sandra being drawn out and set down a peg on film. By keeping us out in public, was Julian trying to gauge my emotional state? The cameras didn't even focus on me at dinner, in case I did break. I started to think my humiliation was just for Julian. He wanted to prove he could demolish me. He didn't want my light to fizzle out in the eyes of the viewer; he was doing this to be cruel. The way Lance and the others glanced at me, they all knew this was being done to put me back in my place.

By the time the cameras were ready to shoot, it was nine at night and freezing. We played volleyball for what felt like forever, especially after I worked so hard climbing the stairs to get back on top of the cliff.

Julian came out of his van every fifteen minutes to switch up the teams. He wore an awful hooded poncho. He kept trying to push my buttons. First, I had to be on Tess's team, and then I had to be against Tess. He'd encourage Ethan to cheer us on from the sidelines. Ethan cheered for me, but I didn't notice and cheered the other contestants on, mostly Veronica while she smoked us all. Positive and pretending, I played like nothing was wrong.

Julian pulled out all his conniving little tricks. He personally interviewed us. No doubt these interviews would be the only thing shown. Sandra lost it a few times, Veronica cried, and Tess snapped more than usual. I pretended to be at a tea party and refocused everything said to me politely. I'd been training for this all my life.

Julian sat me in a chair and put so much light in my face I couldn't see.

"How do you feel about Ethan kissing other women?" He implied Ethan was kissing all the other women and not just Tess. How could I know the truth of such a statement either way?

"Yeah, he's got some game, huh, women all trapped in one place and he's the only guy around. I wonder if he's growing an unhealthy dependence on you. Is he going to need you to pick up women for him the rest of his life, Julian?"

"Go back and play," he said glaring at me.

He pulled me away from the group after another game.

I closed my eyes. I could smell Fritos on Julian's breathe.

"Do you love Ethan, Carrie?" Julian asked, "Can you forgive him for betraying you?"

"He's a judge on a reality show. You're being a little dramatic," I replied with half a laugh.

"I know you love him."

"How?"

"I ... I've spent hours reviewing tapes. I've seen how much you love him."

I stopped for a minute. I'd never admitted my affection for Ethan over a microphone. Did Ethan tell him I admitted it in private? I stammered. That's what Julian wanted, my

321

declaration – to prove he'd bested me, to prove I fell for
Ethan. Or…perhaps…did Julian fancy himself a Cyrano de
Bergerac? If I declared my love for Ethan, did Julian think the
affection extended to him?

Or perhaps, he simply wanted to break me. Like a wild
creature he put in a cage, he wanted me to thrash against the
bars so he could create my dramatic reality until he tamed me
into submission.

What did I say? Say something he'd never air –
something that would break his illusion if anyone ever saw it.

"Carrie, admit it," Julian insisted when I refocused back on
him, "you love Ethan and he hurt you."

"You know, with the camera crew all over the place, and
you feeding us lines most the time, I don't know Ethan well
enough to love him."

Julian glared at me, but quickly wiped it away:

"Tess asked Ethan to invite her down. She's the one who
–"

"It's definitely possible. I don't really believe much of
what you say anymore, though," I said.

"Me? You don't trust me?" Julian said and contorted his
face in disbelief. I couldn't help staring at him. Raw and
unmasked, he honestly couldn't understand why I didn't trust
him. He truly believed himself trustworthy. His seat of self-
dilution lived much deeper than even mine when I believed
love and a reality show could mesh. Julian, as if to prove
himself, said:

"Don't worry Carrie, I'll make this right. I've already set
up some time for you and Ethan to visit your mom Friday

322

afternoon. Richard Blanchard himself helped arrange it with the hospital and will be there."

I only nodded politely. I would never let them into my mother's hospital room. Julian waited for me to thank him. Should I appreciate him turning me, my mother and everyone I knew into reality TV stars? I said nothing.

"Tess won't be there," he said with a wink.

"I don't mind Tess."

"Admit it! You hate Tess!"

I laughed at him, allowing the camera to zoom in to catch my reaction.

"She came on this show to win a million dollars. Seems to me she's the only one who knows what she's doing."

"Ethan loves you. You'll win the money."

"I thought it wasn't about love, Julian. I thought we didn't have to fall in love to win the million dollars."

He rolled his eyes at me and said:

"You can't help who you fall in love with."

"No, I can't, but you can, can't you?" I asked.

"I ... uh," this appeared to make Julian uncomfortable. He claimed he had some editing to finish, no doubt editing me into an emotional mess. He left, instructing Lance to keep rolling while we played.

About midnight I spiked the volleyball hard at Ethan's head. We weren't filming. The cameramen were talking about the bad lighting, and batteries dying. Lance looked from me to the volleyball that rolled to a stop in the sand. Fear sucked through my clinched teeth as my huge eyes locked with Lance. He saw my act crumpling like the ocean eroding away the cliffs until the roots of the cypress stood exposed for

323

the whole world to gawk at. Ethan also saw it and walked toward me.

"Time to go," Lance snapped, "Ethan, can you get your interview over with while we pack up. Ladies, in the bus please," he shouted, sounding more perturbed than I'd ever heard him. We all dropped everything and headed for the bus.

I had to know. Well – deep down I knew, but I had to hear Ethan say it. I stopped. I stooped to tie my shoe. The group pulled ahead of me. As if we'd prearranged it Ethan paused until everyone was out of hearing range, then he walked up to me.

"Look, Carrie I know –"

"That first morning, when we first went running, did Julian call you and tell you where I was?"

"Huh?"

"The very first morning we went running. Did Julian call you and tell you where I was?"

"Well yes, only because he had to warn –"

"That's all I needed to know," I said, jogging away. Julian had set it all up, my manufactured romance.

"Carrie," Ethan called. He followed me.

I caught up to Tess and put an arm around her. She looked sad most of the night. She expected more preference from Ethan after her trip to the bungalow. She wasn't getting it.

When we reached the bus, I stopped so Tess could get on first. Ethan came up behind me but, Lance snapped:

"Ethan, we all want to go. Can you please get the interview done?"

324

Ethan sulked off.

"Remember to show contrition," Lance said to Ethan.

"The volleyball makes us emotional for the interviews. That's what he wanted?" I asked.

"Yeah, Julian likes to find ways to get a little extra drama. You're all kind of a mess like you've lost it."

Lance put one of his thick friendly arms around me to shuffle me onto the bus. Lance held me for a moment too long and putting his forehead to my temple whispered, "I'm so sorry."

I nodded. I couldn't respond verbally. I climbed up onto the bus. Die inside, I told myself when George looked at me with pity in his eyes. Everyone knew – the world knew.

"Smother, pretend – don't admit it hurts. Don't let them see how to use you," I told myself. I sat next to Veronica who put an exhausted head on my shoulder. I stayed stiff and didn't bother making myself comfortable for her. This was all a game.

I didn't go to bed that night. I couldn't. I set up my paints in the bathroom.

Thank God Tess had been there. What would I have forced myself to do to prove Ethan was mine when he wasn't? What if Tess hadn't been there? What if we'd... what if I been with him and then I caught Tess climbing all over him?

Plagued with the memory of Veronica's story, I hated how self-assured I'd been with her. How pathetic I thought her for wanting so desperately to be loved that she gave herself in such a tragic way.

How desperately I wanted to be loved. I, Caroline Carnegie, would have... or no. No, surely, I couldn't have settled for reality show sex. Would I have sunk to the equivalent of the back of a car like Veronica?

Oh, how I owed her an apology. How easy to get sucked into this need to be loved. How easy to lose something so personal. The only thing I was born with that's truly mine to give, and I about gave it on national television. All to appease this need inside me. I hated sex, I hated it. It pushed me to be stupid.

If Tess hadn't been in the bungalow – if I'd been with Ethan – if I'd learned Julian made him love me after I'd had generic reality show sex, what would my sorrow be then? Would it have meant anything? After it was over with, I'd have slinked back to the Manor House isolated, sleeping alone with my shame. Ethan, the actor, would still have kissed Tess. That's not what I wanted.

I sat in the bathroom all night painting my seascape. I threw my sketch away. My bright colors grew dark and shadowed. The only light on the canvas came from the light house. The light glowed brightly where the beam struck through translucent waves. The glowing waves crashed into the rock, angry and determined. The rock grew smooth. The rest of the picture dimmed gradually pushing the corners into shadows.

I added confusion in the form of the mist by rubbing a dark gray into the shadowy distant cliffs. In dark undertones, barely a shadow, I added a Cypress tree hanging off the side of the cliff with gnarly roots exposed. The picture became fierce, a force to be reckoned with. It would not be driven by fear. I would listen to myself. I would control my own life. I would be a lady as Grandfather always told me.

CHAPTER THIRTY-SIX

I heard Patrick the next morning about five-thirty, putting one riser up. We didn't need all of them for the final four contestants. I slipped down and whispered a conversation with him. He told me what happened in the elimination process, and how live we really were. I asked him if he could stall. Find a way to push back the elimination process until we were closer to broadcast time. He agreed to help me.

Everyone slept in late after the exhausting night. When I heard Veronica stir, I lay down and pretended to sleep. She left me alone and I waited in bed for a long time before Lance finally called me to get ready for the eliminations.

After the unbearable preparations, three keys sat on a platter. Lance did his tiresome introduction over and over. Ethan stood by the platter in a black tux with a forest green tie, bouncing a little. His silver-blue eyes had a resolved sort of look in them.

I stood across from him. We all wore pleats this time, and aside from Veronica's funky pleated side cape, we all looked good. I wore an off-white dress that bunched in pleats at my waist and then dropped. The hint of buttercream brought out the warm tones of my skin. My hair was twisted up on the top of my head with tight auburn curls falling back down around my face. My face took on the power I felt.

Even Sandra's beauty, that once intimidated me, dimmed to insignificant standing next to the flame of power I emanated. We waited for more than an hour to start

328

taping. A UPS driver meant to deliver some remote pickup equipment wrote down the wrong city. He wandered around Pacifica looking for the Manor House before he had enough sense to call and ask for better instructions. Ethan stared at me most of the time, but I couldn't look directly at him. Disconnect, that's what he wanted, right?

The delay pushed everything back. We were fifteen minutes into the hour-long broadcast when we started filming the elimination. With little time to re-edit the ending, the viewer saw things almost as they happened.

"Okay, ladies, Ethan, we're live," Lance said.

Lance nodded to Ethan, he didn't miss a beat.

"Carrie," Ethan said.

I walked forward. My creamy heels clicking on the tile until I reached the carpet Ethan stood on. I was first. I couldn't be flattered. I already saw him choose Tess. Whether he preferred her or not, he chose her.

I choked the emotion out of my face. I loved Ethan. I didn't really know if he loved me – if he could love me in such a circumstance. But I knew Julian. Julian would continue to use my love for Ethan to manipulate me until I didn't even know myself.

"Carrie, will you take this key?"

"No, I won't," I said, shaking my head slightly.

"What?" Ethan said, confused.

I didn't respond. I turned from Ethan and walked quickly over to the sitting room where my suitcase sat, one in a pile of four. We always packed before eliminations, but I was careful to grab everything this time. I was leaving. Not because Ethan

329

would eliminate me; Julian would never let him. I left because I chose to!

I carefully picked up the garment bag Becky packed for me. Every designer packed her latest creation up to be sent with whoever was eliminated. It was an unwritten rule that we were to wear the dress on the morning show out of respect for their work. I attached the hook to my suit case and pulled it around.

The other three women looked confused, unsure what to do. Ethan tilted his head toward Lance and said something. He started toward the sitting room, but my only goal was to stay away from his eyes that would make me change my mind.

"Care-" Ethan said as I passed.

I didn't look at him. I kept moving toward the door. I didn't need his eyes. I needed to leave the house before Julian started the elimination process over.

I would leave with whatever dignity I had left – intact. I would not be torn down until some dramatic response spewed from me like Serena. I had to get into the limo before Julian made it across the driveway.

Ethan looked unsure what to do. Then comprehension spread across his face. He ran up to me and glancing over his shoulder to be sure the other women couldn't hear he whispered anxiously, "Please wait. Please stay. You don't understand."

"I'm sorry. This is the only way for me to disconnect," I said. I conquered my emotion, "I totally get this is a game. And I totally get you're supposed to try us all on for size as if we're sweaters in a catalog. I wasn't prepared for it. I didn't realize it was going to be like this. I can't disconnect and be around you. I want someone who wants only me – and there's nothing wrong with that. At the end of the day, I don't want to play games, even for a million dollars on national television."

"Carrie I...I love –"

"Please don't. Please don't say that's what love is to you –

"

"Carrie let me –"

"Explain? Where would you even start? This isn't for me. I can't keep doing this," I said.

He looked at me. He studied my face.

"I understand," Ethan said. He looked at me in such a way I lost the hardened look on my face and a few tears settled in my eyes.

"I have to leave. It's the only way for me," I said.

"No, you're right. You shouldn't have to... Wait for me –"

"Wait for you?" I asked.

"Please I'll make this up to you... don't watch, uh ... four weeks until the reunion show. Please wait for me," Ethan whispered putting his hand on my arm. Maybe he did love me...

It didn't matter. I had to leave.

"Julian's coming. He wants to start the keys over, but we don't have a lot of extra time," Lance said to me nodding at the door. Patrick called from the stairs:

"Oh, that might be a problem. Because of the delay, Julian threatened my job if I didn't have the eliminated contestant out the door without all the blubbering. He worried about getting the limo interview in. I've got her plane ticket," Patrick

331

said. While he spoke, he hit his laptop anxiously like it wasn't quite purchased yet.

"Tell George you have to go to the United Counter at terminal three. They'll have your ticket there," he grinned at me. He was my friend.

"Thank you," I said with as much sincerity as I could muster through my mask.

I allowed one glance back at Ethan. He looked like I gut punched him. He didn't move. He didn't look capable of it through his shock. I turned from him. Moving away from him felt like savagely wrenching my muscles away from the bone. He was that much a part of me. Ethan was my first real love, tragically maybe even my last love. Body and soul. A part of me would always be his, but I had to go.

"Carrie, let me help you out to the limo with that," Veronica said with the urgency that turned my brain back on.

Julian was coming.

"Another limo ride, of course," I said as we hurried toward the door.

Unsure if I would make it to the limo before Julian came, Veronica heaved my suitcase out the door while I held it open. We half ran, scuffling in high heels, pulling the suitcase out to the waiting limo. George looked surprised to see me running toward him.

"We have to go," I called, looking at Julian's pool house. George glanced too. He quickly took my luggage, and motioned to the man who'd tape my exit interview to get in the limo.

"Thank you – I'll see you on the outside," I said. I quickly hugged Veronica.

332

My heart jumped at the sight of Julian cantering toward us. He hurried down the path from the little studio where he worked.

I jumped in the limo. The shadow of Julian hobbled quickly toward me through the back window. George slammed his door shut after me. I turned to see Julian waving his arms at the limo as it left the curb. He cried almost as Hawthorne's misshapen Old Roger Chillingworth: "Thou hast escaped me!"

Before we rounded the hill out of sight, I distinctly saw Julian look at his watch, kick an old olive tree twice, then canter back toward his studio. And I was free.

In my interview I kept it calm. I reminded the cameraman my mom had been in an accident and after much consideration, I felt I needed to be at home with her. When we came to the property line, the cameraman took my interview, my microphone pack and the limo back to Julian. George drove me to the airport in the rental car.

"Thanks," I told him once we were alone.

"Just doing my job," George said, but the mischievous glint in his eyes couldn't be misinterpreted.

"Will you tell Patrick I said thanks for doing his job so efficiently tonight?" I asked.

"Sure will, little Missy," George grinned.

I glanced at him. In that most desperate moment, a dreaded limo ride, two random men – men who had been in the background of my life for the last month and a half – men who hadn't proclaimed love to me – were right where I needed them. They helped me. Julian didn't catch up to me because of them.

333

"Julian cantered for me," I said with a frantic laugh.

"What?" George asked.

"Julian, he spent all his time trying to force us to canter like ponies, but in the end, he cantered down the walk for me."

"I suppose he did," George grinned again. "I think that means you're going to be just fine."

"Yes, it does," I lied. I didn't know how I would ever recover from Ethan.

George dropped me off at the United Airlines sign. He handed me instructions to make it back to the hotel in New York as quickly as possible.

"Good luck on your interview tomorrow," he said.

"Thanks, for everything," I nodded. I climbed out of the car and back into reality.

CHAPTER THIRTY-SEVEN

It wasn't until I made it through security I remembered my fully charged phone would find a signal, and I pulled it out of the bottom of my hand bag.

"Hello."

"Andrea."

"Carrie is that you?"

"Yeah," I said.

"Where are you?" Andrea asked.

"SFO, I'm flying into Newark," I said not even making my request – unable to even articulate I might need something – or allow myself to be vulnerable.

"I'm picking you up," Andrea said anticipating my need. That's how we'd become such good friends. She never made me ask.

"I'll be in after midnight."

"I don't care what time. I'm totally picking you up."

"But I'm supposed –"

"You come here. We'll set up a bed for you. You don't want to go back to your apartment tonight."

"I'm supposed to stay at this hotel by the network building. I have to go on the Morning Show tomorrow – they're actually sending a car for me."

"Who cares? Let 'em. None of that means you have to drive into the city tonight," Andrea said. Her annoyance showed that I tried to be so considerate of the show at such a time.

"They get us an expensive direct flight so we –"

335

"I don't care how much they paid for your direct flight – you're staying here – they don't own you. Seriously we're going to have to detox you – you'd think you were taken over by a cult."

"Oh, rational," I said, feeling real life un-pause.

"Phil's already getting out bedding in the spare room," Andrea said, "give me your flight number, I'll figure out the details."

I read out my flight information from the paper in my hand into the receiver. Andrea finally said, "Okay we'll meet you at the curb under the United sign. Hey, Carrie, I'm proud of you."

"You're the only one."

"I don't care if I'm the only one in America. I'm so proud of you."

"I'm proud of you, too, girl," Phil, Andrea's husband, yelled toward the phone.

"Oh, Phil!" I said. I was free.

"She said thanks," Andrea said in a quick aside. "Okay, I'll see you in a couple hours."

"Was I needy?"

"What?"

"Did I look ... needy, you know pathetic. Or grubbing for... his love like a fool?"

"No, you were the sweetheart of the show. Tess was the –
"

"Please don't. Please let Tess be. The way she is; it's like a compulsion with her. She couldn't help it if she wanted to. Just, did I look cocky, you know, conceited about my name?"

"No, no… honestly Carrie, you were sweet, kind of the class clown. It never showed how smart you are, but everyone saw you as sweet and funny, really funny. You never took on the role of stuck up, or cruel, or even desperate. Considering everything, you held yourself really well."

"Right, a person can't be a lady on a reality show."

"Oh, for heaven sakes! You're so hard on yourself. You went on television, and audiences loved you, like everyone always loves you. It's just for fun. Get over yourself."

"They loved me?"

"Yeah, you have a fan club."

"Julian said people would send me hate mail if I didn't loosen up. Apparently, I'm as uptight as his grandmother."

"What a jerk. Look, don't obsess about every little thing that happened, okay?"

"I don't know how not to."

"Don't worry we'll figure it out," she said.

"Thanks, Andrea. Oh, that's my flight. I've got to go."

"Okay, make your flight. I'm really proud of you. Good-bye."

"See you, Andrea," I said, hanging up.

I handed the TSA guard my ticket. When I finally made it through, I had to run barefoot again to catch my plane.

I slept the whole flight and the stewardess had to physically rouse me when we made it to New Jersey. I walked out of Newark Airport and the heat hit me like a huge, oppressive hand covering my face until I could hardly breathe. Andrea stood next to her idling car. Her long boney

337

arm waved at me to hurry, her blonde hair in a bob of a ponytail, nodding at the cop telling her to leave the curb.

I staggered toward her. Her husband Phil, a large man whose whole face was covered in freckles, came to me and grabbed my luggage.

"Thanks," I said. I almost started crying at his consideration.

Aside from both being tall, everything about Phil contrasted dramatically with his wife. His soft features always looked welcoming where Andrea, with her sharp features, could become barbed wire with just a look. When Andrea wasn't with me at our demanding, sixty-hours-a-week job, she and Phil were always together, so it didn't surprise me to see them both.

"It's so hot."

"I'm sure, after San Francisco," Andrea said, throwing the airport police a dirty look for trying to hurry us along.

I drove back to Andrea's house playing with her daughter Brea's little toes, listening to her soft snores. Neither Phil nor Andrea badgered me. I disconnected so well I had nothing to say. My soul and body ripped apart and were no longer one.

Isn't that what Grandmother, Serena, Julian, even Ethan, wanted from me? To disconnect until I wasn't even a part of the shell of a body walking around? Perhaps it makes the puppet strings easier to manage. Or perhaps that's when they throw the puppet away, because it's lost whatever made it special enough to pick up in the first place.

I stared out the window at the car lights shooting around us. When we reached Andrea's house, Phil lifted Brea out of

338

the car. I watched him cradle her gently into the house, and felt an overwhelming loss.

Andrea helped me to her spare room with my suitcase. I could barely hold my body up. I was so exhausted. I started to cry uncontrollably.

"Are you okay?" Andrea asked startled, hugging me awkwardly.

"No," I stammered through my tears. "I hate everyone, and everything!"

"Well, thank goodness! That's the most human response you've articulated thus far. Carrie, no one's asking you to take a kidney punch and keep smiling."

"Good," I sobbed, dropping my weight into Andrea's arms. "I hate my life."

"That's fine," Andrea cooed into my ear holding me as she would Brea. I sobbed harder. Losing control completely, I jumbled into Andrea's shoulder. "Andi, my daddy's dead," I wept.

"He would have been horrified by that house," I continued, wiping my nose on Andrea's shoulder. "He died and left his little one all alone to fend for herself in a horrible house."

"Carrie, you know he didn't want to leave you alone," Andrea finally said, comforting. "He must have loved you so much. He never would have left you if he could've stayed here."

I sobbed for a few moments uninterrupted.

Andrea was crying softly now, something I thought she never did. Throughout all our conversations in the past, I barely ever mentioned my dad. Something about

339

her tears unleashed everything in me. Why couldn't I
ever find that place where everyone else seemed so
happy. Or was it like living on a reality show? Nobody
was really happy, nobody. It's just the face they showed
the world. Satisfaction, loving relationships – they were
all a sham.

Phil came over and put a hand on his wife's
shoulder. He was so tender with her. Ethan had been
that way with me, but it ended. It died. It faded; he was
gone now. Gone with everyone else. The empty void
sucked him away like my dad, my grandpa, like Gordon
and my mother's strength. I lost every last tenderness.
I felt so alone with no tenderness. And I had no money,
no way to support my mother except to plug along in
the job I hated.

Why had I left again? Why did I leave the
tenderness behind? I sobbed. The void should be
comfortable. I wandered in the desolate wasteland of
void so often I should be capable of taking those steps,
of moving past Ethan, to be alone again, but I felt as if I
might implode like a dying star until the vacuum of a
black hole took me away.

I needed his tenderness. In complete vulnerability I
asked;

"Does he love me?" I couldn't open my eyes again.

"Your dad?"

"No, do you think he'll still want me, or is he in love
with Tess now?"

I vaguely heard Andrea say:

"Of course he loves you. In four weeks, you'll see him again at the reunion show. You were right to leave, but in four weeks he'll come for you."

That little bird, hope, proving I wasn't immune to the emotion, sprang from my heart like a slight trickle of water breaking free above ground.

I had all but fallen asleep on Andrea's shoulder. Phil grunted, lifting my weary body from Andrea's slipping grasp. He cradled me as he had cradled Brea, laying me gently on the bed in the spare bedroom.

CHAPTER THIRTY-EIGHT

I slept in the spare bedroom for a few hours. Andrea woke me long enough to get me into the car so she could drive me into the heart of New York City.

When Andrea and I showed up at the network building, Julian met us at the door. I wasn't expecting him. Seeing him was like being doused with ice cold water. I snapped out of being disoriented. He said:

"Ah, Carrie – Care Bear, you have this ability to disappear that's totally unnerving. Didn't you see the car we had waiting for you at the airport?"

"Missed it," I said swallowing down hard.

"You should have been here. I flew in no more than two hours behind you. Now that you've had time to calm down, we can fix this."

"Nothing needs fixing."

"Next week we'll surprise everyone when you show up on the dinner cruise."

"I left in the manner you said I had to. I will not go back. And if you or anyone from the studio shows up in my mother's hospital room, I'll have you arrested," I said.

"But –"

"Leave her alone!" Andrea snapped.

"You must be Andrea Clover," Julian said. He took a moment to appraise Andrea's cold face.

Andrea nodded, giving him a look that she could eat Julian for breakfast and spit him into the gutter. He took a step back. I'd tried to imitate the look a few times, but couldn't. What a pity.

"I called your house last night when I couldn't find Carrie. I couldn't get through," Julian said.

"I turned my phone off," Andrea said, challenging him with a tilt of her head and strong eyes.

"Well, Carrie," Julian said, "I can't quite comprehend how you inspire such loyalty in the people around you."

"And yet, I can perfectly comprehend how you'd be so confused," I said.

Andrea smirked in an openly hostile manner. Julian preferred damaged women he could manipulate. Seeing Andrea wouldn't canter, Julian backed off. He took us into the studio. He introduced me to everyone, like I was a foreign dignitary, as we walked. So many people with so many titles in this building: I didn't bother to remember anyone.

When I complained about the production crew in the Manor House, Lance assured me that we worked with a skeleton crew. Many members of the crew played dual roles. I hadn't understood until I saw how many people worked together to put on the morning show. When we finally made it to the dressing rooms, Julian asked:

"Becky sent your cruise dress?"

"Yes," I said holding up the garment bag. A stylist showed me where to change. Julian left for a while, but came back when my makeup was almost finished.

"She looks too... her makeup should look softer to match the dress," he told the lady in wardrobe.

343

"Oh, I guess that explains why Becky was dressing me like a victim when everyone else was wearing bright colors." I glowered down at my wispy lavender dress.

Julian ignored me and said to the makeup artist who didn't want his input:

"If she looks wounded it will make more sense that she left the show …."

Did Julian feel it was his fault I left the show? Why did he need me to be wounded? Shifting the blame to Ethan protected Julian?

"I've got this," the woman glared.

"No, don't do it like that. We have to somehow portray to the viewer Ethan wounded her," Julian insisted to the obstinate woman who didn't want to give me soft eyes when they were fiery and meant to stand out. Ignoring Julian, she finished, and then the stage manager took us into the green room. Andrea, talking rapidly on her phone, moved to the far end of the room to put out a fire with one of her accounts. The instant she left, Julian zeroed in on me. He stopped and jumped a little when a man entered the green room and said:

"Julian, this is a pleasure. You don't usually have anything to do with the eliminated contestants."

"Bryan," he said, looking surprised. "You haven't come to see my eliminated contestants since you became the executive producer of the morning show."

"Ah, but this one, this one I have to meet," Bryan said taking both my hands in his. He was a square jawed man with creases in his face almost like dimples. He wore glasses and a vest. He reminded me of Clark Kent.

"Carrie, it is such a pleasure. I'm Bryan Cawlsen," Bryan said, kissing both my cheeks in an overly friendly manner. Bryan addressed me like we were old friends; only I was from an alternative universe and couldn't remember him.

"Thanks," I said, mostly because Julian looked livid.

"Bryan, it's so good of you to take the time out of your busy schedule. I really like this new look you've adopted." Julian went on about Bryan's posh look. He kissed up to this man with such extravagance, my lips grew sore just watching. Bryan interrupted the flow of excessive compliments and said:

"Carrie, you are the first one to ever reject the key on *The Whole Package*. Did you know that?"

"No, not really," I said. He watched me, reading my face. Julian jumped in:

"Yeah, I really chose my judge poorly this season. What he did to her is unpardonable. You should tell Richard that if I had it to over –"

"Carrie, how rude of me. Can I get you anything?" Bryan interrupted, scowling at Julian. That is when I remembered the network studio executive who invested in the Carnegie currency. He meant to come to my mother's hospital room.

345

He meant to get his fifteen minutes from me. No wonder Julian couldn't take the blame for me leaving. No wonder I had to be wounded.

Bryan was cut off at every attempt to damage control me by Julian's attempts to damage control him. Finally, exasperated, Bryan asked:

"You ready, Carrie?"

I nodded and followed him. Julian tried to come as well, but Bryan said:

"I'll bring her back. You can just relax in here."

"Of course. Thanks," Julian said tersely.

Bryan quickly pushed me through the door and looked over his shoulder to be sure Julian wasn't following.

"I can't stand that guy," he said smiling at me.

"Me either," I said warming up to him.

"You know, I've seen a lot of women come through here in the last five years. Before my promotion to executive producer in January, I made the compilation videos for them. I looked through raw footage of what he does to the women on his show. It is unpardonable." Bryan looked at me until I had to look at him. I nodded to show I understood.

"I am so delighted you walked off Julian's show. I took the time to make your video. I know you don't understand the significance of that, I just… I wanted to watch you walk off again and again."

"What did you see in my raw footage?" I asked cringing.

"I saw you… I saw…. Here, take my card," he said, looking embarrassed. "I'd love to take you out."

"Oh," I said, looking at him shyly. He grinned at me.

"You saw everything and are still asking me out?" I asked.

"Yeah, I'm really into you," he said. I blushed.

"And since I value fair play," he said, "I will tell you, Ethan – he watched you all the time. Julian edited his footage, so the viewer never saw Ethan enter a room, because he always looked for you first."

"He… he was watching me?" I asked.

"Yes, but so was I," he said. He grinned at me. I laughed, unsure what to make of this conversation.

"I get you're not really in a place for me to be flirting with you, but I have to take my shot, right?" he asked.

"I guess," I said. I slid his card into a little pocket Becky sewed at my waist. Bryan continued;

"Anyway, even if I never see you again, I want you to know, what you did, leaving the show instead of letting him toy with you, you didn't just do that for yourself. You did that for all the women he destroyed on *The Whole Package*. I am so gratified for you and them."

"Thanks," I said. Afraid he would try to commit me to going out with him, I quickly changed the subject.

"What about the studio guy, Richard Blanchard? Is he mad at Julian," I asked?

"Yeah, and I promise he's watching. You should go into your interview confident, with that fire I saw in you. Make it clear your self-respect was on the line. You're not just speaking for yourself, but all the other women."

"Oh, I have no intention of looking wounded so Julian doesn't get in trouble," I said.

"There she is," he said, putting a hand on my back.

I stood up straighter. I pushed my chin forward. I would control how I presented myself, not Julian. Julian couldn't take responsibility for the role he played in my leaving. He sent me down to Ethan's bungalow, he did that. He overplayed his hand. He no longer has a say in how I present myself to the world. Now, in this last moment, I have to prove I am my own person.

I force myself to be confident. I don't need to be cocky like Sandra, ready to stomp on people like Serena. I will not droop like Veronica. I will be the best, most confident version of me I'd ever been.

"A large number of your fans turned out. We're hoping you'll go out to the plaza and greet them," Bryan said, sounding more professional as we entered the studio.

"Sure," I answer. He introduced me to what he called the camera operator, which looked like Julian's version of a cameraman, and both walked me to enormous glass doors.

I hold my head a little higher for all the other women who never made it out.

I step out into the plaza. Noise erupts all around me.

The End